Through the Wild Gate

Dale Cozort

Chisel and Stone Publishing

This novel is a work of fiction. Names, characters, places and incidents are the products of the author's imagination or are used fictitiously. Any resemblance to actual events, locales or persons (living or dead) is entirely coincidental.

Copyright © 2023 Dale Cozort
Published by: Chisel & Stone Publishing
Interior Design by www.formatting4U.com

All rights reserved. No part of this publication may be reproduced, stored in any retrieval system, or transferred in any form or by any means, electronic, mechanical, recording or otherwise, without the prior written permission of the author.

To My Family and My Online and Real-World Writing Groups

Author's Note:

As with all my writing, this novel is the product of tiny bits of time fit between work and family obligations. It's also the product made possible by my wife, who is also my long-suffering beta reader, and my daughter who respects my writing time, along with individuals in writers' groups willing to read pieces of the original rough drafts and suggest improvements.

Like most writers, I stand on the shoulders of previous authors, borrowing from and expanding on a body of science fiction stories that helped inspire me to write this book.
I would like to especially thank the following groups and people for their help:

The Writing Wombats, the Kansas Novel Repeat Offenders and members of Point of Divergence, the alternate history writers' group and especially David Johnson, Chris Nuttall and Kurt Sidaway for their critiques and suggestions,

If you enjoy the novel, feel free to check out my other novels and novella on Amazon or your other choice of online bookstore or drop by my website and my blog:

Website: www.DaleCozort.com
Blog: https://dalecozort.wordpress.com

Contents

Chapter One: Robinette Throws A Rock 1
Chapter Two: Making Robinette Feel Human 12
Chapter Three: Blackwood Versus Thornburg 28
Chapter Four: Into the Storm 34
Chapter Five: Lion Versus Hyaenas 39
Chapter Six: You're Fired 49
Chapter Seven: Searching for Jimmy Nelson 58
Chapter Eight: Leah Thornburg Plays Nice 63
Chapter Nine: Robinette Lies or Makes a Revelation 76
Chapter Ten: A Dog Collar & A Betrayal 89
Chapter Eleven: Crisis of Faith 94
Chapter Twelve: Back to the Wild 98
Chapter Thirteen: Neolithic Mangi 111
Chapter Fourteen: Mangi in the Suburbs 121
Chapter Fifteen: Thornburg Family Reunion 124
Chapter Sixteen: A Council & A Trap 133
Chapter Seventeen: Getting Ready to Rumble 137
Chapter Eighteen: Bad Luck Times Three? 149
Chapter Nineteen: The Other Shoe Falls 154
Chapter Twenty: Invisible Attack 161
Chapter Twenty-One: Helicopters at Noon 172
Chapter Twenty-Two: Final Confrontation 189
Final Notes 199

Chapter One:
Robinette Throws A Rock

Guarding a rogue Gate is a crap job, scary as hell when it isn't boring. My name is Eric Carter, private eye when I'm not on the graveyard shift guarding Don's Auto Parts. Seedy junkyard. Seedy side of the city. Too seedy even for whores, tattoo parlors and payday loan places. The kind of place where no one asks where you got those catalytic converters. Zoned industrial sewer. Ten-foot-high wood privacy fence so no one has to see where their cars go after they die. Stretch six feet wide around the fence with brown-stained dirt where nothing grows. Paint peeling on the wood fence, but no graffiti.

No graffiti is the only sign that Don's is a front. Robert Bedford Thornburg, head of a powerful Gate family, opened an experimental Gate here twenty years ago when the families were figuring out how to make Gates. They accidentally created a rogue Gate, one that even now still randomly disappears and shows up fifteen minutes or two days later and a mile or two feet away.

When Gates open, pieces of the Wild come through, mostly birds and insects, but sometimes bigger stuff. The bigger stuff doesn't mix with polite society, even when it's arguably human. So, the Gate families pay me to sit on my butt and watch security cameras scattered through a huge junkyard that covers the place where the rogue Gate might open.

Having your own Gate puts you at the top of the hierarchy, above people with yachts the size of World War II cruisers. It also gives you perks almost impossible to get anywhere else. Zero pollution. No antibiotics or pesticides or microplastics in your food and water. Absolute refuge if someone tosses nukes or killer viruses around. When you have everything else, that sort of thing is a nice extra.

I worked for a Gate family, the Thornburgs, fifteen years ago, before they fired me. Golden parachute for an iron clad non-disclosure agreement.

Enough money to last the rest of my life, except I went through it in ten years, got bourbon tastes and ended up with a cheap beer budget.

So, I guard Don's. After a few months, I got used to the constant odor of leaking gasoline and the glaring white florescent lights, both inside and out. As usual, I settled in and got an audio book playing, sound low so it didn't wake Mike Dickey, my shift partner and an off-duty cop. Mike's okay for a squatty five foot eight troll of a guy. He changes wives more often than I get my oil changed and has a herd of mini-Mikes and Mickettes to support, which is why he's always broke and why he works at Don's. I've only got one ex and I haven't heard from her since she moved in with that movie director in LA. Mike claims they broke up and my ex is doing porn now. I don't care enough to check.

Mike's ten years older than me and has a gut, but there is muscle under the sloppy fat and despite being a crap human being, I know he'll have my back. No, he wasn't supposed to be sleeping on the job, but he wakes up full tilt like snapping your fingers if things get hot.

And lights. Camera. Action. Before a Gate opens, it gives a brief light show, shimmering in a rainbow of colors. Then it opens to the Wild, like our reality was a piece of paper and somebody burned a hole in it, the edges still blazing, letting us see what's on the other side. If you're close enough, you sometimes hear what sounds like an elephant-sized wet fart. In this case, I saw moonlit night sky over short grass, nothing unusual except it was framed in still-glowing red and sat among the wrecked cars, actually in the center of a rusted out yellow van.

As soon as Mike woke up, we jumped into our electric cart, I brought up the camera feed on the monitor and raced down a too-narrow aisle between towering stacks of flattened wrecks.

Mike swore. "I don't remember who I was dreaming about, but it was good sex."

"Ever dream about bad sex?"

"When I have the kids over for the weekend."

I eased the cart around a sharp corner, then glanced at the monitor. The Gate was still there, the glow around its edges fading slowly, still empty.

"Maybe the kids remind you that sex sometimes has consequences."

"Nope. That's not it."

Most times the Gate closes before anything comes through. When the Gate closes, it makes an unstoppable guillotine. Cuts through metal or flesh like it's a damp paper towel. Not something to screw with.

Sometimes, bold, curious animals like squirrels slip through. Squirrels, we don't care about. Same species as ours, or close enough. Other stuff matters, especially Mangi and big predators.

Gate families keep the Wild secret from their children and most of their servants. Only a carefully vetted few get to go through the Gates. Even most of the servants who go to the Wild don't know they've been there. Modern, controlled gates open to walled family compounds in the Wild and almost no one goes outside the gate. As far as most people know, they're at an ultra-private rich people place.

Robert Thornburg took me on a hunting trip to the Wild when I was his bodyguard. Hunting is a big attraction of the Wild, for people in the know. Trophies from there are unique, not exhibited publicly, but major sources of prestige among those in the know. It takes skill and guts to hunt in the Wild. Big animals there are almost as dangerous as African game like Cape Buffalo that often turn hunter into hunted. "They've been hunted by Mangi for half a million years," Thornburg said then. "Having people hunt them is burned into their DNA."

I kept one eye on the monitor while I steered through the cluttered junkyard. A Mangi scuttled through, human-like pale white face framed by tangled red hair on a mostly hairless body, standing on two legs. Just one Mangi, thankfully. One Mangi was bad, three times as strong as a strong man. This one was female, breasts clearly visible. She had a deerskin around her waist and moved purposefully, as if the strange sights of the junkyard didn't bother her.

"Scavenger. She's been across before," Mike said. I relaxed slightly. Scavengers come across, grab scrap metal and are rich in a world where hand-axes are high technology, if the Gate doesn't close when they're partway through. I've never seen that happen and don't want to. It leaves a dead near-human and a river of blood.

Scavengers usually know the signs a Gate is about to close. They also know to be afraid of guns, though they attack if cornered.

"Don't get between her and the Gate," Mike said. I nodded. The Gate families would cover it up if we shot a Mangi, but they prefer that we herd them back through the Gate. I've never killed a Mangi, though I've fired warning shots. Sure, they're more different from us than Neanderthals, but they're sort of human.

This Mangi was more human-looking than most. She had her long red hair tied back out of her eyes in a messy ponytail, exposing heavier than human brow ridges, sharp, high cheekbones and an almost nonexistent chin. She wasn't built like Raquel Welch in that notorious caveman movie. Instead, she was all sinew and muscle, with taut, strong legs that were long for a Mangi.

She wasn't gathering scrap. Instead, she strode purposefully through junk cars toward the fence.

"A crosser?" Mike asked. If she was a crosser, we had to head her off, for her own good. Local organized crime knew about the wild Gate. They didn't challenge Gate families for control, and they didn't blab about Mangi. They just shot them with tranquilizer darts, hustled them into vans and put them to work, females as low-rent, dangerous prostitutes and males as labor for companies that would otherwise have used undocumented workers and liked workers they could treat even more like slaves. Mangi make awful slaves, but some people never get that memo.

I turned to cut the Mangi off. She changed course immediately. "Crap! She's tracking our cart by the sound."

That was new and unwelcome. I was surprised she could figure it out with the echoes.

I turned the cart to cut her off again. She stopped as soon as the cart changed directions. My fists clenched on the steering wheel and a surge of frustration sent my pulse racing. I slowed the cart, hoping the breeze whistling through scrap metal would hide the engine whine. I focused on sound, our tires crunching through the gravel, wrecks rattling in the wind, a transformer humming, distant sirens. How could she hear us through all that?

Mike's hand hovered close to his Glock. "That poor little bitch is too smart. It'll get her killed."

"Think we need backup?" I asked. Backup was five minutes away, but they came in ready to shoot and something had better need shooting. A dozen Mangi or Dire Wolves meant something needed shooting. One female Mangi probably didn't.

I split the monitor's view, one view following the Mangi, the other monitoring the Gate. So far only one Mangi. It was night in the Wild too, but any one of half a dozen big predators could show up, none of them afraid of people except around captive Gates, where the families hunted.

I half-wished more Mangi would come through, so we could back off and call backup.

The camera nearest the Mangi went out.

"That little bitch!" Mike said. "She's going to make us kill her."

I flipped to the next closest camera. It went out too. That wasn't a coincidence. She was taking out cameras. I switched to a camera further down the aisle. No luck.

Mike drew his Glock and scanned a half circle toward the broken cameras. "Get the drone up. We need eyes on her."

The drone was recharging and wouldn't have much juice. Still, with this Mangi taking out cameras, we had to use it,

"She's been a servant over there," Mike said. "That's the only way she could know about cameras."

I nodded. Gate families don't take many human servants to the Wild—too many tongues wagging when people come home, so they capture Mangi as slaves, servants or domestic animals. It rarely works out well for long. Mangi aren't stupid. They see that Gate families aren't old and toothless by their late twenties, have enough to eat and stay warm in the winter. They want that, but adult Mangi won't put up with the Gate families controlling their lives to get it, so Gate families mostly use Mangi children. They grow up and want what the Gate families have, but for themselves, without the slavery or servant crap. Families mostly force their Mangi servants back into the wild when they hit puberty. That causes problems because they know about people and are smart as hell. This one seemed smarter than most.

"That poor little bitch probably got old and cranky, and the Family kicked her to the curb," Mike said. "That's a shitty way to treat servants. They give them a taste of our life and then dump them back in the Wild like used toilet paper."

I nodded. "And we clean up the mess."

The drone glided toward the Mangi's last known location. More cameras blinked out. We would have to use guns to herd her back. Tasers don't have the range and tranquilizers kill Mangi way too often. I know that sounds stupid. Use guns instead of tranquilizers to keep from killing Mangi. They'll run from gunshots though, so you usually don't have to kill them.

The drone circled where the Mangi had been. Nothing. I made the circle bigger, my gut clinching. "Crap! Where is she?"

Mike stood up in the cart, one hand on the top frame, his Glock still out, weapon and eyes still roaming, Something rattled behind us. Mike turned and a fist-sized rock smashed him in the nose. Mike dropped the

Glock and slammed back into his seat, splattering blood on his uniform and my arm. He gurgled something angry and probably blasphemous through the blood. I ducked, drawing my revolver and wishing for backup.

I spotted the Mangi. She had another rock poised to throw but stopped abruptly. "Mr. Carter?"

I paused but didn't lower my weapon, trying to see her better in the gloom. Something stirred in the back of my mind, a nearly forgotten memory. "How do you know my name?"

"You saved my life when I was six years old."

The memory flowed in. I don't rescue a lot of distressed damsels, and only one child I could remember.

"Robinette Thornburg," I said. Daughter of Robert. The son of a bitch who'd fired me and the reason I spend my nights prowling a shitty junkyard with Mike instead of living a normal life.

#

Mangi and humans can make babies together. Usually, those babies die in the womb. The ones who survive are sterile, like mules. They say the Mangi got to the Wild's New World half a million years ago. Half a million years is enough isolation that things work different in baby-making between the Mangi and humans.

I mentioned Robert Thornburg. Powerful guy. Harvard grad. Knew all the right people the right way. Inherited a substantial family fortune and supersized it with finance crap I don't begin to understand. Bought and sold billion-dollar companies like they were trading cards. Rented Senators and Federal agencies to pick up his laundry. Jerk sometimes. Screwed anything female on two legs that held still for him. That included Mangi.

Thornburg had islands of decency. My severance package was one. Robinette Thornburg was another. Half Mangi. Half Thornburg. Robert Thornburg had his servants raise her like a human child. And now she was coming through a rogue Gate, half-naked.

Robinette took a step toward us. Mike reached for his fallen Glock. I grabbed his arm. "Leave it. I know her."

He wasn't in any shape to shoot anyway. His nose gushed blood and he looked like he was about to barf. He spat blood, then said in a strangled voice, "Bitch broke my nose."

"She's Robert Thornburg's daughter."

Mike put both hands to his face. "I don't care. She still broke my nose. Oh God that hurts!" He wiped his nose on his shirt and took a deep breath. "Half human? At least I don't feel as much like a perv for checking out her boobs."

Being Robert Thornburg's daughter took shooting her off the table. I tried not to stare at her, but my eyes drifted down to her chest. I shook my head and focused on meeting her green eyes, Robinette shifted uncomfortably and folded her arms across her bare breasts. "I got used to going bare. Can you get me clothes?"

She picked up Mike's Glock, which had fallen onto the gravel beside the cart. "Cheap piece of crap. The families didn't issue you this, did they?"

She climbed over Mike into the cart before he could say anything, not waiting to be invited and pushing in between Mike and me. I felt her bare breast brush against my upper arm as she settled in and scooted over, my butt hanging half off the seat. I stared at her face, trying to see the six-year-old I had known in the woman beside me. I saw the resemblance under the dirt and wild hair. She covered her face with her hands, then shifted an arm back to her breasts. "Don't look at me."

I gave her my shirt, which came down almost to her knees. Once she had it on, she leaned back and closed her eyes. "I made it. I'm back. I can't believe it."

"What were you doing in the Wild?" Mike asked. The question ended in a gurgle. When he stopped coughing, he added, "And couldn't you introduce yourself before you brained me?"

"I didn't know you," she said. "You were waving your dime-store want-to-be firearm around like you were expecting a pack of dire wolves to jump out at you. It didn't seem like an 'introduce myself' situation."

"I spent half a month's pay for that weapon," Mike said. "Can I have it back?"

"I don't know," she said. "Your job is to stop crossers. Planning to keep trying to stop me?"

That brought up an awkward problem. Our job *was* to stop crossers. On the other hand, she was half-human and raised as human. And I knew her.

"So, what have you been up to lately?" I asked, trying for ironically casual.

She smiled as though she hadn't smiled lately. "Oh, the usual. I went to the best private schools, then to Harvard. Nothing but the best for daddy's little girl. I graduated with a near perfect GPA. My bachelor's is in Physics, with a minor in Chemistry. I went home for a long weekend, drank a martini and woke up in the Wild's version of Oklahoma, stark naked, with the sun beating down on me, a pounding headache, my hands and feet tied with enough rope for a bondage convention and with vultures eyeing me from two feet away."

"Any idea why?"

"No, but someone has some explaining to do before I kill them."

Physics. Ivy League. I was impressed. Robinette was six when I left my bodyguard job, took my payout and thought I was done with the Thornburgs. I saved her life back then, which got me Golden Parachute fired. Robinette could have passed for fully human at age six, with red hair, freckles and green eyes. Smart too. Say what you want about Mangi, Robinette was ahead of where a six-year-old should have been in brainpower. College for her didn't surprise me.

Her fitting in at college was harder to see. Even at six, something set her deeply apart from her fully human half-brother and sister, differences in how and when she smiled, how she moved. Her voice was uncomfortably high then and unpleasantly nasal then, but she could sing. God could she sing.

Robinette was also ungodly strong for a little girl. Mangi are three times as strong as men pound for pound and having pulled Robinette off her then twelve-year-old brother, that applied to her. A fully human boy twice her age was no match for her and even I had trouble pulling her off him. If she was still that strong pound for pound, we needed to treat her like cranky old dynamite. She could take out both of us hand to hand.

She looked exhausted, unlikely to fight now. She leaned against me, head on my shoulder and looked up. "God, I want to hug you, but I smell like I haven't had a shower in—" she paused, apparently calculating. "Over two months."

She smelled ripe, but I didn't move away from her. "Two months? How did you survive?"

"Because she's half animal," Mike said through his bloody nose. "Back in her natural habitat."

She gave him a look that should have incinerated him, then smiled. "I was sorry I broke your nose and insulted your little gun. Not anymore."

"What are we going to do with her?" Mike asked. "We can't let her go."

"I spent twenty-one years on this side," Robinette said. "I graduated from fricking Harvard with a near perfect GPA."

"We still can't let you go," Mike said. "They would shitcan us."

"Forcing Robert Thornburg's daughter into the Wild would put an expiration date on you. Use by yesterday," Robinette said. "Besides, you couldn't send me back if you tried."

Mike was an old cop, arrogant, probably twice her weight, but he looked away under her gaze. "Okay. How do we get you out without getting fired? Everything is on video."

"We'll kick it upstairs," I said.

Robinette shook her head. "I don't know who set me up. Until I find out, I don't want anyone else to know I'm back. I'll take care of the video. When I'm done, the video will make you heroes. You chased a Mangi back with your drone." She grinned. "Metal bird make Mangi crap herself and run back through the Gate."

The Gate closed as I steered the cart to the main office. There was a locker room with a shower there. A lot of guys shower after a shift in the junkyard. I let her in and found clothes in the lost-and-found, guys' stuff, but it would do. I stood outside until she came back out, her wild red hair tamed as much as it could be, and a man's shirt cinched around her waist with a belt. The shirt came midway down her thighs and looked like a short dress. She handed me back my shirt.

"I'll get clothes once I get home." She paused. "Except I can't go home until I figure out who did this to me." She turned to me. "You saved my life once. Can you do it again?"

"I got fired last time. I would save you again in a second though."

"I know." She gave me a hug, reaching up to do it. I'm six foot two. She's maybe five feet tall. That's the Mangi side. Five feet is tall for a male Mangi, and females are usually a head shorter. She clung to me. I felt her body under the shirt. She was still strong, but hunger and the Wild had stripped fat and muscle from her body, leaving bones standing out among the wiry remnants of muscles.

Mike smirked. "She cleans up nicely. I wouldn't kick her out of bed for not being entirely in my species."

"You'll never get a chance to," Robinette said.

Feeling her ribcage through the shirt gave me a different view of her. Knowing her when she wasn't even a preteen added an extra helping of 'yuck' to Mike's thought. Even tired and near starvation, though, she was still a very attractive young woman.

"Not the time for your horndog act," I said. "She's been through hell." She also really needed a friend now. She still had her arms around me, clinging desperately hard. I looked down at her exhausted face. "How can I help?"

She stepped back. "I don't know if you can. Dad was away on business when someone slipped me knockout drops, but everyone else in the household is a suspect." She paused and her eyes grew sad. "I suppose Dad is too. Have you heard anything about me being missing? If he didn't want me gone, he would have moved heaven and Earth to get me back."

"Why would he want you gone?" Robert Thornburg violated Gate family taboos by raising Robinette as human. Probably nobody else among the families could have made that decision stick. Island of decency in a hard, arrogant man, remember.

"Maybe I was an experiment," Robinette said. "What happens if you raise a half-Mangi kid as human?" Her lips quivered. "Maybe he took it to heart when I called him a heartless bastard."

"That might do it," I said. "Why did you say that?"

She shook her head, her face suddenly cold. "I had my reasons." She turned away, her shoulders shaking with sobs. When she turned back, though, her face was impassive. "I don't think he did this. He can be a bastard, but if he wanted me gone, he wouldn't sneak around to make it happen."

"Okay. Who else is on your suspect list?"

"My sister and brother dearest would be on there, along with the servants and security people, though they wouldn't do anything unless Dad okayed it."

"Your stepmom tried to kill you when you were six," I pointed out. She got drunk and tried to drown little Robinette in the pool, then accused me of rape when I pulled her off the little girl.

"That was four Mrs. Thornburgs ago," Robinette said. "If I knew they were going to fire you for helping I would have bit the bitch's hand off instead of waiting for you to rescue me."

I had wondered how the drunken woman kept a hold on Robinette. Even at six she was strong enough I could barely restrain her. "Why did you wait for me to rescue you?"

She reddened, then laughed. "You really didn't notice that I had a huge crush on you?"

Actually, I didn't. "I can be clueless. Isn't six a little young for crushes?"

"That was the Mangi side. We mature a little faster." She grinned. "I'll have to be more obvious next time. But that will have to wait. We have an attempted murder to solve and somebody's face to pound my fist through and yank their intestines out their throat."

I was suddenly almost sorry for whoever stranded her.

Chapter Two:
Making Robinette Feel Human

We wrote up the incident for Mike's workers' comp claim, blaming a neighborhood kid for the rock to Mike's nose. I called 911 and our offsite backup as soon as Robinette cleaned up the video and hid.

We had a perfect short time hiding place. A few years ago, a foreman on the first shift hid a large van among the wrecks, fitted it with a bed and used it as a love nest. He got fired for stealing not long afterwards, but the van was still there. We found it on our rounds a while back, but Mike asked me not to report it, probably wanting to use it the same way eventually. We chased squirrels, mice and spiders out of it.

Robinette was still barefoot, so I carried her across the gravel to the van. She leaned her head on my chest and put her arms around my neck. "After two months in the Wild my feet are tough enough to take anything this junkyard has to throw at them, but thanks for carrying me across the threshold."

"It's not exactly a five-star hotel, but it should do." I sat her on her feet. "You should be okay here until the cops and our offsite backup leave."

The cops just had us fill out an incident form about the alleged rock-throwing. Offsite backup was more thorough. They work for the Gate Family Council, not Mr. Thornburg and they asked a lot of questions, viewing the video several times before they left.

Mike made a rude gesture when they left. "The Council Police are the Council's private FBI and an arrogant bunch of pricks."

I'd heard rumors that they're technically actual federal law enforcement. Could the families manage that? I didn't know, though the renting Senators thing might make it possible. One of the founding Gate families had a Senator and an assistant CIA director in their ranks, which also probably helped.

"Think the video fooled them?"

"Maybe, but they may have recognized Robinette."

That left us with a problem. Whoever stranded Robinette in the Wild clearly intended for her to die there. The Council Police probably knew that they didn't succeed now. If they knew Robinette was alive and near Don's Auto, Don's would get a lot more attention when word spread.

"We have to get her out of Don's," I said. "We might not get a chance later."

"Where to?" Mike asked.

That was a good question. Where could we hide her that the Families couldn't find her? We couldn't, not if they were seriously looking for her on this side of the Gate, but they shouldn't be, not after seeing the video.

"My apartment for now," I said.

Mike smirked. "Yeah, I figured that was where she would end up. What will your live-in girlfriend think of that?"

"Clara? She's gone. I had her give me her key last time she came back after disappearing for a week."

"Clara Wolf," Mike said. "If that's her real name. I think she's some rich old guy's trophy wife who comes to visit you when he's out of town. She's way too good for you otherwise. She's definitely trophy wife material. She also looks familiar, You're a private investigator. You should do a background check before her husband shows up and has his security people break your knees."

"No point. She's out of my life."

"Until she decides to come back in."

I didn't bother to respond, just closed my eyes briefly and let exhaustion flow over me.

Clara Wolf. Late twenties. Tall. Almost, but not quite model slender. Brown hair always perfect, even when she got out of my bed in the morning. Face that said, "I'm too good for you," except when it didn't, when it was inviting. Athletic and imaginative in bed. And gone a month now. No contact. I made her leave her key. I pushed Clara out of my mind. Closed chapter.

Graveyard shifts aren't fun. People aren't built to work from eleven at night to seven in the morning. Even after years, my body hates it. I have it down to a routine, though. I eat breakfast at a coffee shop a block from my apartment after I get off work, then sleep five or six hours. I putter around the apartment until nine and sleep until I have to go to work. That lets me sleep at night on my days off.

I smuggled Robinette out to my car, hoping the Council Police didn't have Don's under surveillance. They probably would soon, but hopefully wouldn't have time to set it up yet.

I wanted to go straight to my apartment, but Robinette insisted on spending a little time enjoying civilization before she went into hiding. so I took her to my normal breakfast place, where she ordered enough food for a famine victim. She wolfed it down at first, but quickly slowed.

"I want more, but I think my stomach shrank. I'll have to eat in stages." She fumbled with her knife and fork at first, but quickly got back her old habits. I had to remind her to keep her knees together. She grimaced. "Yes, mom. I need jeans. I guess I'll have to wear a bra too. Ordering food and having it handed to me is great. Worrying about pervs looking up my dress and wearing bras, not so much."

"How did you survive over there?"

"I don't want to relive it," she said. "Figure I'm tougher than hell and smart and hate is a good motivator."

I took her clothes shopping on my dime, knowing it might be her last chance to get out for a long time. I stood and waited while she shopped, with my body screaming for sleep. She was exhausted too, but insisted on buying a toothbrush, makeup and personal items too.

"I can get you a hotel room," I told her when she finished shopping.

"You would have to use a credit card unless you stuck me in a fleabag place," Robinette said. "If you rent a hotel room now it might draw the wrong kind of attention. I'm okay with your apartment. I just want to sleep, and I trust you."

My apartment was the last thing I still had from the bourbon era of my life. It was on the third floor of an upscale apartment building in an upscale neighborhood, with keyed access to the building and good security. It was draining the financial life out of me, but compared to what Robinette was used to, it was undoubtedly a dump. I also had unwashed dishes in the sink and underwear on the floor. I lived alone and wasn't expecting company.

When I opened the door, she took a deep breath. "Ah, the smell of dirty socks. It smells like bachelor."

"Close your eyes." I ran ahead and cleaned up the worst of the mess, then opened a window.

"I've been in bachelor apartments before," she said. "Most of them smell worse." She insisted on brushing her teeth and putting on fuzzy, much too large one-piece light green pajamas that matched her eyes, then grabbed my hand. "I want your arms around me when I sleep. Nothing else, just a bed with someone I trust holding me."

She snuggled under the covers with a huge smile. "Three months ago, I took this for granted. Now, it's way better than sex." She was asleep in seconds, with her arms desperately tight around me, her too-thin body gradually relaxing.

Her hair smelled of cheap shampoo that she probably wouldn't have allowed on her head normally. She looked tiny in the oversized pajamas, like the little girl I remembered. I turned off the light and felt her breathing slow into the regular pattern of sleep, then I was asleep too.

I had the next night off, so I didn't set an alarm. When I woke, she was leaning against a pillow, my smartphone in her hand, searching the Internet.

"I should have asked to use this," she said. "But I needed to get questions answered."

"Get them answered?"

"Yeah, but I don't like the answers. Nobody searched for me. Someone hacked my social media accounts and claimed I was taking a break from social media. They didn't shut down my e-mail, so that piled up. I was job hunting and had five interview requests. That sucks because I'll never get another chance with those companies. I'll have to start job hunting again from scratch. My college boyfriend thinks I dumped him with a text." She grinned. "I planned to dump him, so that's okay. Text dumping is harsh though. He deserved better." The grin faded. "Speaking of relationships, I hope your live-in girlfriend is okay with me sleeping in your bed."

"Why do you think I have a live-in girlfriend?"

"You put the toilet seat down. Guys don't do that unless there is a woman in the picture."

"She moved out six weeks ago and left her key," I said. "Haven't heard from her since."

"She must have trained you well." Her smile flickered, then faded, replaced with grim determination. "Dad is still alive, but he isn't looking for me, which means he already knew where I was. I need to ask daddy dearest a question or three."

"Or run and hope he never finds you," I said.

"I'm not the running type," she said. "I get that from Dad's side."

#

I lounged on my couch, half-watching TV. Robinette sat at my computer, catching up on our world. Maybe I should have pushed her to run, not that she would have anyway. If Robert Thornburg wanted his half-human daughter in the Wild, I couldn't stop him. He might have to step over my corpse to get to her, but I would rather not die in a futile gesture. On the other hand, I liked Robinette a lot, both as a little girl and now in her adult, very smart incarnation. The thought of her going back to the Wild sent a surge of anger rumbling through me.

That anger warred with sleepiness. It was early afternoon, and I was usually asleep this time of day. I stayed up to keep Robinette company, but my mind worked sluggishly, feeling jetlagged.

Robinette had a window open, sitting in the sunlight, the window speckled with drops from a rain that had just stopped. She took a deep breath. "The air on this side sucks, except just after it rains. The Wild smells this good all the time." She stood and paced restlessly. "I have another prospect for person who drugged me. My sister had a boyfriend over that weekend. He's a big, burly guy, probably Irish, with flaming red hair." She pressed a fist against her forehead. "Crap! Why can't I remember his name? It's Marcus something. Marcus McFinney!"

I knew that name. "Head of security for a big Gate family," I said. "Probably the Blackwoods." McFinney used to fight Mixed Martial Arts. Dirty fighter. Yeah, he was a suspect. "And he was in your Dad's house when you got kidnapped? That's probably your answer."

"But why would Dad's security let him drug me and dump me in the Wild?"

"Your dad knew about it." That seemed inescapable. If another Gate family kidnapped her without Mr. Thornburg knowing, he would have searched for her. I thought that Robinette was an island of decency in Robert Thornburg. Maybe he had some other motive, or maybe grown-up Robinette didn't tug at his emotions anymore.

How he could he not be proud as hell of her, though. Smart. Pretty. Tough. Down to Earth. What more could you ask in a daughter? Being fully human maybe and able to give him grandkids. The Gate families are like royalty. They like having spare heirs.

"Is there currently a Mrs. Thornburg?" I asked. Robert Thornburg had to be in his late sixties. He didn't seem like a guy a younger woman

Through the Wild Gate

could twist around her finger, but maybe he slipped in the fifteen years since I saw him."

"Dad's current wife won't last out the year. She's yet another trophy wife. Dad likes to win the trophies but doesn't let them clutter up his life. He always has ironclad prenuptial agreements."

That left Marcus McFinney, plus Robinette's brother and sister. I remembered Leah Thornburg and her twin brother Tom. They were exact opposites of Robinette, tall, blond and vicious. They were six years older and tormented Robinette until six-year-old Robinette beat the crap out of Tom. Humiliating, but he learned from the experience and backed off. Leah, apparently not so much, though she never challenged Robinette physically.

Robinette tensed at a distant siren. "I have to relearn tuning out the routine noises." She closed the window and turned to me. "Got it figured out?"

"No."

"And you won't if you sit there grinding gears. You should take a nap." She put her leftovers from breakfast in the microwave and smiled. "I could get used to this again. I *am* going to get used to it again."

I tried to get my mind off Robinette's kidnapping but kept circling back. The situation made no sense, and I had no idea how to unsnarl it. Gate families don't like private detectives poking around in their affairs and have ways of making their opinions painfully clear. Even asking around was dangerous. Not many people, even in the PI business, know about the Wild and the few who do work with the Gate families. If they want to keep working for Gate families, they keep their mouths shut.

Gate families don't tell their kids about the Wild until the kids are adults. They like having the Wild to themselves and couldn't if word got out . There are rumors about the Gates, but most people class them with Bigfoot and UFOs.

Police? Organized crime? A few people on both sides of the street knew a little about the Wild, rumors or sometimes deliberate bullshit spread by the families.

Asking questions might also tip off whoever stranded her that Robinette was back. What did that leave? I backtracked Robinette's life, using my tablet computer while she worked on my laptop. Did Robinette have enemies outside her family? Was her college boyfriend a psycho? He would have to be a psycho with ties to the Gate families to put her in the Wild. She couldn't remember anything that said he knew about the

Wild and nothing I found online made me think his family was wealthy enough to own a Gate. They were wealthy by normal standards, just not by Gate family standards.

"Randall Dailey. Small town rich, father sells real estate. New rich," I said. "Bet your father hated him."

Robinette shook her head. "Randall's family had enough generations between him and the grubby making money part that being new rich wasn't a problem."

I paced restlessly while Robinette tore into her leftovers. "You planned to break up with him. Why?"

Robinette shrugged. "We were both trying to start careers. We talked about keeping up the relationship, but neither of us wanted to tie ourselves down. I wouldn't have dumped him with a text, but I don't want him back."

That probably made Randall a dead end, but I didn't write him off entirely. If a woman disappears, always look at the husband or boyfriend first. If Randall didn't help dump her in the Wild, my already short list of suspects got even shorter.

Sons and daughters of wealth were tempting targets for kidnappers, but this couldn't be an ordinary kidnapping. Whoever kidnapped her had to get through her father's security and through a Gate. Then they got into her social networks and hid her disappearance.

My list of suspects was down to the Thornburg family and Marcus McFinney, but how could I investigate them? If I tried, they would hit me with restraining orders and high-priced lawyers. People with Gate level money reflexively fight for their privacy, even if they have nothing to hide, and someone here definitely had something to hide.

I'd bet good money Marcus McFinney help kidnap Robinette, but somebody in the Thornburg family had to let him. The Robert Thornburg I remembered ruled his family absolutely.

"What about your brother and sister?" I asked. "They're in their late twenties now. They both used to hate you." I couldn't remember much about Leah, just that even as a preteen she was vicious and sneaky. "Your sister Leah and Marcus McFinney are odds-on favorites for kidnapping you."

"Leah? She would have done it in a second, but she wouldn't dare unless Dad okayed it," Robinette said. "And if he wanted to get rid of me, he wouldn't drug me and strand me in the Wild."

Back to the same crap circle. Thornburg didn't search for Robinette, had to okay the kidnapping. But he didn't operate like that. If he wanted Robinette dead, he would have her killed. No messing around, just dump her body in the Wild. No chance police would ever find it.

#

I hastily grabbed a nap, then got ready for graveyard shift at Don's Auto Parts. That left Robinette alone. I thought about calling in sick, but left her in my apartment, telling her not to answer the door.

Parking garages always creep me out, even ones with guards and good lighting. Odd when I spend nights at Don's Auto. Don's is genuinely creepy but doesn't bother me much.

I headed to my once-expensive ten-year-old sports car, a relic of my bourbon days. I rounded a corner, then stopped. Three guys lounged against my car. Business suits. Expensive. Two bulky guys I recognized as muscle and a thirty-something guy who looked like an accountant until I saw his eyes.

I hate blind corners. I was too close to walk away.

"Eric Carter," Mr. Accounting with the cold eyes said. "We need to chat." His face smiled while his eyes stayed cold. "Just business. Don's Auto stuff."

"You don't want to mess with Don's," I said.

"Of course not," Mr. Accounting said. He pointed to himself. "Zane Marburg here. We have an understanding with Don's. Odd people come out of it. We find them jobs where they don't draw attention. In exchange, we don't ask why high-level feds watch a junkyard, or where people come from that don't know anything about the world. We don't bother Don's. They don't bother us. We make strange people into earners. Don's doesn't bother our earners."

That was sort of true. The Gate families could have taken back crosser Mangi, but even they were wary of battling organized crime and creating a vacuum around Don's.

"Recently, though, Don's took one of our best earners," Marburg said. "We want him back and we want to make sure Don's honors our arrangement. I request this, in deep respect for our partnership."

So this was the guy who forced crosser Mangi into prostitution or other unsavory jobs.

"I just work for Don's," I said. "Haven't heard about my bosses taking people back once they get outside." Marburg looked displeased. I hastily added, "I'm a private eye. If you have a missing person, I'll look into it."

"That's a generous offer," Marburg said. He put a big envelope on the roof of my car. "Money, pictures of our missing earner and what we know about him. I'll be in touch."

He walked away, with his two guys in tow before I could figure out how to say no without getting the crap beaten out of me. The envelope held a wad of large denomination bills and a picture of the biggest Mangi I had ever seen, not tall by human standards, maybe five foot nine, but with muscles that would make a silverback gorilla wary and make a bodybuilder up his steroids. Weirdly, a tattoo on the Mangi's oversized bicep said, "I heart books."

The Mangi went by Jimmy Nichols, according to a sheet under the picture. He fought on some underground circuit. He had been on our side of the Gate over ten years and was married to a human woman, with a son. How did a full-blooded Mangi pass for human? I studied the picture. In a wife-beater T-shirt and blue jeans he stood out, but mostly because of his muscles. His head was longer front to back than a human's, but he looked more homely than non-human. Clothes and haircuts make a big difference.

I crammed the picture and money back in the envelope. Local organized crime thought they had hired me. I could use the money. On the other hand, did I want to risk drawing Gate family attention with Robinette in my apartment?

Why would the Gate families grab a Mangi fighter after letting him stay on this side for years?

I decided to cautiously check on Jimmy Nichols. Poke around. Talk to his wife. Maybe the Gate families had nothing to do with Jimmy's disappearance.

Or poking around could put me in front of the eighteen-wheeler Mike talked about.

Mike was back at Don's, face bruised, nose bandaged. He grinned at me. "Sleep with the half-Mangi bitch yet?"

"Call her that to her face and you'll end up with more than a broken nose."

"She's five foot nothing. I'm not afraid of her."

I remembered how she faced him down the night before. Yeah, he was afraid of Robinette. Would he keep his mouth shut about her? If he was smart, yeah. We were both fired if he talked.

I tossed Zane Marburg's name out casually. Mike shook his head. "When a mob boss looks like an accountant, you know he's a nasty piece of work. He knows not to mess with the Gate families, though."

"He called them heavy duty feds."

"You've chatted?"

I told him about the parking garage.

He winced. "It's not enough to hide little miss hot as hell. Now you want into a pissing match between the Council Police and organized crime. I'll sit that one out."

"You're sitting out Robinette's problems too."

"Unless you send her over to try out my king-sized waterbed."

"Why do the Gate families put up with Mangi on this side?"

Mike shrugged. "Above my pay grade, but most crossers happened early, when Thornburg was experimenting. Now that the feds are involved..." His voice trailed off. "And you didn't hear that. I thought you knew."

The Council Police acted like law enforcement. I circled back to that rumor. Did the Gate families get them law enforcement powers? The idea seemed absurd, but if they could rent Senators, why couldn't they set up their own police force? The idea shook me more than Mangi or the Wild.

"I've heard rumors," I said. "But if they're true, holy crap."

Mike grinned. "Shakes your world, doesn't it? You worked for the Thornburgs," he added. He slouched in his usual chair in front of the monitors. "You never told me that, but I figured you knew more than you do."

"Non-disclosure agreement with teeth like a beartrap." That was putting it mildly. "And they didn't tell me everything. You never said how you got involved with the families either."

"No. That I didn't." He paused as if he wasn't going to say anything more while I glared at him. Finally, he went on. "I was on a case years ago. A prominent married businessman disappeared. I worked on the case for a while, and found out that he knocked up Patricia Blackwood, daughter and heir to Jericho Blackwood. The businessman told her he was going to divorce his wife, but after he knocked the Blackwood girl up, he dumped her. That put the Blackwood family high on the suspect list, but when I followed up, my boss told me to back off. I was young and stupid, so I kept picking at the case on my own time until the Blackwood family grabbed me and offered me silver or lead. This job is their idea of silver." He leaned back and yawned. "They were serious about giving me lead if I kept pushing. And I do odd jobs for them that pay better money than I get here, though they haven't handed many out lately."

"And the businessman?"

"He's never been found." A shadow flitted across his face, then he went expressionless. "The guy was a jerk and a fool. There are families you don't mess with." Mike shrugged. "Maybe he deserved what he got."

Mike as a young, idealistic cop pushing a case when his boss told him to stop? Hard to see that guy in the Mike I knew.

"Ever meet Jericho Blackwood?" Mike asked.

"No, but I've heard about him."

Blackwood family: Goes way back. Current generation started with three brothers. The senator and the bigwig in the CIA are both dead. Surviving brother: Jericho. Big finance guy. Founding member, Gate family. Same age as Robert Thornburg.

"First time you meet him, he'll tell you his family came over on the Mayflower, direct ancestors on both sides," Mike said. He grinned. "One of my ancestors walked across the Bering Strait ten thousand years before that crappy little boat, but you don't hear me bragging about it. I have a bigamist and a horse thieve ancestor too. Same guy."

Something moved on the monitor. I turned away when I recognized the gait. Raccoon.

Mike lowered his voice. "The Thornburgs may be on their way out. I hear the Council Police shut down their Gate." He mimed spitting after he mentioned the Council Police.

Don't know much about the Council. Robert Thornburg mentioned them a couple times, usually with disgust. How could anyone give men like Robert Thornburg orders? No idea, but the Council Police made them do things they didn't want to do, put tight restrictions on what the Gate families did in the Wild. No industry. Strict limits on how much household help could be in the Wild. The Wild was a place for the ultrarich to play and the Council kept it that way.

"How can the Council force Robert Thornburg to do anything?" I asked. "Guy rents Senators and government agencies to do his laundry."

"How they made him shut down his Gate is way above my pay grade," Mike said. "Maybe they didn't. Just a rumor I heard."

I didn't press him, though I wanted to. If the rumor was true, it was significant. Maybe the Council forced Robert Thornburg to let someone strand Robinette and closed down his Gate so he couldn't rescue her. But why would they do it two months ago, after letting him raise her and send her through college? Maybe the Council was cracking down on Mangi on this side and Robinette and Jimmy Nichols both got caught in the crackdown. Mangi were a huge security risk. Their DNA would be hard to sweep under the rug, even for the Gate families.

Maybe Thornburg was slipping, looking vulnerable, and his enemies attacked him through Robinette. If that was true, though, what could I do about it? Probably nothing. I couldn't fight the Gate families. I probably couldn't hide Robinette from them long.

I curse myself for our brief shopping trip. The families could probably get to store security cameras and my credit card records. Hopefully, they wouldn't since they still thought she was in the Wild. 'Hopefully' isn't a strategy, though.

Mike grinned. "Like I told you, if Thornburg's little half-ape daughter gets tired of your apartment, you can send her my way. I have a King-sized waterbed."

"How is your broken nose healing?"

"Not well. I'll probably snore the rest of my life." He touched his cheek near his nose, winced, then leaned back. "What *are* you going to do with her?"

"No idea."

"You could give her supplies and slip her back to the Wild next time a Gate opens."

Might work, but she would be at the mercy of the gate's randomness, and even with modern equipment it would be a short and crap life for her. Could I even get her back into Don's? Council Police would be watching Don's now, looking for Robinette coming out, not going in, but I couldn't count on them being sloppy.

"What if they took over Don's, like they took over the Thornburg Gate. Then she's stranded again."

What if I went to papa Thornburg and told him she was alive? If he let her get stranded, he had already lost a lot of power. If he didn't fight when the Council stranded Robinette, or lost then, he probably couldn't win now.

I needed to know more about the Council and Mike apparently

didn't know much more than I did. Who was on it? How could it control wealthy, powerful, egotistical families who could buy and sell police and even Senators? Were there factions we could exploit? No clue, Way above my paygrade.

"You're even more boring to work with than usual," Mike said. "Trying to figure out how to help Little Miss Broke My Nose But is Still Sexy as Hell?"

"Thought crossed my mind."

"There is a bump right where you turn into the parking lot here. You have as much chance of helping that girl against the Gate families as that bump has of stopping an eighteen-wheeler."

That was probably true. I shrugged. "I knew her fifteen years ago. Not looking to lock horns with the Gate families."

"You may not be looking to, but I bet you let that girl stay in your apartment, and I bet she ended up in your bed. That will put you in some powerful crosshairs and Robert Thornburg doesn't have the juice to get you, or his daughter, out of them anymore."

That might also be true, based on what happened to Robinette.

"You can't save her," Mike said. "You may already be so far in that you can't save yourself. Keep going and you may pull me down with you."

"What do you want me to do?"

"Tell her you have a plan. Get her down here, slip something in her drink and push her back through next time the gate opens. Give her food and water if you think it will help and maybe a knife. She made it for two months over there. With some help she might make it longer. She won't last long on this side."

"You really think I'm going to do that?"

Mike shook his head. "I've worked with you long enough to know that you won't. No common sense. No survival instinct. A moral code. In this business, any of that shit will get you killed."

"Would you put her back over there if you were in my place?"

He grimaced. "You did have to ask that. I'm not sure. I've crossed a lot of lines, but I'd like to think I wouldn't cross that one."

How was this different from looking away when he knew the Blackwood family murdered a man? Maybe because this was a young woman who didn't do anything wrong, and he would have a direct hand in murdering her. I didn't ask him, figuring that if he saw a line there he didn't want to cross I should let him keep seeing it.

"You plan on telling the Council Police?"

"Nope. I hate those bastards. Don't ask me for help, though. If the families find out, I'll claim that Robinette threatened to sic her father on me and broke my nose. Maybe they'll buy me being afraid of Mr. Thornburg. I'm not though, not anymore." He sneezed, then swore. "She, on the other hand, is scary as hell."

"I thought you said you aren't afraid of her."

"Maybe I am. Who wouldn't be? That would make the sex even better though."

"You're a screwed up human being."

"That's what ex-wife number four used to tell me, but she was the one who threw dishes at me. Toaster oven too, once. We still have sex once in a while. Ex-wife number two stops by every couple of months too, when her new husband is away on business."

I didn't entirely trust that Mike would keep his mouth shut, but I didn't have a lot of choice but to take him at his word. Threatening him wouldn't work. Killing him? The thought crossed my mind, but I quickly ruled it out. I'm a fighter and if someone threatens a client when I'm bodyguarding them, I wouldn't hesitate to take them out. Killing a coworker because of what he might say? That's a whole different thing, even if the guy is a disgusting human being.

We settled in for the shift, which meant that Mike put his feet up, put on one of those neck pillows people use on long trips and was snoring inside five minutes. I turned on my audiobook, not bothering with headphones, and settled into watching the monitors. There wasn't much point in staring at them because alarms would tell me if the gate opened, but teenagers sometimes snuck in to make out in the back seats of wrecked cars, so I had to keep half an eye on that, too. We had motion sensors but had to turn the sensitivity way down to keep from getting constant false alarms from raccoons and feral cats.

Security systems are only as good as the bored guys monitoring them, something most rich people don't understand. Some high-end systems use artificial intelligence, but they aren't as good as motivated humans. Of course, we weren't exactly motivated humans.

Something moved on a monitor. I nudged Mike, then moved a camera to focus on it. It was on the edge of a blind spot, where the cameras probably wouldn't have reached before Robinette's rock-throwing. The replacement cameras had slightly wider fields of view. I eyed the area closely. Something moved again, too big for a raccoon. It was at the fringe of the light and of the camera's coverage. I couldn't get a good look at it. Whatever it was moved again, into what should have been another blind spot, but wasn't quite anymore. Once in a blind spot could have been a coincidence. Twice? Probably not.

Mike was still asleep, despite my nudge. I thought about waking him up, but decided to find out more. The drone was charged this time, so I sent it up. It used thermal imaging and quickly showed a human-shaped figure picking its way through the junkyard.

Good thermal imaging can show a lot, but ours was crap at picking up features. I could tell this was a person, big, probably a man. He was moving purposefully, looking down. I caught glimpses of a flashlight. He was looking at the dirt, not the car parts.

I turned off the audiobook and poked Mike, "Someone coming in."

Mike groaned but put his feet down. "Crap. Why do things always happen when I'm dreaming about sex?"

"Do you ever dream about anything else?"

"Not that I remember."

He eyed the drone monitor. "Not teenagers looking for love in all the creepy places. Doesn't look like he's looking for auto parts. Think we should ask him what he wants?"

I nodded. "And how he knows where our cameras had blind spots."

We headed toward the guy in our cart, watching him on the drone monitor. He looked up, apparently when he heard the cart.

"They need to get us something quieter," Mike whispered. "The families can afford it."

The intruder kept sweeping his flashlight across the ground, though I was certain he heard us. I slowed the cart. "Let's hang back and see what he's up to."

Another couple flashlight sweeps, and the intruder suddenly seemed more intense. "That's where we picked up Robinette," I whispered. The intruder probably knew about her kidnapping. I had a sudden urge to punish whoever it was. "On foot, then tasers."

Mike shot me a sharp glance. "He's probably from the families. Really want to play it that way?" He shrugged. "Just call you Mr. Speedbump."

He stayed in the cart, watching the drone feed. I got closer, one stack of crushed car bodies away. My pulse hammered, loud enough I was sure the intruder would hear it. He kept swinging his flashlight though. I took a step around the crushed cars, then stepped on something metal. It clanged against the car bodies. The intruder straightened and swung his flashlight toward me, reached for a pocket. I recognized him just before I tazed him. *Marcus McFinney.*

Chapter Three:
Blackwood Versus Thornburg

I've never been tazed, but it didn't look fun, especially in a junkyard with metal crap to bang into while you're convulsing. McFinney slammed his head into a bumper and kicked a rusty car hood that slammed down across his legs when the current went through him. I rolled him over and cuffed him before he recovered, grabbed a hideout .38 from his waistband and impulsively yanked his shirt up over his head from the front as an improvised blindfold.

He struggled to his feet. "You just signed up for a beating, whoever you are."

"Private property. I could shoot you."

Legally, probably not. The families would cover for me, though, even if I shot one of their own. I suddenly wished I had shot him, but I couldn't have done it in cold blood, with only a suspicion that he helped kidnap Robinette. At least he was bleeding from a long cut across his forehead and down one leg from thrashing into debris.

"I'm head of security for the Blackwood family," Marcus said. "Get these cuffs off me."

"The Blackwood family doesn't own Don's," I said. Hopefully, that was still true, though if Robert Thornburg lost enough power the Council might take Don's away from him. I hustled Marcus back to the cart. "We'll sort this out at the office."

Mike pulled me aside and whispered, "Is that Marcus McFinney?"

"In the flesh."

"Oh hell no! I wasn't here. I had nothing to do with this. It's entirely on you." He took a couple steps away from the cart. "You're determined to be a speed bump, aren't you?"

He helped me load McFinney in the cart, though, putting McFinney in the seat next to me and taking the rear-facing back seat, distancing himself from my actions.

Through the Wild Gate

I deliberately drove to the area McFinney had searched. I couldn't read anything from the tracks. I tried to remember if the Council Police searched out here. I didn't think so. If you're going to do something sketchy, do it on third shift. Low men on the totem pole get third shift and no matter how long they've been at it, they aren't as sharp as people on day shift.

I stopped the cart and tramped across the area where we met Robinette two nights ago, looking down as though I was figuring out what McFinney was looking for, then hopped back in the cart and turned it around, driving over as much of the scene as I could without being obvious.

Mike leaned back so I could see him and rolled his eyes but didn't say anything.

"Screwing up the scene won't work," Marcus said. "We can look at the cameras."

That settled it. He suspected that Robinette came through here and was looking for proof. We should have faked the tracks to match the cameras the night she came through. Amateur mistake. I was surprised Robinette or Mike didn't think about the tracks and surprised the Council Police didn't catch us.

When we got back to the office, Marcus said, "The longer you string this out, the more trouble you're in. Get the cuffs off me."

Mike spoke up for the first time. "I didn't tase you and wouldn't have, but I figure this is something between families. I'm bucking it up to Mr. Thornburg."

"He doesn't need to get involved," Marcus said.

"This is his property," Mike said. "Another family's security breaks in and tries to avoid the cameras. Where this goes from here sure as hell isn't my call."

Technically Mike was right. Was it smart to get Robert Thornburg involved though? If he was in a weak position, he might have to let the other families search the junkyard, which would weaken his position even more. We didn't have much choice that I could see, though.

"When someone hands you a hot potato, you hand it to somebody else," Mike said. "That's the only way not to get burned."

He called Mr. Thornburg secretary before I could decide whether involving Mr. Thornburg was smart. Robert Thornburg himself called back a few minutes later and showed up with a crap ton of security people within the hour, two dozen men and women.

We pulled Marcus's shirt down from over his head before we let

Mr. Thornburg in. Marcus glared defiantly at us. He sneered at Mike. "The Blackwood family got you this job. Good luck getting anything from us from now on."

Mr. Thornburg walked in, looking confident, in charge. He left his security people outside the office.

He had aged well, at least physically. He still stood straight, with his tanned skin wrinkled a little, like old leather, his stomach flat and his arms well-muscled. His perfectly tailored suit looked out of place in the cramped office, with its cracked floor tiles, too-white fluorescent lights and ever-present smell of engine oil.

"Is this about what I think it's about?" Mr. Thornburg asked.

"If you think your half-Mangi daughter tried to come through here, that's what I'm trying to find out," Marcus said.

Mr. Thornburg turned to us. "Did Robinette Thornburg try to come through the Gate?"

"A Mangi came through the Gate," Mike said. "They saw the drone and ran back through. It's all on video."

He brought up the video. Mr. Thornburg's fists clenched when he saw Robinette, but he didn't say anything.

Marcus studied the video, hands still cuffed behind his back. "That's her. Lost some weight. Looks like she went back to animal fast."

Mr. Thornburg hit him in the jaw, the punch slewing McFinney's head around and slinging blood from the cut on his forehead. Marcus swore, then smiled coldly. "Try that again when my hands aren't cuffed, and you don't have your security outside."

"Try touching Robinette again when she isn't drugged," Mr. Thornburg said. He didn't raise his voice, but somehow it lashed out like a whip.

Mike flattened himself against the wall, staying as far away from the two as he could. My fists clenched but I stayed back.

"You caused this," Marcus said. He leaned forward, as though he was about to charge Mr. Thornburg, despite the handcuffs. "She was about to blow our secrets out of the water. What you tried would have screwed us all. How did you think you could get away with it?"

"Robinette is not a threat," Mr. Thornburg said. "Who is going to investigate us? Who would believe it if someone blew the whistle on the Wild? It might make the supermarket rags next to Bigfoot and Elvis sightings, but it probably wouldn't."

"You got careless," Marcus said. "And you hid it from the Council." He turned to us. "Thornburg is a sinking ship. The Council closed his Gate for six months and suspended him from the Council. They'll kick him out altogether eventually."

Mike raised his hands in an elaborate shrug. "Not my fight. The Blackwoods put me here as a favor to Mr. Thornburg. When they tell me to leave, I'm gone." He looked Marcus over. "You have a tetanus booster in your future. Rusty metal wounds can get nasty."

I wanted to ask what Mr. Thornburg supposedly did to start all this drama, but reluctantly kept my mouth shut.

Mr. Thornburg summoned a security guy. "Take him to a friendly precinct and have them slow roll booking him for trespassing and giving him his call. Make it take all night." He turned back and grinned at Marcus, before adding, "If they have a biker gang in custody or a bunch of belligerent rednecks, put him in with them."

Marcus shrugged. "I can handle myself. You just made it personal, though. You won't like it when it's personal."

Thornburg's security people took him away.

When he was gone, Mr. Thornburg turned to us. "Neither of you are stupid, so you've probably figured out some of what's going on."

"I know enough that I don't want to know more," Mike said. "I'm going to sit the rest of this out."

He sat down in his chair, but at the front edge of it, warily.

"Robinette's grown up since I left," I said inanely. "I didn't recognize her."

"She's the best of me," Mr. Thornburg said. "Without the alley cat part. I thought she was dead, but I will get her back. If she can make it four more months..." He broke off abruptly, then said, "You didn't hear any of that." He grinned, "Except the alley cat part. That's not a secret."

One of Mr. Thornburg's security guys rushed in. "Jericho Blackwood is outside. He wants to talk to you."

"Did you get McFinney away before he showed up?"

The security guy shook his head.

"Let Blackwood in."

Jericho Blackwood. Tall. Dressed all in black except for a white bow tie. Three-piece, tailored suit. Watch that cost more than I make in a year. Shoes I couldn't afford even at the peak of my bourbon days. Haircut that cost a month of my salary. Walked with the confidence only old money can bring. Closest thing to royalty we have in the US.

He nodded to Mr. Thornburg. "Hi Robert. I hear you had issues with one of my employees."

"Nothing I can't handle. You didn't need to come just for that," Mr. Thornburg said.

"I actually came to head off the problem," Jericho said. "I'll need to look at your video."

I thought Mr. Thornburg would say 'no' but he gestured toward the screen. "Feel free, but I won't be watching. Once was enough."

Mr. Blackwood watched the doctored video twice, then turned away. "Unfortunate. Living in the Wild is tough."

"She is starving to death," Mr. Thornburg said.

"Six months is effectively a death sentence," Mr. Blackwood said. "Four more months puts her into fall, with nights near freezing." His voice was matter of fact. "People don't understand how quickly you can die of exposure when you can't get inside, and temperature gets down even to the low fifties."

"You need to get her out of there," Mr. Thornburg said.

"Not my call."

"You're chairman of the Council."

"But not dictator," Mr. Blackwood said. "You know the rules. You set them up."

"I'm why Gates exist," Mr. Thornburg said. "I set up the Council, brought you and the others in. I should have done it all myself, kept complete control."

"You brought us in because you needed us," Mr. Blackwood said. "Me for government connections, other families for money or technology. You did what you did, and we are where we are."

"I still don't know why Robinette is in the Wild."

"We preferred to handle it informally, not get the Council Police involved. They get heavy-handed."

"Handling it informally means my daughter dies."

"She was always an experiment, Robert and always a risk. The Council ended the experiment and ended the risk." He made a cutting gesture with his hand. "Since we know she's nearby, we'll have the Council Police redouble their patrols around the perimeter." He turned to Mike and me. "Your job is to send crossers back, no matter who they are. Keep doing that." He turned to Mr. Thornburg. "Have anything to add?"

"She's still alive," Mr. Thornburg said. "She's smart and tough as hell. What will you do if six months go by and she's still out there?"

"That's never happened and won't this time unless she has help," Blackwood turned to me. "I know Mike, but I don't think we've met. Jericho Blackwood here. Yes, from that Blackwood family. Ancestors on both sides came over on the Mayflower."

I tried to look impressed until he left, then shot Mike a glance.

"Told you," he said.

I wanted to ask Mr. Thornburg how the Council could force him to do their bidding. He had seemed as powerful and decisive as ever until Jericho Blackwood came in, an unstoppable force. Now he seemed defeated, resigned. I wanted to tell him that Robinette was safe in my apartment, but that might trigger a confrontation he would lose.

Chapter Four:
Into the Storm

"We should have told him his daughter isn't over there," Mike said. "We should dump the problem in his lap where it belongs. We're holding the hot potato again, between Thornburg and the Council Police."

I might have agreed if Robinette was some random Gate family brat, but she wasn't. "She really is the best of the Thornburgs, maybe the best of the Gate families," I said. "We can't let them kill her."

"Best of the Gate families is a low bar," Mike said. "They're mostly scum in ten thousand-dollar suits."

That I could buy. "She's worth saving."

"I'm already in way too deep. Taking sides in a fight between families is a terrible idea, like playing chicken with a train."

Mike was right about not taking sides in a Gate family fight, but what choice did I have?

The Council Police were going to have Don's under a microscope. That wasn't all bad. It meant backup would be closer, at least. The rogue gate was always dangerous. Scavengers came through often enough that the local Mangi had to know that the Wild where Don's Gate opened was a source of wonder. Did Mangi fight for the right to scavenge from Don's. Probably. Whoever controlled access to the Gate could be rich in a world where nobody else had metal. Why didn't scavengers come through every time a Gate opened? Maybe control of the Gate got Mangi killed by jealous neighbors.

The Wild was dangerous on its own. The times I went over with the Thornburgs, I was with well-armed hunting parties and even they weren't completely safe. Animals in the Wild had enough experience with Mangi that they were wary of us and tricky, unpredictable. If an animal always does the same thing around humans or Mangi, we can counter it. Human or Mangi hunters probably select for unpredictable.

Through the Wild Gate

"You put us in this position," Mike said. "You should tell Mr. Thornburg. Dump the hot potato in his lap where it belongs."

He was probably right but I promised Robinette that I would keep her secret and I didn't want to risk her life by breaking my promise.

I suddenly, fiercely didn't want to tell Mr. Thornburg that Robinette was back. Was it because I was afraid of what would happen to her or because I didn't want our time at my apartment to end? Both, and I wasn't sure which was more important. Robinette seemed to be enjoying her time in the apartment, a brief vacation from a dangerous world, but it would end. It had to end. Then what? Maybe she would go back to her world as a Thornburg. Maybe that world would send her back to the Wild.

"My apartment doesn't smell like dirty socks anymore."

Mike grinned. "That's how they get their hooks into you, that and sex."

The night dragged. A thunderstorm roared in, with wind gusts and driving rain. Rain and wind in a junkyard clear the gas/oil/antifreeze odor out of the air, but they set the junk creaking and banging ominously. At least the rain wiped out Robinette's tracks.

Midwest thunderstorms come with high winds and hail or even tornadoes often enough to add spice to the experience. Ten minutes into the thunderstorm, a Gate opened at the far end of the junkyard, as far from the office as it could get.

"Well crap!" That didn't even begin to express my feelings. I grabbed a rain jacket and hoped nothing came through the Gate.

Something moved in the fading gate glow, sending a dog-shaped shadow across the grass. We both swore and headed for the cart.

I headed the cart into the driving rain. "Probably a coyote, but could be a dire wolf."

"Yeah," Mike said. "Most likely a coyote and just curious. Doesn't look like it's raining in the Wild."

I couldn't get a good look at it on the cart's monitors, couldn't rule out dire wolf. Dire wolves: bigger than the biggest timber wolves. Mean. Not a part of the Wild we want coming through. Nothing a modern rifle couldn't handle, but sneaky too.

I was soaked when we got close enough to the Gate to get a good look at what was thinking about coming through. Coyote. I relaxed a little, then lightning hit close by. The cart's rear tires both exploded, sending the coyote loping back into the Wild, ears back and yipping.

The cart veered into a ten-foot-tall pile of smashed flat car bodies. We jumped off while car bodies slid down on the cart.

"The cart's on fire," Mike said.

With buckets of rain still sleeting down, I didn't think the fire would last long. Wrong. Fire got to the battery and the rain made as much difference as spitting into a blast furnace. Heat forced us back. The lights all over Don's went out, maybe from another lightning strike, maybe from the fire.

"Perfect! What's next? Rain of frogs?" I asked. At least the Gate closed.

Rain knifed into my face, pushing the raincoat's hood back while the wind shrieked down the aisles of junked cars, pushing against us. The slog back to our office went on and on, with the office emergency lights stubbornly far away. We finally flopped into our chairs, soaked and breathing hard. My teeth chattered, while my heart pounded. Adrenaline fought exhaustion and lost, leaving overstressed muscles shaking.

"That could have gone better," Mike said.

"You think?" I pulled the raincoat off and wasn't surprised that my clothes were soaked. The power came back on, along with the air conditioning. I hastily turned the air conditioning off, wiping the water off with paper towels, my hands shaking from cold and left-over adrenaline. "What do we put in our report about the cart?"

"Lightning strike?" Mike asked. "Better than crappy driving."

"Crappy driving? Next time I'll let you drive in the rain on two blown tires."

"We could claim something went wrong with the batteries and distracted you."

The cart used lithium batteries and they sometimes catch fire if you mishandle them. And, as we found out, they'll keep burning even in a cloudburst thunderstorm. We thought about fighting the fire, but the thunderstorm redoubled its fury. The cart was already toast and the rain would hopefully keep the fire from spreading, though lithium fires don't go out easily. With the lightning hitting way too close and the electricity iffy, we decided to let the off-site security handle it. The phone system was down at first, but we got it working.

The fire was still burning when off-site security got there and the cart was a total loss, fused and melted so badly that they didn't poke around it much once they finally did get the fire out. They didn't ask to look at the video before they left.

"If you do something shady, a thunderstorm is a good time to do it," Mike said. "They investigate it just enough to check off the boxes, then go home."

"I didn't do anything shady."

The thunderstorm reinforced the third shift bit about shoddy investigations I mentioned earlier. Hopefully that was the end of the night's adventures except for my aching back and muddy clothes. Once the lights came back on to stay, I showered and changed clothes, then put my feet on my desk, sipping coffee.

"That's more than enough excitement for one month." Mike slipped his neck pillow on and tossed me a pen. "You get to fill out the incident report."

The chilling rain and the thunderstorm slapped me in the face with how tough it would be to make it in the Wild. Get caught in a downpour like that with no chance to dry off and you were in trouble, even in the summer. Your body would pour energy reserves into keeping vital organs warm. If it ran out of reserves, they would shut down, then you would die. I thought of how Robinette's body felt when she hugged me, still strong but painfully thin. No reserves. Getting caught in a night like this would finish her. "She was near the end of her line," I said. "On a downward spiral, with her body eating muscle to stay alive."

"Our ancestors were tough suckers," Mike said. "Can you imagine living that way? Having kids, waddling around pregnant, trying to catch food after you twisted an ankle or trying to prove that you could still earn what you ate when your knees went, and you couldn't keep up."

"Old is probably thirty-five, if that, for Mangi," I said. "And forty is like a hundred and twenty for us. We could help them, but the families want to keep the Wild the way it is, their private playground."

"I side with the families on that," Mike said. "Try to help the Mangi and they would fall apart. Look what happens when we contact remote tribes in South America. They mostly die, even if we are really trying to help, which a lot of the time we aren't."

He had a point there, but it was still sad to think of Mangi women dying in childbirth or wearing their bodies out before they were thirty, pregnant or nursing infants. That could have been Robinette's life, minus having kids, if Robert Thornburg hadn't raised her as his daughter.

"Lots of wasted lives out there," I said. "How many potential Harvard graduates live and die in the Wild?"

"Probably none," Mike said. "Robinette is half Mangi. The human part is the smart half."

"Maybe. How many full Mangi have had the chances Robinette did?"

"Probably none, but if they were smart, they would have changed. Our ancestors started out at the same place and ended up building cities. The Mangi kept running around bare-assed and throwing rocks at their dinner."

The thunderstorm finally passed, and the sky lightened with approaching dawn. "You didn't get your nap tonight," I said. "Won't you be cranky for your day job?"

"I'm always cranky for my day job. I work with the scum of the Earth, guys who would stab me in the back and laugh while I thrashed out my last minutes of life," Mike said. "And that's the police. The criminals are even worse."

Chapter Five:
Lion Versus Hyaenas

Robinette was wearing one of my white sleeveless t-shirts when I got home, her arms and legs bare. She stood on her tiptoes to hug me, then handed me a plate with pancakes and scrambled eggs, grabbed one for herself and sat on the couch with me. She studied my face. "You look like you've had an adventure. I had one too, but it can wait."

She insisted on hearing about my night first.

"If adventures are mostly about being cold and scared and wet, I had an adventure." I told her about the night's events while we ate.

Robinette was already looking stronger and healthier, her legs and arms filling out. I marveled at her toughness. A dozen hunters with modern weapons would have been hard-pressed to make that trip, even on horseback, but she did it alone, on foot.

Whoever stranded her must have had some inkling of her toughness to send Marcus into Don's. My money was increasingly on Marcus as the strong arm behind stranding her, though not the brains behind it. I mentioned the encounter in the parking garage and my new private eye job.

"A full Mangi male in underground fighting?" Robinette asked. "Who would be dumb enough to fight him?"

"Three or four big guys might have a chance," I said. "Or a couple full-grown male gorillas. Any idea why the families don't round up crossers?"

"If they've been here long enough, they would know too much," Robinette said. "If you sent them back to the Wild they would bring that knowledge with them."

"So either kill them or let them stay," I said. "The families are ruthless enough I would have bet on them killing crossers."

"There are pockets of good in them, especially dad."

I thought about my 'islands of decency.' "What did your dad do to start this crap avalanche?" I asked. "Is he slipping? He didn't look it last night, but Blackwood made him back down."

"I bet Blackwood was polite about it. You don't back dad into a corner, even if he did something to unite the hyaena clan against him." She grinned briefly when I looked puzzled and added, "Dad's a lion. The rest of the Council are hyaenas. They only tackle the weak."

"Yet they forced your dad to close his Gate with you in the Wild."

"I have no idea how they did that," Robinette said. "I just know Marcus was in on it and so was my sister dearest. I wonder which one I should kill first."

I grinned suddenly. "I did tase the crap out of Marcus. We have video of him twitching and knocking pieces of long dead cars down on himself."

She smiled. "You'll have to show it to me." Her smile faded. "I want my revenge hands-on though, up close and personal."

I had no idea how to get to that and I don't think she did either. I wasn't even sure I knew who was behind the stranding. Marcus and Leah alone couldn't defy Mr. Thornburg, so someone powerful must be backing them.

"You said you had an adventure," I said. "How did you manage that?"

"By prowling around your computer," Robinette said. "Someone hacked you as thoroughly as someone can be hacked. Every keystroke and mouse click logged. Audio and video recorded, even when you thought the computer was off."

"Your dad? The Council Police?"

"Probably not," Robinette said. "I wouldn't have found anything they installed. This was a step above script kiddie hacking, but not professional. And they installed it from inside your apartment. How much do you trust your ex-live-in?"

"A lot less now." I swore. "Do they know you're here?"

"I don't think so. They store files on your computer and upload when you're at work, so you don't notice a slowdown."

"Can you get that crap off?"

"I already did."

I was exhausted, but too angry to sleep. My apartment was a refuge, where I shut out Don's, the Gate families and the private eye world, but someone wired it for sound using my own computer. I paced. "What did they want?"

"The hack dates back six months, so it isn't about me." Robinette said. "Any big money cases in your PI business?"

"Do I look as though I have big money cases?" That came out sharper than I intended. "Sorry. Long night."

"The apartment looks as though you had upper-middle-class money, but not lately," she said.

That was close enough to hurt.

"Was your ex-live-in jealous?"

"Didn't seem to be. If anyone was jealous it was me. She came, stayed a week or two, then left, four or five times. I finally told her not to come back. She didn't beg to stay." I shrugged. "She's not important. You are. What if we told your dad you're alive and on this side? He has more resources than us, and he does want to help."

She shook her head. "We can't trust him. The Council forced him to shut down his Gate and look the other way when they stranded me. Whatever they used to coerce him, it's still there."

What other choices did we have? For now, Marcus thought Robinette tried for the Don's Auto Parts Gate but lost her nerve. How long could we keep them thinking that?

"How good is your video fakery?" I asked.

"Good enough unless an expert looks at it pixel by pixel. It won't stand up to that."

The families would have plenty of experts. Would they look at the video that closely? Would Mr. Thornburg give them copies? He wouldn't have any reason not to, unless he suspected the video was fake. I saw no evidence he did, but Thornburg had a good poker face.

With all the attention focused on Don's Auto Parts, Marcus might look into my background. He probably knew me by reputation. The world of Gate families was like a small town composed of the very rich and their servants.

Nothing in my background or Mike's showed a talent for video editing. Did Robinette's? Did it matter? Marcus might come after me because I tazed and humiliated him. He probably wouldn't let that go and it might lead him to Robinette.

"I don't know if you'll be safe here after what I did to McFinney," I said. "He may come looking for me and find you."

Robinette folded her arms across her chest. "If he finds me, I'll take him out of the gene pool."

"He may not come alone."

"Know of anywhere safer?"

I didn't.

Were we back where we started? Not really. I knew more about the mysterious Council, and I knew Robert Thornburg wasn't okay with Robinette being stranded in the Wild. Robinette filled in some of the gaps. The Council, as I thought, had twenty-one members, one per Gate family. It also had a five-person standing committee that made most of the decisions. How did they enforce their decisions? Robinette seemed to know more than she would tell me, but she offered some clues. The Council owned all the Gates and the properties they were on. Council members bought their positions on the Council with a huge deposit, even by Gate family standards and the Council could keep the money if they kicked someone out. Would even those barriers stop Robert Thornburg if he wanted something badly enough? Maybe. What about the Council Police? What authority did they have and how could they use it against Mr. Thornburg, who had his own well-armed security people and plenty of lawyers to tie up hostile legal actions in court?

Marcus claimed that something Mr. Thornburg did brought the Council's wrath down on him, something involving Robinette that might expose Gate family secrets. What could that be?

"Was he planning to make you his heir?"

That shook her. "Wow. That could unite them against him. He wouldn't do it, though. I'm sterile. I can't continue the line. I wouldn't want it anyway. It would turn me into someone I don't want to be. My brother isn't a possibility. I think I broke him when I beat the crap out of him all those years ago. Sister dearest is the logical candidate. She has a street whore's taste in men, but she's sneaky and vicious, traits she would need to run a Gate family. I'm a lot smarter and she'll never forgive me for that, but I'm not her rival for heir."

"Your dad said you're the best parts of him."

She smiled. "I almost forgive him for letting me think I could have a normal family." The smile faded. "I can't forgive him for leaving me stranded though. That was a death sentence. I only survived because I wanted revenge bad enough to keep pushing myself. And I'll have it."

A lot of people are down on revenge, but if anyone ever deserved revenge, Robinette did. How could we get it for her though?

#

I ate breakfast, then dozed on the couch for a while, but kept waking up. Too much cycling through my head. I thought about shivering in the summer rain at Don's and wondered again how Robinette made it through those two long months in the Wild with no shelter.

She was lounging at the computer and glanced back at me. "Trouble falling asleep?"

"Wondering how you kept from dying of exposure when it rained."

"It wasn't easy, but I knew a lot of old camper's tricks for emergency shelter," Robinette said. "A lot of them assumed you had a knife or an ax or string, but I improvised. God, I could have used camping gear The drops to treat water so it doesn't give you the trots would have been near life savers. Or toilet paper. They could have left me one roll. I would have still killed them, but I would make it quick and painless. Antibiotic cream. Even a nail clipper. Do you realize how many times I had a hang nail and worried about ripping it off?"

Despite her words, she seemed happier now that her dad had opposed, though ineffectively, stranding her in the Wild. She fixed a huge sandwich, but only nibbled at it, sitting on the couch next to me, her head against my shoulder. "They say to start with small meals after you come close to starvation. Eating a lot will screw you up, maybe kill you. I don't know if 'they' know what they're talking about, but my brain wants to wolf down this whole sandwich, while my stomach wants a couple strips now and more later."

She looked noticeably healthier now, with color returning to her face and her movements more animated. "I wasn't quite at famine victim level, but I was headed there. I was the kind of hungry where my body was eating my muscles to keep itself going and the only thing I thought about was food."

She put her arms around me, still painfully thin but noticeably stronger. She still felt fragile though, like I needed to be careful not to break bones when I hugged her back.

"You'll get it back," I said. "Everything they took from you."

"We don't know how to get from me hiding here to me living a normal life," she said. "We can talk about getting it back, but we can't get there." She turned her head away, but I saw tears trailing down her cheeks. "I was strong for all those months in the Wild, but I'm not sure I can be strong anymore." She held onto to me desperately tight, sobbing quietly. I held her gently, her red curls brushing my cheek. Finally, she wiped her eyes. "Wow. I had to wait until you were here before I melted down. That'll cost me my tough girl badge."

"You're human," I said. "Nobody human could handle what you went through these last few months without it getting to them."

"I'm human? A lot of people don't think so. Toss me out in the Wild with no clothes or weapons and it's just 'returning me to my natural habitat.' Just another Mangi. Something halfway between human and animal."

"People who think that don't know you," I said. "And if they know you and claim to think that, you're a threat to them."

I wondered briefly if that was what the stranding was about. The Council tolerated Mr. Thornburg raising Robinette as human. It tolerated him sending her to private school and college, but when she graduated with outstanding scores, maybe they wouldn't tolerate her in the human world anymore. Did college make her and other Mangi too human to them? The Gate families did things to Mangi in the Wild that would be illegal if they did them to humans. I heard whispers about special hunts that targeted Mangi when the ones near Gate family mansions in the Wild got too bold. If Mangi were human, hunting them was murder.

Would the Gate families care, though? They could do anything they wanted in the Wild, even to normal humans. I remembered Mike's story about the businessman who crossed the Blackwood family and disappeared. Did he wake up in the Wild like Robinette did, naked and weaponless? Maybe he even woke up and found he was the prey in a more interesting than normal hunt.

Yeah, in case you haven't figured this out, the Gate families were scum.

#

Robinette was happy to lounge around my apartment for the next few days. I had those days off but kept my normal third-shift schedule as much as I could, sleeping in two stretches, one in the morning and the other from around nine in the evening until my normal time to go to work. Graveyard shift isn't fun. It isolates you from normal people with normal lives, leaves you prowling around the Internet or watching crap TV when everyone else is asleep. Robinette slept almost normal hours, falling asleep shortly after dark, and waking before dawn. Okay, not normal except compared to me.

I cautioned her not to get on social media, not that she needed the reminder. Still, she was twenty-one and until a couple months ago had been as obsessed with her smart phone as most twenty-somethings. I would hate to have Marcus McFinney track us down because she posted something.

We talked about getting in touch with Mr. Thornburg, but neither of us followed through. I felt comfortable having her in my apartment, content. After a couple days, though, Robinette got cabin fever. She obsessively cleaned or paced quietly while I slept, trying not to wake me, but not always succeeding. I never sleep as deeply as people on a normal schedule. When I woke up around noon the second day, she had ordered food and timed the delivery for just after I got up.

"Food here is crap," she said abruptly. "It's easy to get and my body craves more of it, but my taste buds are recalibrated. This is second-rate food with the crappiness hidden by salt and sugar."

"At least you didn't have to chase off a mountain lion to get it."

"That is true. And I probably won't have to eat bugs here," she said. "Still crap is crap. The food at home spoiled me."

Food from the Wild is one of the many perks the Gate families get. It's as organic as organic can be, sheltered from pesticides and every other kind of pollution. The Thornburgs sell food grown in the Wild to a small, exclusive clientele. You don't have to be a Gate family to buy their stuff, but at the prices they charge, if you buy the food, you probably own a yacht.

"Here is something weird," Robinette said. "Dad encouraged me to do things that helped over there, rough camping, rock climbing, which helped me climb to shelter at night, jogging on rough ground, finding wild plants for food and martial arts. Did he expect something like this and get me ready for it? I'm even good at archery, though I couldn't make a usable bow over there."

That put yet another twist to this mystery. Maybe Mr. Thornburg enjoyed doing those things with his daughter. Maybe he was afraid the Council would send Robinette to the Wild. Maybe he spent the last twenty-one years fighting against sending her back but did the training in case he lost.

"No amount of training would be enough for the Wild," I said. "Maybe if you did wilderness survival with military snake-eaters you would have a chance, but I don't think even those guys could make it there for two months without modern weapons."

"So, you're saying I'm pretty special, aren't you?" She grinned, then went serious. "I want to talk to Dad, tell him I'm here. I also want to go out like we did that first day and pretend that none of this happened, that I'm just a college graduate taking her time finding a job and spending Daddy's money."

That brought up a problem. I was spending for two and with my income I couldn't do that for long. Robinette had credit cards in her name, but using them would be stupid, even if she could do it, because it would leave a trail. She had a hefty bank account, but the families probably had that watched too.

I thought of yet another mystery to stack on top of the others. How did Marcus McFinney know to look at Don's Auto Parts when he did? Was he getting every report of intruders there? Were they tracking Robinette in the Wild? That wouldn't be easy. The families don't allow anything that runs on fossil fuel over there. Electric cars are cool but don't have much range going cross country in the Wild and the Council rules won't let people use them more than a mile away from a family compound anyway.

"Did you ever think you were being followed over there?" I asked.

"Yeah, because I was being followed. Mangi stalked me half a dozen times. So did bears and big cats. A coyote-looking thing followed me most of the way and tried to grab scraps from anything I caught. I can see how wolves turned into dogs. This one was begging to be tamed."

"What about our kind of people?"

"No sign of them the entire time. I saw a Mangi with a Swiss Army Knife on a string around his neck. I wanted to catch him asleep and grab it, but he was with thirty of his closest friends."

I told her what was bothering me. She didn't have any idea how the families could have tracked her. "I don't think they could have. Not sure why they zeroed in on Don's the night I came through."

Mike called later that evening. "Plenty of excitement here. The gate opened again."

"Anything come through?"

"A coyote/wolf thing, or maybe a Gate family stray dog. It acted tame enough to be a dog, but it looked like a coyote. We shot near it, and it ran back through."

Through the Wild Gate

That gave me the glimmering of an idea. Did whoever stranded Robinette somehow train a Wild canine to follow her? Why would they do that? A tracking device on the coyote?

I stared into space, trying to remember my glimpses of the coyote. I couldn't remember a collar. Why would there be one? Why not put the tracker on Robinette herself? I swore under my breath. I should have thought of trackers as soon as she came through, I would be surprised if they didn't put one on her. But if they did, they would know where she was. No need to investigate Don's. They could simply come to my apartment.

What kind of trackers would the families have? The very best, maybe injectable, the size of a grain of rice, powered by body movement and transmitting intermittently to make it hard to detect. I couldn't buy anything like that, but if the technology was possible, the Gate families had it. What kind of range would a tracker that small have? Probably no more than a few miles. Maybe the families were monitoring Don's Auto Parts because they knew about the gate there. If they got the signal there, but only once, that would put a lot of pieces together.

I hastily finished the call and turned to Robinette. "Did you notice anything that might be an injection mark when you first got to the Wild? I would be surprised if whoever stranded you didn't put a tracker on you. You're genius girl. How can we find out if they put a transmitter on you?"

"They didn't," she said. "I'm physics girl too, and the laws of physics won't let a grain of rice-sized transmitter send a signal far. Antenna would be too small. Even if the tracker was right under my skin, the signal wouldn't go much outside this room. Maybe halfway to the street, at best. The limitation isn't the power of the transmitter. It's the size of the antenna and the wavelength it can generate." She paused and grinned. "You aren't buying it, but you should. I had a near-perfect GPA at Harvard, including physics, remember?"

I set the tracker issue aside for the moment. That still left the issue of the coyote or dog. Was it a coincidence that it came through so soon after Robinette did? Maybe. Coyotes are curious and adaptable. This probably wasn't the same one that followed her and even if it was, maybe it was young, just separated from its mother and lonely. Friendships between canines and humans probably happened for thousands of years before wolves became dogs.

"Sometimes I overthink things," I said aloud. "Maybe I'm jumping at shadows." I didn't tell her about my wild idea that the coyote followed her because of the families. "None of this makes sense. Stranding you in the Wild, especially tied up, should have been a death sentence. If someone wanted to kill you, why didn't they slit your throat too?"

Maybe they wanted to taunt Mr. Thornburg or humiliate him. Stranding Robinette in the Wild alive might be a more effective way of demonstrating their power than killing her outright. Maybe stranding her was the Council demonstrating their power over Robert Thornburg. Letting him know his daughter was in the Wild while taking away his Gate was vile but forcing him to let it happen showed their power. Still, tying her up should have been a death sentence anyway and how would Mr. Thornburg know if they killed her?

"If your dad gets a chance, he'll rip this Council out by the roots, burn it and sow salt on the ruins," I said.

She nodded. "I don't know why he hasn't already done that. If he doesn't, I will."

I didn't doubt her determination, but if Robert Thornburg couldn't take on the Council, we certainly couldn't. I remembered Mike's comment about having about as much chance against the families as a bump had of stopping an eighteen-wheeler. He was probably right. I got ready for my next shift at Don's, silently trying to figure out what to do next.

Chapter Six:
You're Fired

Don's Auto is, when you come right down to it, creepy as hell at night. Wind whistles or howls through the stacked wrecks, sending the piles creaking and shifting, filling the aisles with ever-changing noises and moving shadows. Not all the shadows and noises are from the wind and wrecks. Raccoons, opossums, enormous rats and feral cats, among other small, adaptable night creatures, hole up in the junkyard. Believe it or not, you can get used to all that, tune it out. We go out on foot on security rounds at least twice a night. At least I do. Mike always has a reason he can't do his foot rounds. I don't mind too much. The walking keeps me in shape, while my mind usually filters out the creepiness, giving me peaceful time to think.

On my round, my legs were on autopilot while my mind was on Robinette. A cold, realistic part of my mind insisted that we would lose, that the families would send Robinette back to the Wild. If that was true, what could I do about it? I toyed with taking food or supplies through the Gate next time it opened, but what could I take that the local Mangi wouldn't pillage? I couldn't carry enough food to matter much anyway. Camping gear? Maybe, if I could put it something the Mangi couldn't get into. The \Mangi would undoubtedly find whatever I took over and try to open it with all their ingenuity and their crude stone tools. They probably couldn't open a safe, but I wouldn't take any bets on that. I couldn't put anything over there that would give the Mangi dangerous ideas if they got it A bow and arrows? Robinette knew how to handle a bow. Would including a bow be dangerous? Probably not. Getting good with bows takes a lot of work and building a workable bow would take a lot of effort and experiments. The Mangi probably couldn't use an existing bow effectively or make their own.

Would stashing a bow and camping gear in the Wild work?

Probably not. I would have to smuggle it past the Council Police and get it through the Gate. Then Robinette would have to survive long enough to get from wherever the families stranded her back to Don's anyway and the families wouldn't make that easy.

I felt bad about not telling Mr. Thornburg that Robinette was on this side of the gate, but the reasons not to tell him still stood. Mr. Thornburg seemed unable to fight the Council,. His security people were still stationed around Don's Auto Parts, though discreetly. I wondered what would happen if the Council Police tried to take it over. The Thornburg people would probably stand down. If they were going to fight the Council, they would have already.

Mike watched the monitors while I was out on rounds. He paced restlessly when I got back. "We're on a powder keg. I'm surprised it hasn't already blown."

I didn't know enough to even guess what was going on among the Gate families. From what I remembered from working for the Thornburgs and from what Robinette picked up, the Council operated under strict rules, with lawyers debating what those rules meant, and the five-person core council operated according to those rules, or at least in ways they could justify under those rules. That probably meant they rarely moved fast. If they searched Don's without Mr. Thornburg's permission, it would be after a hearing. If they seized the junkyard, they would do it according to their rules.

How many days since Robinette came through the Gate? I had to think about that. Third shift work screws with keeping track. "Four days." I said that aloud, drawing a quizzical look from Mike. "Since the kids broke your nose."

"Since somebody broke my nose," he said. "It still hurts like hell and I'm getting a cold. You can tell your little friend that I'm going to sneeze myself into an aneurism because of her."

"I'm sure she'll be appropriately sorry."

"And I'm sure she'll laugh her cute little ass off."

"You do have a way of pissing off women."

"That I do, but I still get plenty of sex, so oh well."

Yeah, he's a jerk. The PI business doesn't show you the good side of society. Neither does being a cop or working security at a rogue gate. Intact families, loving couples and poor but honest people doing the best they can? I like to think they exist, but if they do, they usually don't need private eyes or cops, especially ones like Mike who took Family money and let the Families get away with murder. Remember islands of decency? I had to settle for them. Robert Thornburg was a chauvinist, vicious, arrogant piece of crap, but he loved Robinette and I think he regretted not fighting for her, whatever the odds. Mike took favors from the Blackwood family to let a disappearance, almost certainly a murder, go unsolved. He was a lazy, slovenly, chauvinistic piece of shit, but he claimed there were lines he wouldn't cross. I hoped to hell that was his island of decency, because if he went to whoever stranded Robinette, she was screwed and so was I.

"Still think the Thornburg's are toothless?" I asked.

"Robert Thornburg has teeth," Mike said. "But he's smart enough to know he can't fight all the other families. If he tried, he would still lose his daughter and he would lose everything else too. You, on the other hand, aren't smart enough to know there are fights you can't win, so eventually they'll stomp you."

Sometimes you have to avoid a fight because you can't win. Other times, the fight is coming and the more you back away from it, the weaker you get. Ask the British after Munich. I kept my mouth shut about that though and steered the conversation to the Council. Mike didn't know much more about it than I did, but he added a few tidbits. "The Council can move fast if they want to. Don't be surprised if they have people here within a day or two," he said. "They may show up tonight. Hope you're ready for a few days off and maybe job hunting."

The prospect of losing this job, crap though it was, added to the general suckage. Despite all our talk about taking on the Council, Robinette and I had as little chance of beating the united power of the Gate families as we did of flapping our arms and flying.

"The Gate families are vicious, greedy pieces of crap who would steal pennies from a blind beggar," Mike said. "But they act like they're nobility, like the old kings and counts and knights. They talk a lot about honor and how everybody does things by the rules." He got a sour look on his face. "I hear they even brought back dueling. Nothing to stop them in the Wild and fights to the death can be great entertainment. Rumor has it that Marcus McFinney has killed four or five men in duels over there."

That didn't surprise me. The Council probably had rules about who could challenge who in a duel, but no laws could stop the families from doing what they wanted in the Wild.

"I've heard that some younger family members play something like Russian Roulette over there," Mike said. "Six guys each put money in a pot and all six names go in a hat. They pick a name, and that guy goes into the Wild buck naked, with the others hunting him. If he makes it for a week, he gets the pot. If someone shoots him, they get the pot."

I was skeptical that the Council and older family members would let that happen, at least not to heirs, but law enforcement couldn't stop them. "The Gate families have way too much power."

"That they do," Mike said. "And we don't want that power coming after us. That's why you need to talk little miss wild and sexy into dumping your butt and climbing into my bed."

"How would that keep the families off of us?"

He grinned. "Because I know how to keep her from being found. Cops make the best criminals. Don't worry. You'll thank me later. Think about it on your next patrol."

I did the patrol. When I got back, I stopped abruptly at the office door. There was no sign of Mike. Marcus McFinney was sitting at Mike's desk, with a couple burly security guards behind him.

"Eric Carter," McFinney said. "It's been too long but I'm happy to say that the Council has taken over Don's and you're fired."

#

The security guys grabbed my keys and hustled me to the main gate. Marcus strolled along behind them. More security guys prowled the yard, searching it.

Mike was standing by his car, looking grim. He shrugged, though. "I've been fired by better people than this over muscled Irish shitburger. Want to go get roaring drunk? I'm buying."

Marcus gave us a small, ironic wave. "Bye bye. God, that felt good!"

I wanted to go back to my apartment, but I let Mike talk me into a drink. Marcus stood watching us, grinning.

Mike hopped in the car and spun his tires going out of the parking lot, slinging gravel. I gave Marcus a one-finger salute and followed Mike to the nearest bar, Marv's Place. Marv's was a bar where the bouncers got a lot of bouncing experience, and the furniture was cheap or bolted to the floor. Someone had barfed recently, and a sullen-looking waitress was cleaning it up. I walked around the mess and found Mike. "Nice place."

"Cheap beer. Hookers. Bar fights. Everything I like in a bar!" He motioned for me to sit across from him. "I didn't expect the Council to take a hand so soon."

"But they control Don's now, and we're fired. How is that even legal? Does the Council own Don's too?"

Mike didn't know. "Possession is nine-tenths of the law. They have possession and it will take lawsuits to get them out. Unless Mr. Thornburg has leverage I don't know about, we won't see the inside of Don's for at least a year, if ever. Hope you had money saved."

"I'll make it." I wasn't as confident as I sounded. Money was tight already. Bourbon tastes, remember. "And you?"

"I'm still a cop and the Blackwood family will still need me for special jobs, if my friends there can sneak them past McFinney," he said. "I can send jobs your way if you need them, but you may have to cross some lines."

"I hope I don't have to go down that road."

"I would love to be a fly on the wall when this Leah Thornburg bitch figures out that she doesn't really have any power, whatever Marcus McFinney told her to get her to go against her dad," Mike said.

"You think she turned against her dad?" That thought had crossed my mind too. If McFinney and her were a couple, they were probably working together.

"McFinney will use her and dump her," Mike said.

"You don't think she can handle him?"

"Hell no. He'll chew her up and spit her out like the traitorous little piece of shit she is."

I thought about my experiences with Leah Thornburg and wasn't so sure. Even fifteen years ago she was scary good at manipulating people.

"You underestimate women," I said.

"And you respect them. That's why I get laid a lot more than you."

Yeah, chauvinist pig in more ways than one, but right now Mike was the only ally I had except Robinette. How much could I trust him? I had no idea.

"You're in the wrong business," Mike said. "Private Eye isn't a job for decent people, and you're decent." He paused to watch a waitress in tight blue jeans and platform heels wiggle past. "Your job would eat you alive except you're big and have that resting thug face thing going." He grinned. "First night we worked together you scared the crap out of me.

You looked like you were figuring out which of my knees to break. After a couple nights, I realized that you were harmless."

"Harmless isn't how I would describe myself," I said. "Does Robert Thornburg know what happened at Don's?"

Mike shrugged. "Probably not. He won't be able to stop it, not if Leah is playing for the other side. He looks like he's losing, so everyone stays quiet or joins the winning side. Profiles in courage, aren't they?" He paused to watch an argument a couple tables over get loud. It didn't turn into a fistfight, though, and he turned away. "We didn't exactly fight for Thornburg either. Is he worth fighting for?"

"He raised Robinette as his daughter. That makes him okay to me."

"Yeah? What did he do with her mother?"

I felt the color drain out of my face.

"You never thought about that, did you, tough guy?" Mike shrugged. "I bet she went back to the Wild and died of old age when she was twenty-five, just like all the other Mangi women. That's the kind of guy we work for. I guess I should say 'worked for.'"

I wished that I didn't believe him, but I did. Robert Thornburg's Island of decency probably didn't extend to Robinette's mother. I certainly never heard anything about her. "You don't have to convince me. He's a bastard."

"No, but you keep convincing yourself that deep down he has a spark of good," Mike said. "And maybe he does, but it's just a spark in a cold, hard, ruthless man. If he wasn't a bastard the other families would have taken his power away long ago. So, remember the kind of guy you're fighting for." He suddenly grinned. "Speaking of fights, want to start one?"

"Beating up random rednecks? Not tonight. I already have a headache."

"Oh come on. I challenged your tough guy status. Now is your chance to prove yourself. What about beating up a couple of McFinney's thugs?"

"They're here?"

"God, you're a crap PI." He pointed them out. "Watch this." He eased over to a table full of big, boisterous guys in shit-kicker boots and denim jackets with the sleeves cut off, then slid back to our table. "Let's see if they give us fifty dollars' worth of entertainment."

The big guys wandered over to McFinney's security guys and stood around the table. One of them poured a pitcher of beer over the nearest security guy's head and said an obviously insincere "oops." The bar went quiet, with everyone turning toward the brewing fight.

Mike grabbed my arm. "Head for the door. This will get ugly fast."

It did, starting at the table and spreading rapidly, as if everyone in the bar was waiting for an excuse to hit random people around them. I ducked a roundhouse punch from a five-foot-nothing woman in a ridiculously short miniskirt, then sidestepped a flying chair. Mike plowed through the crowd, whooping and knocking people aside, starting new clusters of fights. We got to the door and glanced back. McFinney's guys were trapped in the fight, taking damage, but dealing out more.

Mike gave me a fist bump. "At least they got a few bruises."

There wasn't much more to say. I slunk home, feeling like a beaten puppy despite the fight. I wondered how I was going to make it without my job. I hoped Robinette would be asleep so I wouldn't have to tell her about getting fired, but she was still up, watching videos. She looked up when I came in. "What happened?"

I told her. When I finished, she asked, "Do you trust Mike?"

"We don't have much choice on that."

"But do you trust him?"

"Not enough to tell him where you are." He certainly suspected she was here, though. Where else would she be?

"They'll figure it out," Robinette said. She sighed. "Too bad if Leah is going against dad. She made everything a competition, even when I told her it wasn't. I didn't care if my grades and scores on the standardized tests tromped hers. I didn't even tell her about them. I didn't rub it in that I always beat her. She found out anyway and every time I won, she hated me more."

"She's the heir, either her or her brother. Why should she care if you're smarter?"

"I'm half apewoman. Of course it drives her nuts that I'm head and shoulders smarter. She got into Harvard because she was a Thornburg. I got in because I was smart."

I wondered about Leah's twin brother Tom. The brief, one-sided fight with Robinette seemed to leave a big impression on him, and the rest of the time I was with the Thornburgs he left Robinette alone. He still treated the servants and security people like crap. I wondered if he eventually learned the wisdom of not hacking off his dad's workers.

"Does Leah still treat servants and security people like dirt?" I asked.

"Tom and her both," Robinette said. "The security people hate him. Her too, but they're afraid of her. If you think Dad's security people will go against her, you're wrong, not unless Dad is there and even then, they will probably try to stay out of it. He can be vicious but she's sneaky and way more vicious."

I thought about calling Mr. Thornburg. He gave Mike and I his direct line when he visited Don's. If he didn't already know about the Council's move, though, he was slipping enough that it probably wasn't worth calling him.

Just as I had that thought, he called me. "Did you see any more of Robinette before the Council got there?"

I glanced at Robinette sitting beside me, then lied. "No. The gate opened, and a coyote tried to come through, but no sign of her on the other side."

"Too bad but maybe we can still salvage this." He asked me how often the Gate at Don's Auto Body opened and how long it stayed open. When I finished, he said, "Good. Unpredictable enough they probably won't put an expedition through. I thought it might have settled down enough that they could."

I hadn't thought of it, but an expedition through that Gate made sense if Robinette was hanging around the other side of it.

I wanted to ask him why he was letting the Council act against him but didn't know how to ask without hacking him off. Diminished power or not, I didn't want Mr. Thornburg angry at me.

I glanced at Robinette. She was glaring at the phone as though she wanted to reach through it and wring her dad's neck.

"You're still employed," Mr. Thornburg said. "I still control the bank accounts, so you're on paid vacation for now." He paused. "You're a private detective. I may be able to use one I can trust. What do you think of my daughter Leah?"

"She's dating the guy who just tried to shitcan me, so I'm not a fan."

"You didn't like her when you were my bodyguard, though you tried to hide it."

So much for my acting ability. When I feel something, it shows on my face. Not a good thing for a private eye. "She's your daughter, so what I thought of her didn't matter. I would have taken a bullet for her the same as I would have for you." Actually, there might have been a little hesitation for Leah or her brother Tom, maybe enough that the bullet would have hit the intended target. Mr. Thornburg didn't need to know that, though.

They say that a professional bodyguard doesn't have to like the person they're guarding. I don't believe that, not if they're guarding a big enough prick. That's something anyone who hires bodyguards should keep in mind.

"Anything I can do for you now?" I asked.

Mr. Thornburg hesitated, then said, "Hang tight. You may be back at Don's in a couple days."

Going back to Don's that quick didn't seem likely, but I didn't say so. Robert Thornburg was a wounded lion, with hyaenas closing in for the kill. *And the hyaenas won't forget I was on his side.*

Chapter Seven:
Searching for Jimmy Nelson

I finished my morning nap and spent the afternoon in private eye mode. I found Jimmy Nelson's house. He lived in one of Chicago's middle-range suburbs, still nice but going seedy around the edges, with big city problems edging out there. Last place you would expect a Mangi underground fighter, but that probably made it easier for him to pass as human. It was a two-hour drive from my apartment, but I impulsively drove to his house without calling ahead. Robinette wanted to join me, but I talked her out of it. The trip would probably be like a lot of private eye work, a lot of boredom with no payout at the end. That described a lot of my life, come to think of it.

Jimmy Nelson married well, though he and his wife must have made an odd-looking couple. His wife kept her last name, Powell, Evette Powell. She was a tall Jamaican woman in her late twenties, at least six feet tall, with long legs and arms, pretty in light green shorts and a sleeveless white t-shirt that left her slender midriff bare.

She opened the door to the ranch-style house that she apparently shared with Jimmy, but stood in the entrance and didn't invite me in. "You know something about Jimmy?"

I shook my head. "Only that he's missing. One of his business partners asked me to find him." I handed her my card. "I'm a private detective, working for..." I paused, not thrilled to admit I was working for an organized crime boss.

"The gang? Zane?" Her lips tightened. "They're finally getting off their asses. Amazing. He disappeared over three months ago. He went on some big mysterious fight trip he claimed would make us rich and never came back. I thought he was dead. I don't trust the men he hung out with just before he left." Her face went angry. "He'll wish he was dead if he was catting around all this time with me sitting here worrying."

"From what little I know of the case, he probably couldn't come back," I said. That was pure guess, but it sounded as though the Gate families lured him back to the Wild, maybe for one of their hunts or maybe simply to kill him. That probably made Evette Powell a widow, but that was total speculation on my part.

"Is he hurt?" She asked. "If anyone touched a hair on his head, I'll cut out their heart and stomp on it."

"I'm just getting started looking for him, but he may be on the run from someone. He probably can't call without bringing them down on you."

She studied my face, then abruptly stepped back. "Come in. We need to talk."

When we were inside, she put a finger to her lips and wrote on a notepad. "Guys in a gray panel truck watching. Have directional microphone."

The watchers showed up around a week after Jimmy disappeared. Jimmy's gang friends spotted them and pointed them out to Evette. According to the gang members, the watchers weren't local cops. They had good equipment but weren't stealthy enough to be feds.

That probably meant they weren't Council Police either. The Gate families only bought the best, people or equipment.

Who was watching Evette, then? Was there yet another player in this already convoluted game? Yet another mystery? The timing of Jimmy's disappearance was suspicious, far too close to when Robinette was kidnapped for me to be comfortable with the coincidence. The watchers showed up around a week after Jimmy disappeared. Why?

Jimmy left, supposedly for a special fight, with a lot of money at stake. Before he left, Evette met a couple of the guys involved, but couldn't describe them well enough to be useful, beyond that they were young and wealthy but trying to hide their wealth, wearing blue jeans, but also watches and shoes that cost six months of a working person's salary. Rich people trying to hide their wealth usually forget about the little things—shoes, watches, belts and pens. I notice those things, could afford the rich people versions back in my bourbon days. Evette had enough contact with wealth to notice the expensive trinkets too.

I tried to get some idea what happened to Jimmy. Maybe someone tricked him into a Russian Roulette hunt with him as the hunted. A Mangi fighter with years of experience in our world? Hunting him would not end well for the hunters unless they were very smart and experienced. I wondered if the hunt ended with dead family members.

What, if anything, did Jimmy's disappearance have to do with Robinette? Probably nothing, though the timing put it within a couple weeks of when Robinette got stranded in the Wild. Coincidences do happen and you can drive yourself nuts trying to make sense of them. A Russian Roulette-style hunt with Jimmy as the hunted explained several mysteries, but probably put them in a different puzzle from Robinette.

The Mangi hunt theory didn't explain why someone was watching Evette. Were they afraid she would start a search for Jimmy? She wouldn't go to the police when Jimmy made a living in underground, illegal fighting.

Did Evette even know where Jimmy came from? She didn't mention the Wild and I didn't bring it up. Where did she think Jimmy was from if she didn't know about the Wild? Humans are a diverse lot, but Mangi are way outside the normal human range. Jimmy was tall for a Mangi, though, and a lot of the other differences were subtle, things an anthropologist would notice, but the average person would miss, especially if the Mangi dressed like a human and hid the more obvious differences.

Why would the Blackwood family tolerate a Mangi making his life on this side of the Gates? Probably because he kept a low profile and had ties to local organized crime. Gate families were overwhelmingly powerful, but even they avoided clashes with organized crime. Why fight thugs with guns and bad attitudes if you didn't have to?

The Gate family young bucks might not share that wisdom, though,

Evette offered to make sketches of the rich young men but wrote that it would take a few days. "I'll get it right, though."

I got Evette's cell phone number before I left and gave her my number and email address. She wrote a final message on the notepad before I left, "Get him back. My son needs a good man to look up to, and Jimmy is a good man."

I promised to try, then left. I watched for anyone following me when I left and wasn't surprised when I spotted a tail. I didn't try to lose them. If they were from the Gate families, which they almost certainly were, they knew where I lived.

#

Robinette embraced the modern, like the Internet and TV, for the next few days but she never slept deeply, something I noticed more now that I wasn't working.

I gave her plenty of space. sleeping on the couch while she slept in the bedroom, but traffic noise and electric hums made her restless now that she wasn't sleep deprived. I turned off everything electronic in the bedroom and everything I didn't have to have running in the rest of the apartment, which helped. Amazing how many sounds you don't notice after a while.

I kept my usual crazy schedule, staying awake during my normal shift hours and watching videos with headphones on. I was restless, though. I was used to patrolling the junkyard regularly, alternating foot patrols and using the cart. Mike usually found some excuse when it was his turn to patrol on foot.

It's amazing what you get used to. Walking around a dimly lit junkyard in the small hours of the morning, winding through a maze of wrecked cars, tired enough that the eyes play tricks on you, making you think you see movement. Most times it's nothing, but just when you think it's imagination, you stumble across something real, like a stray dog with a broken chain wrapped around wreckage the dog is about to pull down on himself, or a forty-pound snapping turtle that crawled under the fence and wedged itself under the bumper of an old Chevy. That snapping turtle was a bitch to rescue, too stupid to realize we were trying to help, but strong and incredibly fast with its bite. Mike got twelve stitches on his arm from that adventure and the doctor told him he was lucky the turtle didn't bite off a finger.

All that and I missed the place.

Robinette came out and sat by me, leaning her head on my shoulder. "I'm sorry you're semi-fired and wrapped up in family crap over me."

"You were desperate and probably didn't know I would be on the other side of the Gate."

"I sort of did know," Robinette said. "A few months ago, I asked Dad what happened to you, and he told me about the rogue Gate. That was the only reason I knew it was there. Finding it from the other side took a lot of thinking and even more luck."

I tried to imagine what that trip was like, walking alone for months, not sure where she started from, with only the stars to tell her the direction, hiding from hostile Mangi during the day and big carnivores at night.

"You're incredibly tough and lucky as hell."

"Mostly lucky and I used up a dozen lifetimes worth of luck in those two months."

Robinette knew a little more about other Gate families than I did, but never paid much attention to her dad's comments about his competitors and colleagues, many of whom were probably from Gate families. Those names were part of an adult world she didn't care about as a teenager, then she was away at college. Some of her fellow students at Harvard probably came from Gate families, but they wouldn't know about the Wild until they turned twenty-one. I did get a few more names from her.

How did the Gate families keep the Wild out of newspapers and Internet blogs? I sensed that Robinette knew more than she would tell me about that, but I guessed that they owned most of the media outlets and were major advertisers in the rest, so leaks to major media never made it far. The Internet was harder, but they didn't have to keep the Wild completely off it. They just had to put it in the same realm with lake monsters, bigfoot, and secret rich people cities on Mars. They may have even spread that last meme deliberately to compete with leaks about the Wild.

I thought about exposing the Wild or threatening to. Robinette's blood or saliva would prove our story to anthropologists, or at least prove that her origins were very unusual.

The Gate families could squelch anything we did, though, force any anthropologist who published about her DNA to retract the story, or retract it for them while sending the anthropologist to the Wild.

All our paths were blocked, not because the families were smarter than us but because they were so powerful. Outwitting the nine-hundred-pound gorilla is meaningless if you can't hurt it and it can end the fight with one punch.

"You're getting discouraged," Robinette said. "Is this whole thing hopeless? Should I get in a few more good meals and go back to the Wild? If that's where I'll end up anyway, why drag you and my dad down with me?" She paused. "I don't care about the cop bastard you work with, but I worry about you. Sometimes Dad too, though he's a lot of things that I wish he wasn't."

"You wouldn't really go back, would you?"

"No. I guess not, but I don't want to drag you down with me."

I thought about asking her what happened to her mother, but she was already feeling bad enough. That question sat in my mind though and sapped my respect for Robert Thornburg.

Chapter Eight:
Leah Thornburg Plays Nice

Just after breakfast the next morning, Leah Thornburg called me from Don's Auto Parts.

I recognized the number and hesitated before I answered.

She introduced herself, then added, "I'm sorry you got fired. I may be able to help."

"Your boyfriend shitcanned me," I said. "Why should I talk to you?"

"Because you're sitting in front of a freight train of bad and I can help you get off the tracks."

"And are you driving the freight train?"

"No. I'm trying to stay out of its way and salvage something for my family. Want to meet and chat?"

"No." I hung up.

I never liked Leah as a preteen years ago, though I tried not to show it. She was my boss's daughter after all. My attitude must have filtered through despite my efforts. I was surprised she even remembered me, though.

"At least I left an impression."

"She called you eye-candy," Robinette said.

"When I was a bodyguard? She was twelve. I don't know whether to be flattered or feel like barfing."

Leah called again seconds later. "You're in this. The only question is can you survive?"

I hung up again and didn't pick up when she called a third time.

"It wouldn't hurt to listen to her," Robinette said. "She isn't that bright. You might learn something."

"But it's so much more fun hanging up on her." I finally picked up after a couple rings when Leah tried again. "Your boyfriend didn't want to talk last night. What changed?"

"I'm not Marcus," she said. "Meet me over coffee and I'll tell you what is really going on."

I gave her the name of a coffee shop, figuring I could stand her up if I decided to. "I'll be there in half an hour."

After I hung up, I turned to Robinette. "Why would she want to meet me?"

"Maybe she knows I'm here and wants you out of the apartment so they can try something."

That thought had crossed my mind. "Too obvious."

"Curiosity is a powerful motivator," Robinette said. "You think it's a trap, but you still want to go."

"Will she even be there?"

"Probably. If someone grabs me, sister dearest won't be here to watch. She knows what I can do. She'll send half a dozen big guys, but she'll be somewhere else."

"The families can send as much muscle as they need," I said. "If Leah knows you're here and wants to get you, we've lost. Doesn't matter if I'm here."

I was curious, as Robinette suspected. The meeting smelled like a trap, but I wanted to go. I normally wouldn't worry about security. My apartment was a remnant of my bourbon days, upscale, with keyed entry, security cameras and armed guards onsite. It was also too expensive for me, gradually draining my savings; Against the Gate families, that security was worthless. If they wanted Robinette, they could take her, whether I was there or not. If this meeting was an excuse to get me out of my apartment, it was pointless.

I called Mike and told him about Leah's call, adding, "She may try to search my apartment while I'm out."

"I'll find some reason to drive by while you're gone. Can't have Leah Thornburg rooting around in your underwear drawer."

He didn't ask about Robinette, but probably figured she was there. I was putting a lot of trust in Mike, with little reason to trust him beyond his talk of lines he wouldn't cross. He sold out the police and a probable murder victim to work for the families. Why wouldn't he sell me out? Still, he was the closest thing to an ally we had.

I turned to Robinette after I hung up. "Know how to handle a gun?" I asked.

"Rifle and pistol," she said.

Private eyes don't usually shoot people in real life. Police take a dim view of private eyes and when private eyes kill people, police check out the circumstances carefully. If they aren't satisfied that it was self-defense, the private eye loses their license and probably goes to jail.

Still, being a private eye is a tough business, so I have guns, not just the ones from Don's. I brought out a semi-automatic shotgun. "This thing kicks like an elephant, but it's the only thing I have here that's good for close-up work." I showed her how to use it. "Use it only if you're in imminent danger of dying."

Robinette had a burner cell phone with my number on speed dial, so hopefully I could get back to help if someone tried to grab her. "You know the drill. Don't open the door or let anyone know you're here. I'll have the key and I'll say something through the door before I use it."

With that I left. It was a sunny morning, warm but nice enough I wished I could focus on the day instead of gearing up for a confrontation. Robinette and I were wandering in the dark, with a crap storm howling around us, though. Leah Thornburg probably knew what was going on. I couldn't trust what she said, but the most convincing lies are mostly true so I might learn something even from her lies.

I made a wide circle around my apartment, watching for tails, ready to head back if Robinette called. I didn't see Mike, but he was good enough that I probably wouldn't. I didn't see anyone following me either, but the families would use professionals, and I probably wouldn't spot them.

After a couple circles, I drove to the coffee shop. It was broad daylight, in an upscale part of town and I chose the spot, so a trap seemed unlikely, but the families had enough power to grab me from a crowd and make the incident disappear, though they were usually more discreet.

Leah was alone at a table near the door, sipping a latte. She smiled a warm and apparently genuine smile when I came in. "I thought you were standing me up."

I didn't return the smile and didn't sit down. "I almost did. I can't imagine anything we have to say to each other."

"Robinette is my half-sister. I don't like her much, but I like what my dearest daddy wanted to do to her even less."

"And what was he doing to her?"

"That's not my story to tell, but he planned to screw with her in a way that makes getting stranded in the Wild look pleasant."

"I've been to the Wild. Nothing would make stranding in the Wild look pleasant." I almost added, 'for two months' but caught myself just in time. What would I ask if I just saw Robinette briefly before she ran back through the Gate? "Did you leave her with food or weapons?"

"I didn't leave her in the Wild," Leah said. "Was she carrying weapons when you saw her at Don's?"

I was pretty sure Leah was lying about not having anything to do with the stranding, but then I was lying too. She was a smooth, accomplished liar, with no tells I could spot and an answer ready for everything I asked. I sparred with her verbally for a while, then said, "You asked me here for a reason. What was it?"

"I want you to stay out of this and I'll pay you to do it. You'll get three months' severance pay, and I'll keep you in mind for future jobs, but you have nothing to do with Dad and stay away from Don's. If Robinette somehow gets through and comes to you, tell her I urgently need to talk to her."

I sat down across from her. "The severance is nice, but you promised me answers. Not getting any yet."

"Dad risked everything the families have built up on something that wouldn't work anyway, so the Council voted to make his plan impossible. They couldn't kill Robinette without getting the Council Police involved, but they could return her to the Wild."

"Return her? Has she ever even been to the Wild? 'Returning' her to the Wild is a death sentence." I carefully avoided mentioning that they left her there tied up.

"The only other choice was to go to the Council police, and they would kill her outright." Leah took a sip of latte, "I don't like my half-sister and I hate it that Dad screwed her half-ape mom, but she is sort of family, so I would rather see her have a tiny chance than no chance."

"But you can't tell me what Mr. Thornburg was trying to do."

"I could, but I'm not planning to. You can figure it out yourself. Dad paid her last Harvard boyfriend to get close to her. Find out why and you'll figure out the rest."

Was that true? I had no idea. I tried a shot in the dark. "Was your dad trying to make Robinette his heir?"

"A hopped-up ape sitting on the Gate family Council? Do you think the families would stand for that?" She smiled coldly. "Even the great Robert Thornburg couldn't ram that down their throats. I'm the heir, not officially, but I vote his seat on the Council when he can't make it. There isn't anybody else."

"Your twin brother?"

"Tom knows not to get in my way."

That, at least, I could believe. Sometimes it isn't an event that changes someone, but the way they react to it. Tom Thornburg wasn't the same after I pulled Robinette off him. He lost more than that fight. Self-confidence maybe?

"Is there anything else?" I asked.

"How does it feel to be poor?" She asked. "Driving a crap car? Wearing last year's clothes? Working weird hours at a creepy, boring God-awful job?"

"It's a life."

"Not much of one." She handed me her card. "You don't owe my dad any loyalty. When you realize that, give me a call and I can make your life suck less. I'm trying to save the family after Dad put it in jeopardy. The Council could take away everything. I'm not going to be poor because Dad's an idiot."

I walked back to my car, half-expecting someone to jump me, but no one did. I called Robinette's burner phone when I got to the car. "Everything okay?"

"Quiet here. What did sister dearest want?"

I walked her through the conversation. "A lot of nothing. Why does she really want me on her side?"

Neither of us had an answer.

I tried calling Mike when I got to the apartment, but the call went to voicemail. What would I have told him anyway? Did Leah Thornburg call him too? If she didn't, why not? Maybe she called him and convinced him to switch allegiance.

At least Robinette was recovering from her ordeal in the Wild, resting and eating the food her body needed so badly. Her cabin fever got worse, though. She hadn't been outside since the first morning after she came through the Gate and probably wouldn't get out again anytime soon. I bought groceries on my way home from meeting Leah, picking up female-specific items using my dwindling supply of cash and stashing them in cloth bags to make them less obvious. That might be paranoid, but I didn't want to underestimate the Gate families. Could they get my credit card records? Sure. I would if I was in their position.

Maybe Mike was acting when he exchanged insults with Marcus. That sounded paranoid, but why not? Maybe his sponsors in the Blackwood family told him to support Marcus. I knew he was bribable. Why would he stay loyal?

I mentioned those suspicions to Robinette. She shrugged. "If he switched sides, he knows I'm on this side of the Gate, so Marcus and probably Leah do too. They can figure out where I am. Why would they leave us alone?"

I didn't have an answer for that. I was probably reading too much into one unanswered phone call. I circled back to Leah's comments about Robinette's college boyfriend, Randall Dailey. "Remember anything weird about him?"

"Not really. He was an upgrade from the other guys I dated. I can't stand stupid guys, but I like some muscle too. I tried jocks but they realized I was stronger than them, even when I tried to hide it, and they hated it. So, I mostly dated guys who had brain power, but not as much muscle as I wanted. Randall was the total package, brains and muscle. I should have been head over heels, but I never felt close to him, and he wasn't that into the relationship, though I don't think he cheated on me. That would have been a very bad move."

Leah hinted that Mr. Thornburg pushed Randall toward Robinette. Why? Was there something in Randall's family background that caused Mr. Thornburg to want him with Robinette? Would he merge some key financial interest with the Thornburg family empire? Gate families operated a lot like the old European monarchies, pushing their kids into marriages that added to family power. But what would Randall bring to the table? Would something about that relationship turn the Council against Robert Thornburg?

That was useless mental thrashing without more information.

Robinette sat beside me on the couch, our knees touching. "Your brain is going a mile a minute. What are you thinking?"

I didn't share all my thoughts, but I asked, "Did Randall say anything about his family? Any ties your dad would like or object to?"

"He had one grandparent from India, but Dad isn't prejudiced that way."

"Are the other Gate families prejudiced? Aren't they mostly Anglo, mostly 'trace their line back to the Mayflower' types? Would they have a problem with India ancestry?"

She shook her head. "If he was Black, Irish, Jewish or Italian, that might be a problem, though I doubt it. One-quarter India Indian? They wouldn't care. New rich parents might set them off, but his family has been moderately wealthy for generations. I don't think he's the problem. Dad pushed a half-Mangi daughter through the Council. They wouldn't balk at me marrying a full human over ethnicity."

Another dead end. I told myself we were eliminating possibilities, zeroing in on the right answer, but we seemed to be eliminating all possible answers.

"Leah was screwing with you," Robinette said. "She's good, at least at that. She dragged Randall into this as a distraction."

"And I'm grasping at straws, so I went for it." I leaned my head back and closed my eyes. Randall could easily be a distraction, in which case meeting Leah was a total waste. "Whatever the reason, though, the Council had to be involved, right? No one else could shut your dad's Gate down."

If the Council was working against Mr. Thornburg, something caused the break. It must have involved Robinette, or the Council wouldn't have stranded her. What could it have been? I could ask Mr. Thornburg, but he might not answer or might not tell the truth.

#

Mr. Thornburg called later that afternoon. "I hear you met my daughter Leah."

I felt a brief flare of resentment. Mr. Thornburg must have people watching me. I pushed the resentment aside. In his place, I would have people watching me.

"She called me and claimed to have information I needed. When we met, she danced around, hinted that you were up to something the Gate Council didn't want, then sort of offered me a job."

"Did you take it?"

"No," I said. "It wasn't anything solid, and if she wanted me to work for her, she shouldn't have let Marcus fire me."

"Don't worry. Marcus can't fire you."

"I'm not worried," I lied. Until the next check was in my bank account, I would worry. I didn't have much of a cushion, though the money for tracking down Jimmy Nelson helped.

"Do you mind if I ask what happened to bring this on?"

"You can ask, but I don't know myself." He paused. "All of this blindsided me and not much in life does. Leah stabbed me in the back in the Council, which makes no sense. If she wanted power, all she had to do was wait. I was getting her ready, letting her fill in for me at the Council, giving her more control. A few more years and I planned to fade into retirement. She had all the power she could handle and knew she would have more."

"You weren't planning on making Robinette your heir?"

"Hell no. Robinette is smart and tough, but the Council would never accept her. Even if the Council was okay with her, being head of a Gate family isn't the life for her. She's a good person and the Council is no place for good people. She's better off without it. I have a trust fund set up, enough for the rest of her life." He laughed bitterly. "Make that, she would have been better off without it. She has to stay alive until we straighten this out." He cleared his throat. "Everything I just said is confidential. This conversation never happened."

"I understand." I didn't know what to think. Mr. Thornburg was tough, reserved, but he didn't come off that way this time. Was he at the end of his rope, sharing his fears or was he trying to win my sympathy? Why would he bother? Why would any of the Thornburgs care what I thought?

"We need to get her out of there," he said. "She needs food. She looked half-starved."

I glanced at Robinette, who was nibbling on a roast beef sandwich. An almost overwhelming part of me wanted to tell him she was safe, but the reasons we didn't tell him before still applied. I wondered why he didn't yell at me for supposedly scaring her back into the Wild. I would have.

"I'll be busy cleaning up Leah's mess, so you may not hear from me for a few days," Mr. Thornburg said. "But if you find out anything about Robinette, call me, any time, day or night."

I filled Robinette in on Mr. Thornburg's end of the conversation as soon as he hung up. "He claims he doesn't know why Leah turned against him or why the Council sided with her," I said. "If he really doesn't know, how could we figure it out?"

"Leah is vicious and not very smart by my standards," Robinette said. "But if she knew she was the heir, she wouldn't rock that boat."

"Maybe Marcus McFinney talked her into doing something stupid," I said.

"She likes bad boys, and he is definitely one, but she uses them, not the other way around."

I had my doubts about that. McFinney struck me as bad boy grown up and supercharged, not someone Leah Thornburg could easily use. Then again, I could be underestimating Leah. If Mr. Thornburg thought she could hold her own in the Gate family Council, there was more to her than I had seen so far. I remembered her warm, sincere looking smile. She was certainly a good actress.

"Did your dad try to get her to drop McFinney?"

"No. McFinney is bad news, but she's an adult. She can handle herself."

Again, I had my doubts, both about her handling herself and about Mr. Thornburg letting the relationship develop. McFinney was bad news and he also worked for a rival family. Would Robert Thornburg really take a hands-off approach when McFinney started seeing his daughter?

The conversation trailed off with no further revelations.

I called Mike again, and this time got through. I barely recognized his voice when he said, "Hello."

"Are you okay?"

"Hell no. I'm in the hospital with my nose rebroken."

"The Gate families?"

"Probably not. My airbag went off from a fender-bender. I might have been okay if your rock-throwing hottie hadn't already broken my nose." He coughed, then swore. "I'm out of action a couple days and you need eyes in the back of your head. Learn anything from Leah Thornburg?"

I told him about our conversation, ending with, "A lot of nothing. And you ended up in the hospital."

"I'll add it to your tab. Meanwhile, the second shift nurse's body goes in and out at just the right places. I wonder if she comforts patients in a special way. Go all out for the men in blue."

"She'll probably end up poisoning you."

"I do have that effect on women."

After he hung up, I turned to Robinette. "There goes our one potential ally."

"Somebody trying to poison him? I can help. He's a crap human being."

"You're more of a kick them in the groin and slam their heads against the wall kind of girl."

She grinned. "You know me well. Still, if someone poisons him, I won't get in their way."

#

Randall Dailey, Robinette's last college boyfriend, was probably a dead end, but I didn't have any other leads, so that afternoon I did a deep dive into his life, using social media and public records.

Another thunderstorm rumbled through, bringing buckets of rain sheeting against the windows. How did Robinette survive in the Wild without shelter when the rain and wind and lightning slashed down at her? I wanted to know more, but she withdrew into herself while the storm roared, curling up in a blanket with one arm across my chest.

I kept digging, even checking court records for any hint that his family had ties to organized crime. That last bit was a long shot, but organized crime would dearly love to control Gates. I circled back to that. Gates would be incredibly useful to the cartels or even a big street gang, giving them a perfect, undetectable smuggling network and a perfect place to dump bodies. Toxic waste and landfill too.

Why would Mr. Thornburg be in touch with Randall if his family was involved in organized crime, though? For that matter, why would he be in contact with the kid at all? Was Randall secretly Robinette's bodyguard, hired by her father without her knowing it? Maybe, but if he wasn't a bodyguard, his relationship with Mr. Thornburg was a mystery and solving it might be the thread that unraveled the overall mystery. I had no idea how to solve it, though, and Leah might have made up the relationship to screw with me.

Mr. Thornburg didn't talk much about the Council when I worked for him, but he said enough that I pieced together some of what it did. Gate families were rich enough they could treat the Wild as am unspoiled playground, far more pristine than any place on our Earth. Whatever else you could say about them, the Council wanted to keep the Wild pristine.

At least that was true fifteen years ago. Was it still? No matter how much money and power you have, it is never enough. Maybe some families wanted to exploit the Wild more. There were plenty of ways to make money in the Wild. Smuggling and hiding bodies were easy ones, but the Wild also had scarce natural resources for the taking. The richest gold and silver mines were untapped there. Oil still seeped out of the ground in some places, like it did on our Earth before we started using it. Diamonds still sat untouched where they were found on our Earth, waiting for someone to pick them up.

All of that required changing the Wild, making it less pristine, introducing pollution. Even picking up diamonds meant getting to them, either by creating more Gates or crossing the Wild, flying or going cross country. Enriching yourself in the Wild meant changing it, and the Council saw even small changes as a slippery slope toward turning the Wild into another polluted, messed up version of our Earth. They had selfish motives, but I was with the Council on that one. The Wild needed to stay the way it was.

Even people as rich as Gate families get in financial trouble, though. Fortunes don't last forever, no matter how big they are and no matter how many Senators and congressmen the families rent. Eventually, generations come along that take power and wealth for granted and it slips through their fingers. What if Gate families ran out of money? The Wild would be a huge temptation, or maybe organized crime got their tentacles into a Gate family.

How could any of that get Robinette stranded, though? Was the Thornburg family in trouble? If Mr. Thornburg partnered with organized crime to keep a veneer of wealth, he would hide that bargain from the other families, and if they couldn't figure it out I certainly couldn't. I tried anyway, researching Thornburg companies I remembered. I asked Robinette if she knew of any financial problems, not just in the Thornburg companies but in any Gate families. Nothing.

"Did you see any sign in the Wild that somebody was doing more than vacationing there? Any sign of trucks or airplanes? Mangi with anything unusual?"

"I mentioned the Mangi with a Swiss army knife," Robinette said. "I also saw one with an honest to God rusty sword. I would have given my trust fund for that thing."

She didn't know what kind of sword it was and also didn't recognize it when we searched for it on the Internet. "It's sort of like quite a few broadswords, but not exactly like any of them."

So, we had yet another mystery, or maybe another piece of the same mystery. The mystery sword might not be important. Maybe someone in a Gate family had it custom made and lost it on a hunting trip. One sword didn't prove anyone was smuggling through the Wild. Robinette made a sketch of it anyway. Maybe someone with historical knowledge could recognize it. Then what? Probably nothing unless we traced it to a specific family. Even then, why would a lost sword in the Wild matter?

"Everything's a dead end," I said. "I'm a crap detective."

"Gate families are good at keeping their business private," Robinette said. "Most people don't even know they exist."

"Does the Council let you make money in the Wild now?" I asked.

"Not usually. If you need to make money there, you aren't rich enough to be a Gate family." There were a few exceptions. Families raised vegetables and meat animals in the Wild and sold their surplus to a very exclusive circle of friends and family members for very high prices. Beyond that, almost no businesses were allowed there. Even sewage from Gate family mansions on the other side was rerouted back through the Gate, as was exhaust from heating and cooling systems.

"Keep it pristine," I said. "They don't mess around with that."

On the hunting trips fifteen years ago, we went by electric cart, stayed within two miles of the compound where we started and made sure every cartridge case was accounted for. No cars or trucks or planes over there, not even electric cars with over twenty-five mile ranges. From what Robinette saw, the Gate families were still just as strict. "If you lose something over there, even a plastic bag, you pay a huge fine," Robinette said. "The Council takes inventory every month and you have to account for everything you take over there, down to chocolate wrappers and spare underwear."

Those tight controls had to grate on wealthy, entitled people like the Gate families. There had to be friction between the Council and some families. If there was, how would I find out about it, though? More importantly, what would it have to do with Robinette?

I would have been more impressed by the Council's dedication to keeping the Wild clean if they didn't dump their crap in our version of Earth. Granted, it didn't add much to our garbage, but dumping was just another way they made the rest of us wallow in their crap while they didn't have to.

Did any of this relate to Robinette? Probably not. I was mostly venting. I found the Gate families annoying even in my bourbon days and more so now.

I paced restlessly, with my body clock screwed up by not working third shift. If Robinette ended up stranded in the Wild because of inter-Family rivalry, we would never figure it out and Mr. Thornburg didn't know or wouldn't tell us. What did that leave? Only what Leah said, and I couldn't trust a word of that. Still, she wanted me to think the stranding had something to do with Robinette and her college boyfriend.

That brought me back to Randall Dailey. I tried to get a sense of who the guy was. He apparently wasn't broken up about getting dumped by a text. He didn't even mention it on social media. He wasn't currently in a relationship. Robinette was no longer listed as a friend. I looked at his friends and family. His grandparents were still alive and on his friends list, along with three of his great-grandparents. He was now working for a Thornburg-owned company. Did that mean anything? I asked Robinette.

"Dad doesn't usually do hiring and Leah probably wouldn't hire Randall, so it probably isn't important."

"No." I closed my eyes and tried to make sense of the many puzzle pieces swirling around the central mystery of who stranded Robinette and why. The more pieces showed up, the less sense they made, though.

The faint sound of a key turning in my apartment door's lock, almost lost in the thunderstorm, sent my hand streaking to my sidearm. Clara Wolf walked in and flipped on the lights. My ex-girlfriend looked calm, with no water on her clothes and not a hair out of place.

Robinette sat up beside me. "I thought she left her key."

"I made an extra copy," Clara said. "I didn't expect to get replaced this fast. Is she legal?"

I turned to Robinette. "This is my ex, Clara Wolf."

"Clara Wolf, huh?" Robinette grinned. "I knew her as Clara Thornburg. Hi stepmother dearest."

Chapter Nine:
Robinette Lies or Makes a Revelation

"Wolf is my maiden name," Clara said. "I went back to it after the divorce."

"I can't remember if she was the fourth or fifth Mrs. Thornburg," Robinette said. "I was a freshman at Harvard and didn't pay much attention. other than being disgusted by dad sleeping with someone not much older than Leah." She turned to Clara. "You screwed Eric and put surveillance crap on his computer to get dirt on dad so you could break your prenuptial agreement."

It all made sense now. Mike nailed the trophy wife part, except Clara was an ex-trophy wife instead of one cheating on her husband. "I guess I should feel used." I didn't, though. Our relationship felt purely physical from the start. The physical part was good though. "What did you expect to find out from me?"

"Enough to prove the Wild exists," Clara said. "Then he can't discard me like a used Kleenex. He'll have to give my daughter her fair share of the inheritance and give me enough money I don't have to date rich old men."

"Try blackmailing dad with the Wild and you'll end up in an off-the-books federal prison," Robinette said. "Do you understand what the Wild is?"

"It's a different reality where superrich people go to play."

"It's also legally a top-secret part of the federal government's continuity of government program," Robinette said. "Supposedly, top government would go there in a nuclear war."

Clara and I both stared at her. Clara shook her head. "That can't be true."

"Why not?" Robinette pulled her legs under her on the couch. "Dad and his friends rent Senators and spy agency bigwigs. Why not make their playground a perfectly legal secret part of the federal government, complete with its own federal security force? Mansions in the Wild are legally part of the continuity of government program. Exposing that program will get you dead or in jail."

Was that true? Clara didn't seem to buy it. "How would you know that?"

"Sons and daughters get read in when they're twenty-one."

"But not wives?"

"Not dad's trophy wives," Robinette said. "He changes wives more often than he changes his oil. I'm surprised you even know about the Wild. Dad wouldn't tell you."

"I have ways of getting information," Clara said.

"I can imagine," Robinette said. "If pillow talk doesn't work, you hack computers." She stretched and ended up with her arm around me. "If you're smart, you'll leave the Wild alone."

"I don't believe your continuity of government crap," Clara said.

"Either way, the families have a big secret," I said. "And they will smash you like a bug to keep it."

"That I believe more than her crap about government secrets," Clara said. "I won't be as easy to crush as you think."

She leaned in suddenly and kissed me on the lips, then turned to Robinette. "I was here first." She walked away, hips swaying. At the door, she paused. "I'll leave my spare key, and I will be extra careful, in case anyone cares."

When she closed the door, Robinette said, "She'll be back. She left her cellphone. I may have helped it fall out of her pocket and put a tracker on it. That's payback for wiring your apartment for sound."

#

Cabin fever is a real thing. After several days cooped up in my apartment, Robinette and I alternated snapping at each other with apologies and retreats to opposite ends of the apartment. She craved sunlight, opening the balcony door and sitting in the evening sun. She couldn't sit outside because she would be too visible.

I kept going over what we knew, trying to put the pieces together. Robinette refused to confirm or deny what she told Clara about Continuity of Government, saying, "You don't need to know."

If everything the Gate families did really was legal, with the federal government's backing, how could anyone stop them? Revealing their activities would be treason. If congressional or law enforcement investigations got off the ground, they would find only legal activity with good reasons to stay secret. The families could even use federal money to maintain their mansions in the Wild, a line item in some secret budget. It made sense, but I had trouble accepting it.

Part of the reason I was skeptical was that Robinette and I remained untouched and apparently undetected. I took reasonable precautions against normal opponents, but not against federal law enforcement. How could they not know Robinette came through? Her video editing of Don's cameras the night she came through looked flawless to me, but the feds should have experts who could see through it. If the Gate families wanted me dead or in the hospital, they could make it happen, even if I never left my apartment.

Mr. Thornburg called, breaking my spiral of thoughts.

"Go back to Don's Auto Parts tonight," he said. "The Council people are pulling out. Watch yourself, though."

I wanted to cheer, but also felt wary. Getting out of the apartment would be good, but what would I be going back to?

"Mike is in the hospital," I said. I told him why, at least part of it. I couldn't remember if Robinette's edits included her hitting Mike with the rock, so I left that part vague.

I wondered what me going back to Don's meant. Was Mr. Thornburg regaining power in the Council? I wanted to think so but knew not to depend on that.

Mike and I handled most midnight shifts at Don's, with part-timers, retired cops in their early sixties, pulling our days off. "Who will be filling in?"

"We'll line up somebody for the shift," Mr. Thornburg said. "Watch yourself though. My security people will be close, but some of them may have forgotten who signs their paychecks."

A shift at Don's meant leaving Robinette alone all night, but I couldn't tell Mr. Thornburg that. "Mind having someone keep an eye on my apartment? I don't want to come home to booby traps or bugs."

He agreed to arrange security, though with loyalties in flux, that might not mean much. I asked him to keep his people outside the apartment, officially because of uncertain loyalties, but actually so they wouldn't find Robinette.

Going back to Don's seemed too easy and a strong part of me feared a trick. What kind of trick, though? If the Gate families knew Robinette was in my apartment, they could take her. If they wanted to kill me, they could. Don's Auto Body was an ideal place to kill someone, but the families didn't need to be sneaky.

I'm tough. Robert Thornburg's doesn't choose wimps as bodyguards. I'm not as tough as I was fifteen years ago, but I kept up my skills. Still, I knew how little chance I would have against the guys the Gate families could throw at me, or a Gate family sniper. Despite what Mike said about me, I tried to be realistic. The Private Eye business knocked the idealism out of me along with any illusion that being good with my fists or a gun made me a superhero. I couldn't give up on Robinette, but I knew how outclassed we would be in a fight.

I watched for anyone following me on my way to Don's, though, the people I worried about already knew where I was going and when I would get there.

You can get used to almost anything. I had pulled into Don's Auto Parts parking lot hundreds of times. After a while, I stopped noticing how creepy it was, an almost empty parking lot, with the lights by the door and by the parking lot entrance tiny patches almost lost in the darkness. If Mr. Thornburg's security people, or Marcus's, were around, I didn't see them.

Nature loves parts of a city without many people, so Don's had a lot of nature hanging around. A possum scuttled across the parking lot in front of me, short legs moving fast and body moving slow. It stopped in my headlights and glared, not a great survival move, though it hurried on when I honked at it.

Possums and other small animals go back and forth through the Gate. At first, Gate families tried to keep animals from the Wild from crossing at Don's, afraid DNA analysis would show differences in their genes. At some point, they gave up on the smaller animals. Animals from the Wild can't handle traffic as well as ours, so they quickly die out. Our animals don't last long in the Wild either. More predators there, especially hawks and eagles.

The second shift guards were waiting to leave when I got there. They let me in because I didn't have my key. One of them, Roy Duncan, said, "Your keys and badge are on the desk. We don't have a new cart yet, so our rounds are all on foot. Thanks a lot for screwing up the cart."

"The other guy here?"

"Yep, and you'll never guess who he is."

"So tell me."

"Tom fricking Thornburg, from the big name Thornburgs. They own this place. I never knew that. Why the hell would they own a junkyard? And why would a Thornburg want to sit on his butt here?"

If he didn't already know the story behind the rogue Gate, I wasn't going to fill him in. As to why Tom Thornburg was here, I had no idea. "They probably bought the corporation that owned Don's because it owned something else that was worth buying. Any Gate openings since last time I was here?"

"A couple, but they didn't last long. A coyote came through but turned back when I buzzed it with the drone."

I paused outside the office. Why *was* Tom Thornburg here? Did Mr. Thornburg trust him? That would be a mistake. Maybe he was a compromise, someone the Council and Mr. Thornburg could both accept. Either way, I didn't look forward to working the long graveyard shift with him.

I reluctantly pushed the office door open. I would have recognized Tom Thornburg anywhere, despite the fifteen years since the last time I saw him. He was an inch or two taller than my six foot two, skinny, with blond hair cut short and wore jogging shorts with a sleeveless T-shirt, both of which fit too well not to be hand tailored. He was in my chair, feet on my desk, showing off tennis shoes that would have cost me two months' salary. He didn't look up from his smartphone.

"I didn't expect to see you here," I said.

"Slumming. I'm supposed to keep an eye on the Gate and handle it if my dearest half-sister tries to come through again."

I slumped down in the chair across from him, Mike's chair. "And what does 'handling it' mean?"

"That's a great question. There is no way to handle it without getting Dad or the Council hacked off at me." He shrugged, eyes still on his phone. "So, they dumped an impossible assignment in my lap. Fortunately, you're here, so I can dump the mess in your lap."

"If Robinette tries to come through, I'll let her," I said.

"And the Gate family Council will stomp you like a cockroach," Tom said. He finally glanced up from his phone. "They sentenced her to six months in the Wild."

"Why?"

"Ask them. I don't get invited to Council meetings." His voice was flat, unemotional.

"Does she know she's sentenced to stay over there six months?"

"Probably not."

"Six months is effectively a death sentence."

"It probably is, but the Council can't sentence Gate family people to death directly, so they did it this way. I'm surprised they didn't play the 'she's not human' card."

"She's as human as you are." I felt my fists clinch. "And you're okay with them killing your sister."

"Half-sister. We were never close, certainly not close enough for me to go against the Council for her."

"If she comes through, what am I officially supposed to do?"

"Dad says help her. The Council says send her back. I'll be interested in how you manage to do both. I'll be busy staying out of it."

I tried to keep anger off my face. Fortunately, the situation wouldn't arise since Robinette was already on this side. "You guys aren't great at employee relations, are you?"

"The Gate families? Actually, they're pretty good at it. The key to managing employees is to bring in subsistence farmers from some crap country, pay them what they think is big money for a few jobs, then send them back before they figure out how much their labor is worth here."

"Sounds enlightened."

"It's better than slavery. For both sides, actually. The cheap labor goes home thinking they got a great deal, and the Gate families know they got a great deal because they know what the labor is worth. And we don't have to pay them when they're having babies or when they get old."

"Not trying to use Mangi as slaves?"

"Mangi make horrible slaves, though I could make it work. Nobody listens to me though."

"You're really bragging that you could make slavery work?"

"I could, but I wouldn't." Tom steepled his hands behind his head. "Too expensive. If we needed Mangi slaves, we would have to catch them young, no more than four or five years old, and raise them ourselves. In their culture, giving adults orders is a deadly insult, which they'll try to kill you for eventually. You can phrase the orders as suggestions and get some work out of them if you offer them big enough rewards, but they won't work more than a few hours at anything. We would have to replace that entire culture by raising young Mangi ourselves. Ripping off subsistence farmers is a lot cheaper. We just make sure they don't know where the Gates are."

"Bringing people in is a change. Mr. Thornburg had strict limits on how many people he could bring through the Gate when I worked for him."

"The Council changes when it has to," Tom said. "They don't change much, though. Still no cars or planes in the Wild. They allow drones, but you can't fly them more than a mile from your property, and you can only claim a square mile of the Wild."

"Anybody trying to change the rules?"

Tom shrugged. "People talk, but nothing will happen until the next generation takes over. Even then, I don't think much will change because the next generation doesn't agree on what should change."

"What changes would you want?" I asked.

"Put satellites up so we'll know more about the Wild. We don't know anything about that world outside North America. There could be a super-civilization in Europe that decided to keep North America as their playground and hasn't noticed us yet. More likely, their Europe is a few centuries behind us and gearing up to pull a Columbus on the Mangi. They might already have colonies on the coasts. We wouldn't know until they blind-sided us."

I had never thought about the Wild outside of North America. "The rest of the Wild is probably like the parts we've seen." I sounded more confident than I was. "Anything else you would do?"

"Tune the Gates. We know about the Wild. Is it just one of dozens or hundreds of realities we could get to? We don't know because the council won't let us check."

"I'm with the Council on that one," I said. "Some rocks shouldn't be turned over."

"But then you get surprised when something on the other side of the rock turns it over themselves."

That was getting quite a distance from Robinette's issues. I leaned back in Mike's chair and wished for his neck pillow. Was it worth steering the conversation back? Did Tom Thornburg know anything that could help? Maybe, but he seemed poised, unlikely to tell me anything important. "I haven't seen Robinette in fifteen years," I said finally. "How did she do as a human kid?"

"She reverted to Mangi as soon as she got a chance," Tom said. "You can send a Mangi to Harvard, but she's still a Mangi."

"She went to Harvard?" I tried to sound surprised. "That's impressive."

"Dad could send his goldfish to Harvard, and it would get gentleman's 'C's," Tom said. "Ivy league schools have a smart poor people track and a rich people track. Rich kid track is about meeting other rich kids and cementing ties so their parents hire you and your parents hire them. That didn't work for her. She's half animal. What would you expect when you put her in a school with next generation's movers and shakers?"

And yet she did well in her classes there. How much of what he said about Harvard was true? I had no idea. Ivy league was so far from my aspirations I couldn't imagine going there. "She was a brilliant little girl."

"Book smart, yeah. She's not people smart, though. Being book smart gets you middle class jobs at best. People smart and connections get you to the top."

"So, you're going to the top?"

He laughed shortly. "Do you know what happened to the king's brothers and sisters back when kings mattered? The inheritance went to the king and his family. It didn't take many generations before his brothers and sisters' kids were basically peasants. Leah is the next king of Thornburgia. My kids or grandkids will be peasants like you. No offense."

Some offense was taken, but I kept my face impassive. "So back to kings and nobles. I heard that the younger generation plays something like Russian Roulette."

"That we do. I've had my name in the hat. I didn't get the kill, but I would have shot if I had the chance. We knew what we were doing when we put our names in the hat. In the Wild, the Council makes its own laws, sometimes by looking the other way. They don't officially allow Russian Roulette hunts, but don't stop them unless somebody too important gets involved. They allow duels but only between social equals and only if certain kinds of insults are involved. Even then, they can stop a duel if they want to. Usually, they don't. We love our spectacles and duels to the death are spectacles only we get to see. We would probably do jousts except everybody is crap at riding horses. They won't let us take horses over there anyway. They don't want to give the Mangi ideas."

"Jousts and duels. Sounds positively Middle Ages," I said.

"Kings and nobles are the natural order of things, even if we don't call them that. The middle class pushed back and set up the system the way they wanted it in the US and a few other countries, but the middle-class ruling isn't natural or stable. Gate families are the way people are hardwired to live. Rulers and ruled, with enforcers like you in the middle."

I mentioned that the Private Eye business doesn't put you in the best of company. Working for the Gate families adds an extra level to that. I wondered if Tom Thornburg had islands of decency. He didn't show any yet, other than apparent candor. How much of what he said was true? Duels and hunts to the death among young aristocrats I believed. What little he said about Robinette didn't help solve the mysteries surrounding her. His ideas about workers and how society should work were crap, but not surprising given the wealth he was born into. He was clearer eyed about the Gate families than I expected and more willing to talk about them.

"Dad seems to trust you," Tom said. "Do you buy the Robert Thornburg myth? He's as big a sociopath as the rest of them. He set up the Council rules. He's been a member of the inner Council almost forever. He didn't get there by being a nice guy."

He didn't have to convince me. "I was his bodyguard. I know him."

"Whatever you think you know, double or triple it. I'm his son, the spare heir. I know fifteen more years of him than you. The man is utterly selfish, uses everybody around him, including Leah, me and especially Robinette."

#

After that burst of conversation both of us retreated to our own thoughts, or in Tom's case, to his phone. I wanted to get my audiobook out but hesitated to do it in front of my boss's son. Without my usual distractions, the hours crept by, especially when I started watching the clock. Great way to make time go slow, but I couldn't stop glancing at it.

I went on my rounds, on foot. Tom Thornburg refused to go when it was his turn. "It's bad enough that I have to sit here. I'm not wandering around a junkyard in the middle of the night."

I did one of his rounds to make the time pass faster and left the other one undone. The rounds were mostly to make sure the guards stayed awake anyway.

The burned-out cart was now stacked on top of the squashed down remnants of a low-slung sports car that hadn't been low slung enough to go under a big truck.

Mike sometimes made macabre bets on whether the driver survived when we got a new wreck. He would have bet against the sports car driver. Looking at the wreckage, I figured he would have been right. Somebody died in that car, and it felt weird walking past it as though it was just another wreck.

I had a sudden impulse to call Mike. It was three in the morning, but if he had the same habits I did on his days off, he would be awake. I dialed before I had a chance to change my mind.

He answered on the second ring. "This had better be an emergency."

"It isn't, but I thought you might want to know that I'm back working at Don's."

"You really need to watch your back. That's a convenient place for murder. Just stash the body and toss it through next time a Gate opens."

"If the Gate families want me dead, I'm dead."

"True, but Don's is a great place to get caught in their feud too."

I told him about Tom Thornburg.

"So, if Robinette came through, you would automatically be on Robert Thornburg's shit list, or the Council's," Mike said. "Built in scapegoat. Sucks to be you."

"I know something they don't."

"True."

Did the families really not know Robinette came through? I wouldn't have been sure if I was in their place. Still, Marcus McFinney saw the video that first night and seemed convinced by it.

"Sometimes I overthink things and run in a circle."

"That's true," Mike said. "And sometimes you try to do the right thing. That's when you really get yourself in trouble. You're in the wrong career to have a conscience."

My radio came to life. "A Gate is opening," Tom said.

"I heard that," Mike said. "Want to let me listen in?"

"Listen in, I guess," I thumbed the reply button. "Where is it?"

Tom tried to give me directions, but they were so muddled I wasn't sure I was going the right direction at first. "Am I headed the right way?"

I was, so I kept going. "Anything coming through?"

"I see motion through the Gate, but nothing on our side yet."

I turned a corner and spotted the Gate, then tensed when I saw footprints, Mangi or bear. From the monster size, probably bear. I had my taser and sidearm, but my rifle was at the office. I thumbed the radio again. "Can you get over here with a rifle?"

"No. I'll let you handle whatever it is."

I wanted to kick myself for not bringing a rifle. I don't normally carry a rifle on foot patrols because the rifle is cumbersome, and Mike can get anywhere in the junkyard in less than a minute to back me up. Mike wasn't there, though.

"If a bear comes through, I'll climb on something big and let it rampage," I said. "You really want to handle a bear from the Wild on your own?"

"If a bear comes through, I'll be in my car and down the highway before it gets all four feet on our side."

Whatever else I thought of Mike, he would have backed me up. I turned back to the phone. "You heard that?"

"Yeah. He's a weaselly piece of crap," Mike said. "I told you going back was a bad idea. Do you actually see a bear?"

"Just pawprints so far. They look fresh, though." Actually, I wasn't close enough to tell how fresh the tracks were, but given my luck, they probably were fresh.

The radio blared, "Something coming through."

I looked for something to climb. There were piles of wreckage but climbing them was a good way to pull scrap metal down on myself. Camera poles? Maybe, if I could shinny up fifteen feet of smooth pole. I saw a moving shadow by the Gate. Was it a bear? At first, in the dim light I thought so, but when I aimed my flashlight at the movement I saw a coyote-like animal. It cringed away from the light but kept coming. It sidled toward me, sniffing the air. It paused, seeming uncertain, then whined and lowered its head, rubbing it along the ground. Was it begging? Probably.

Robinette said a coyote followed her and begged for food. Was that common for coyotes in the Wild? Maybe they begged for food from the Mangi too. Maybe they were a species ready to be domesticated when the Mangi had enough food to spare.

The coyote didn't make those footprints, though. Maybe the coyotes over there used Mangi as protection when bears got too close.

The bear moved into view, blinking at the junkyard's dim lights. It was skinny for a bear, with a long, rangy body that looked almost catlike.

It looked fast, despite its size. I recognized it from the pictures and knew that though it was rangy it could weigh a ton.

"Short-faced bear," I said into the radio. "Not much use running away from it. They're built for speed." They were also built for chasing and eating animals, far more than our bears. I eased my sidearm out, not that it would stop the bear.

"You're on your own, my friend," Tom Thornburg said. "I'll call in support once I'm down the road a bit." He sounded amused.

I turned to the phone. "You heard?"

"You need to get the hell out of there."

The bear stood near the gate, a dark silhouette in an irregular hole in reality, with a full moon behind it. It growled, but the growl seemed tentative. The strange smells and lights of the junkyard must have made it wary. Good predators are curious, but even the biggest ones are chickenshit, because strange situations can be dangerous, and injuries can mean starvation. They only survive if they're fast and tough enough to keep killing their supper.

Every minute it didn't come through the Gate was a plus for me. The Gate wouldn't stay open forever. I yelped when something brushed my leg, then glanced down to see the coyote beside me, tail tucked between its legs and looking comically submissive. I wanted to tell it I couldn't stop the bear if it came through.

Primal fight or flight urges made my heart pound and made me impatient to do something, run, which would be stupid, or attack, which would be massively stupid. I kept the flashlight beam close to the bear, but not directly on it, ready to shift the beam to its eyes if it charged. What would I do if it charged? Try to blind it? Shoot my sidearm at it? Probably just make it mad. Tase it? Even if the taser took it down, those monster paws could kill me while it flailed.

"Beat feet to the nearest junk mound," Mike said. "You can't outrun it, but you might out dodge it."

Or the bear might shove the pile over on me. I muttered. "Worth a try."

I held the phone to my ear with one shoulder, while I braced the flashlight and sidearm in front of me the way they teach you in cop school. I was so keyed up I kept my finger off the trigger, afraid I would shoot if the bear moved. How long had the Gate been open? I had no idea. This would undoubtedly be a long Gate, given my luck.

I took a deep breath and let it out slowly, wondering if Tom Thornburg was watching me through the camera and laughing. Probably.

The bear growled again, sounding less tentative. I willed myself not to move and hoped the coyote by my leg would have enough misplaced faith in me not to run.

The bear seemed disturbed by the Gate. It was like an irregular door with a view into the warehouse. If the bear circled to get a better look, its view of the junkyard went away entirely. The Gate must look like a cave entrance, but with no cave behind it. The bear snorted and swung a paw the size of a dinner plate at the Gate, then jumped back. I don't know what it saw, but it didn't like it.

Finally, the Gate started its closing light show, the edges sparkling like stars, then the sparks spreading around the entire irregular Gate shape. A few more seconds, I thought. The light spread from the edges to the center, then faded. When they went dark, the Gate and bear were gone.

I glanced down at the coyote. "My friend, you're on the wrong side."

Chapter Ten:
A Dog Collar & A Betrayal

The coyote was still uncomfortably close to my leg, but apparently it felt uncomfortable too, now that the bear was gone, because it moved away. It backtracked where it came in through the gate, paused when the scent trail ended and looked almost comically puzzled before following its scent trail again and ending up at the same place. It looked back at me as though I could give it answers. Instead, I tased it and got an improvised muzzle around its mouth before it recovered. That wasn't recommended, but we normally kept tranquilizer guns and muzzles in the cart. All that stuff was back at the office and Tom Chickenshit Thornburg wasn't going to bring it to me, because he was probably in his car racing away.

Regulations said I had to secure predators from the Wild if they were over twenty pounds, so I wrapped my belt around the coyote's neck and pulled the end through the buckle, making an improvised leash, then paused. The animal already had a collar, cleverly disguised so I wouldn't have noticed it if I hadn't put my belt around its neck. I took the collar off, rolled the coyote onto a flattened cardboard box and dragged it to a dog crate near the office. It had its act together enough to snap at me and struggle by the time I got to the crate. By that time, my body came down from the adrenaline burst from when I was way too close to the bear. My hands shook and my muscles felt weak. At least the crisis was over.

Off-site security arrived, along with Marcus McFinney. I turned the operation over to them, and felt tension flow out of my body while I took in big gasps of crappy junkyard air and wished I had managed a couple gulps of air from the Wild. That air didn't smell of gasoline, antifreeze and partly burned rubber. I stuffed my hands in my pockets until they stopped shaking.

I couldn't relax too much with McFinney there, but compared to the bear he didn't seem all that formidable.

Marcus straightened up from the crate. "Where did you put the collar?"

I pulled it out of my pocket. "Yours?"

"Not yours." He grabbed at it, but I moved it out of his reach.

"Why would a coyote from the Wild have a collar?"

I wanted to examine it but that would start a fight. I wondered which side the off-site security guys would take.

"I hope you make me take it from you," Marcus said. I didn't doubt that he would enjoy trying. Could I take him in a fair fight? Fifteen years ago, I could have. Now, I doubted it. And the fight wouldn't be fair, of course.

"We have a Thornburg in the vicinity. Why don't we let them decide?" I asked.

"Tom Thornburg?" Marcus laughed. "Sure, if you can get him back. Last I saw his car was doing a zero to ninety in five seconds peel out. Great car. Too bad the driver has no balls."

Tom walked through the door behind him in time to hear that. Raw hatred flickered over his face for a second, then was gone, replaced by a cold smile. "You confuse being stupid with having balls. I bet all the first graders were scared of you when you in third grade." He turned to me and waved toward the crate. "Your bear shrunk when it came through the Gate."

"There was a bear," I said. "You must have seen it on the monitors."

"I'm not saying there wasn't," Tom said. "Are we done with excitement for the night?"

Marcus shrugged. "Maybe. Mr. Private Eye here has something I need. If you tell him to give it back, I won't have to beat the crap out of him. On the other hand, he tased me, so I would enjoy knocking his teeth out." He grinned at me. "Your call."

I wanted to slap the smug off his face and a few teeth with it, but instead I handed Tom the collar. "It's out of my hands now." I turned to Marcus. "You can still take a swing at me if you feel lucky."

I braced myself, but he laughed and turned to Tom. "Going to give me the collar?"

Tom turned it over in his hands, then dropped it on the desk. "Sure. No use to anyone now. I take it you were monitoring my half-sister with it. Probably trained a half-coyote/half dog to follow her. A dog collar could have a transmitter with enough range you could know if she got close to a Gate. Ingenious, but you must have lost her after she tried to come through here."

"As long as she doesn't come through a Gate, we don't care where she is," Marcus said. "She's probably in that monster bear's lower intestines by now." He turned to me. "You're a crap private eye. You didn't figure out why ape-girl Thornburg was in the Wild, even after Leah Thornburg spoon fed you the answer. I'll spell it out for you. Robinette went off on her dad when she found out she couldn't have kids, so Robert Thornburg decided to give her kids."

"That's not possible."

"Probably not, but if you throw enough money at a problem sometimes you can solve it. He planned to harvest her eggs and have some genetics lab screw with them until they got a viable fetus." He grinned. "And here's the kicker. He wanted to do this without her knowing. I didn't put knockout drops in her drink. Her daddy dearest was going to get the eggs harvested while she was out, but we found out and diverted her. The Council, minus old man Thornburg, approved our decision. Can't have those genes wandering around over here."

I shook my head. "Robert Thornburg would never do that. Almost zero chance of making it work and if Robinette found out she would rip his spleen out through his nose." I turned to Tom. "Do you know anything about this?"

"Even less than you do," Tom said. "Dad likes Robinette a lot, and says she got the good genes from him, but I can't imagine him trying to make it so she could have kids. The Council would shit itself and Leah would see Robinette as even more of a rival than she already does. I think Dad would see how bad an idea it was." He shrugged. "But he is getting up there in years. Maybe he's slipping."

"It's all true," Marcus said. "We have the receipts. The Council wouldn't have gone along with Leah if we couldn't prove it."

I didn't want to believe McFinney and most of me didn't, but if he was lying, why would the Council shut down the Thornburg Gate? I remembered something else. Robinette's last college boyfriend, Randall Dailey, was quite a specimen, both physically and mentally, plus three out of four of his great-grandparents were still alive, the perfect genes to mix with Robinette's.

"And Randall Dailey was going to be the father," I said.

"Now you're starting to get it," Marcus said. "The Council had no choice. The Council police would have killed her outright if they found out, but the Council likes to take out their own garbage, so they exiled her to the Wild for six months. That's a death sentence anyway but doesn't trigger their bullshit regulations on killing Gate family members."

It all hung together, except the part about Robert Thornburg actually trying to do it. If nothing else, Robinette would hate him if she found out. Harvesting someone's eggs without permission is as close to rape as you can get, a huge violation of her essence. She would never forgive him, even if the process worked, which it probably wouldn't.

"It's sort of plausible," I said. "But I don't believe he would do it."

"I have my doubts too," Tom said. "He would do it in a second if he thought it would work and that he could get away with it, but I can't see him taking the risk. My apish sister's genes would give away everything about the Wild to a gene specialist. We could keep it out of the papers, but we would have to kill everyone who looked at those genes or they would spread the word, informally around the water cooler to their colleagues if nothing else, and we would have a whole new class of people who knew stuff we don't want known."

Marcus shrugged. "All you're saying is that Thornburg is an arrogant old fool. He planned to do it." Marcus turned to Tom. "Do you think he's too ethical to do it? Do you think he values Robinette's rights too much? He thinks all his kids, Leah, you and Robinette are ways of passing on his genes. He would do this in a second. After all these years of getting away with crap, using people like pieces on a chessboard, he got too arrogant. He would have gotten it done, or at least tried, if Leah hadn't pieced his plan together."

"Or maybe she invented the whole thing," I said. "She's in charge now if the Council believes her."

"Leah was happy to wait until old man Thornburg retired," Marcus said. "She had a lock on inheriting before this started. This weakened the family she'll inherit. She'll spend years getting back what her dad squandered."

"I didn't think she was getting impatient," Tom said. "But she loves to lull people and then blindside them." He grinned wryly. "You don't want to get on her bad side."

I didn't say it aloud, but I still thought Leah might have set Mr. Thornburg up. This scheme got rid of Robinette, who she hated, and gave her the inheritance she would have had to wait years to get. Still, if she faked this, she had to fool not only a Council reluctant to act because they wouldn't want to encourage their own younger generation to stage coups, but also lawyers and other experts, who would scrutinize the evidence she presented. Mr. Thornburg might have done exactly what they accused him of. If so, it was strong evidence that he was slipping. It also explained why he claimed not to know why the Council turned on him. I felt almost physically sick. I didn't want to pass this along to Robinette, but how could I keep it from her?

"It's sinking in, isn't it," Marcus said. "After all the shit you've seen daddy Thornburg pull, why does it surprise you that he pulled this?"

Chapter Eleven:
Crisis of Faith

I drove back to my apartment that morning without figuring out if I believed McFinney and without figuring out if I should tell Robinette what he said. I didn't want to tell her, because the story was corrosive, eating away at my disbelief even when I told myself it wasn't true.

The most convincing lies are mostly true, I knew from long, sad experience, and the lies are hard to separate from the truth around them. What did I know was true? Robert Thornburg was a ruthless, manipulative bastard. He was proud of Robinette and who wouldn't be? Their big, recent fight came when she found out she couldn't have kids. A normal father wouldn't go from an angry daughter to genetic experiments, but Robert Thornburg wasn't an ordinary father. He got what he wanted, overriding moral considerations and people who tried to stop him.

If McFinney was right, what could we do about it? Not much. The Council already condemned Robinette to death, without having the guts to do it directly. If Mr. Thornburg tried what McFinney accused him of trying, he was dangerously detached from reality. Robinette would never forgive him, and the Council would never give Mr. Thornburg another chance at his daughter. The danger from her DNA was too high.

Would Robinette still be at my apartment when I got back? I was cautious when I opened the door, but Robinette was there, making pancakes and bacon for breakfast. She smiled at me, then studied my face when I slumped into a chair across from her. "Someone had a bad night."

"Gate opened with a monster bear by it," I said. "I was on foot, without my rifle and your gutless brother Tom was my backup. He ran to his car instead of helping." I took a deep breath. "And things went downhill from there."

She poured me a glass of juice. "My brother? Why was Tom there?"

"Supposedly keeping an eye on the place for your dad and Leah. He

Through the Wild Gate

was so busy trying to stay out of the drama that he dumped everything on me."

"That's my brother," she said. "So, did the bear come through?"

"No. It didn't like the lights and wrecked car smell."

"Bears are smarter than people that way. You said it went downhill from there. What happened?"

I closed my eyes and let the smell of pancakes and bacon wash over me. "You don't want to know."

"You'll tell me eventually. Why not now?"

"Because breakfast smells great and I don't want to ruin it for you."

She sat beside me on the couch, her dark red hair still wet from a shower, dressed in a green and white T-shirt and green shorts. She leaned close. "I made it through two months in the Wild. I can handle whatever this is. It won't ruin breakfast."

I told her, my words stark and emotionless. When I finished, her fists were clenched so hard I expected blood to seep out where her nails cut into her hands. "None of it is true. Leah set Dad up. He wouldn't do that."

I hated to ask but I had to. "How sure are you?"

She turned away. When she turned back, tears coursed down her cheeks. "Close to a hundred percent."

"Then why are you crying?"

"I have my reasons. It's time Dad and I had a heart to heart."

I thought that was a horrible idea, partly because Robinette would probably rip her dad's heart out if the story was true. On the other hand, we had a better idea why Mr. Thornburg didn't come to her rescue, assuming we believed McFinney.

"Why are we wasting time on this ridiculous story?" I asked.

"Because it isn't ridiculous," Robinette said. "I did blow up at dad when I found out I couldn't have kids. I never wanted them before I found out I couldn't have them, but after that I wanted them a lot. That doesn't mean dad tried what McFinney said he did, but I gave McFinney the perfect club to go after dad. Leah may actually believe it's true. Me with kids has got to be her worst nightmare."

She put together breakfast plates, her movements carefully controlled. "I'm not going to let my piece of crap sister and her latest bad boy ruin breakfast the way she apparently ruined the rest of my life."

I tried to find flaws in the story. If it mingled truth with lies, how could I tell the difference?

"Did the Council really decide this was true?" I asked. "If it did, why wouldn't your dad know what he was being accused of?"

That was a place where I might nail down truth or lies, but how could we know what the Council knew or decided? I wasn't even sure the Council shut down Thornburg Gate. Mike claimed it did, but he was just repeating rumors. I tried to remember if Mr. Thornburg confirmed that his Gate was shut down.

"Did you try to go to your dad's Gate," I asked.

"It was closed," Robinette said. "I went there first. Our mansion in the Wild was stripped bare. And when I say stripped bare, I mean down to taking the barbed wire off the walls around it, taking the plumbing and electric wires, pulling plants from the gardens up by the roots and taking the furniture. They even took down the interior doors. I nearly got cornered there by Mangi, but they were just using the building as shelter. It was stripped before the Gate shut down." She shook her head at the memory. "I must have walked a week to get to that Gate and thought I was saved, but then nothing." She shivered and grabbed my arm. "I almost gave up. If I hadn't been running from the Mangi I probably would have."

I squeezed her arm. "But you made it back anyway." The stripped Thornburg mansion, unfortunately, confirmed one part of McFinney's story. The Thornburg Gate was shut down and the shutdown wasn't temporary. "And only the Council could force a shutdown?" I asked.

"Dad would never do it voluntarily," Robinette said. "It's not just a place to get away from this world's crap. It's a symbol. Gate families have Gates and mansions in the Wild. Take that away and they aren't Gate families."

That was true. It also probably meant Leah wasn't lying. If she took over the family now, it would be much diminished. Why would she move now when she could have the family and Gate intact in a few years?

"Enough swirling this crap around in our heads," Robinette said. "We have Dad's private number. Let's call him."

While I pondered that, Mr. Thornburg called. I thought about confronting him with McFinney's story, but he steered the conversation another direction.

"I need you to find someone in the Wild," he said. "We have a narrow window of opportunity. I'm sending a car to pick you up."

He hung up before I got a chance to say anything. I turned to

Robinette. "That was your dad. He's sending me on an expedition, maybe to find you. Want me to ask about McFinney's story when I see him?"

"No. I want to be in on that conversation," Robinette said. "Go along with what he's doing if you can and see if you learn anything."

Chapter Twelve:
Back to the Wild

Mr. Thornburg traveled in a convoy with five carloads of security people, though the convoy was loose enough most observers wouldn't realize the cars were together. The cars didn't look particularly new or fancy, though they were all immaculate and rode a little lower than normal on their suspensions, which meant they had armor. I rode with Mr. Thornburg. His car had a lot of custom suspension work to make it ride smoother.

"Lots of things have changed since you left," Mr. Thornburg said. "Among them, the Gate Family Council has an official police force, with guns and badges."

I wondered how that got past the proudly independent Families. Maybe as part of their guise as a federal continuity of government operation. "I take it that the Council police shut your Gate down."

"No. Leah did that, but the Council police kept me from reopening it." He grinned. "But what the Council police take away with one hand, they give back with another. I did background checks on most of the ranking members and some of them had things in those backgrounds only I know."

"If you control them, why didn't you send them to look for Robinette?"

"Control is too strong a word," Mr. Thornburg said. "It took a lot of horse-trading to get them to temporarily open my Gate and I had to agree not to try to find Robinette through it."

"What the point of reopening the Gate, then?"

"To find a crosser Mangi, Jimmy Nelson," Mr. Thornburg said. "The official mission is to find him and ask him how he ended up back in the Wild. I want you to get him alone and ask him to find and protect Robinette. He grew up in the Wild. For enough money, he can protect Robinette for the last four months of her exile. If she is still alive after six months, the Council can't touch her without taking steps they don't want to take."

Through the Wild Gate

I wished again that I could tell him that Robinette was safe, but I couldn't, not until I knew more about what had happened to her and who was behind it. Robert Thornburg almost certainly wasn't, but he probably couldn't protect her.

"You'll have Council Police with you," he said. "You'll have to cut them out of the conversation long enough to hire Jimmy. He can help her survive. Then we'll figure out who is behind this and knock the wheels off their cart."

Gate locations are secret except to Family members, so I wore a hood when Mr. Thornburg's men drove me to the Gate he now secretly controlled. I left Robinette with plenty of food, some cash and numbers for grocery delivery places.

We drove a couple hours. When Mr. Thornburg took the hood off, I was in a windowless hall. A man and a woman in Gate Council police uniforms stood beside me. Both were tall, the woman huge for a woman, an inch taller than me and probably weighing not too much less. Not fat, just big. She had blond hair and dark eyes. Her features had a hint of Latin American to them. The guy was light skinned, prematurely balding and wiry, like a distance runner.

The woman looked tough and competent, but I got the feeling she had something to prove. They both had experience in the Wild, but in large hunting groups, not on their own, with limited firepower. Both were experts with rifles and handguns, according to Mr. Thornburg.

The guy held out a hand. "Jerv Elder here. The extra-large cop lady is Captain Indigo Wagner. I call her Captain Wagner, or boss when I'm in a hurry." He pointed down the hall. "Somewhere along there we'll step through the Gate. You won't feel anything. I hear you guard an early Gate, where it flickers on and off and moves. Modern Gates are under control. They don't close or move around. If you shut one down, it takes a week to bring it back up, so they don't get shut down much."

He paused and Captain Wagner interrupted smoothly. "Jerv is a great cop, but he rarely shuts up. He's working on that. Maybe being in the Wild will help." She didn't smile or offer to shake hands, just turned and strode down the hall.

"We're wasting daylight," she said, without turning. She had a faint accent, but I couldn't place it. Hispanic? Maybe, but that didn't seem quite right.

Jerv kept talking while we walked, confirming that he was a distance runner, a top-notch cross-country runner in high school and college.

The Gate Hall led to a walled Family compound in the Wild. I recognized the huge main house, a separate gym and a mechanical building, with a concrete wall surrounding the compound and now barren gardens interspersed between the buildings. Robinette wasn't kidding when she said the compound was stripped. Carpenters were rehanging interior doors while a disgusted-looking man in Council Police uniform shoveled Mangi crap from the swimming pool into a wheelbarrow.

"They had to chase Mangi out when they reopened the Gate," Jerv said. "Mangi used an Olympic-sized swimming pool as a latrine. There has to be a metaphor there someplace."

When I was here fifteen years ago, the mansion left me awed. Mr. Thornburg poured money into this place. It looked like a castle, with towers and gargoyle sculptures.

"The core of the mansion is still here," I said. "It just needs cleaning."

"And rewiring," Jerv said. "And restocking. They normally keep huge supplies of long-shelf-life foods here, but they took that when they shut the Gate."

Was the large food stock evidence the mansions really were for continuity of government? Maybe, or maybe the Gate families were afraid Gate technology would fail, or some disaster might hit our side of the Gates. Maybe the Gate families really would bring government officials to the Wild if something nasty happened to our Earth.

"This one is fancy," Jerv said. "It makes the other one I went to look crude, a 'mansion' with prefabricated cement, astroturf and crushed gravel."

Four light-weight black all-terrain vehicles sat in the courtyard, already packed, with rifles in long holsters in easy reach of the drivers. One ATV was a two-seater.

Captain Wagner handed me a semi-automatic shotgun and a 9-millimeter handgun. "The sidearm won't stop all the animals we could run into, but it may make them back off or pause long enough for you to grab the shotgun. You were a bodyguard, so you know how to use it."

I checked the weapons and nodded. Two Council Police guys were already outside, checking their gear. They didn't introduce themselves, just got in their ATVs and waited while we walked out.

"Friendly bunch, huh?" Jerv grinned at me. "We'll probably be out at least a day or two even if we find this guy right away. I like to know

Through the Wild Gate

who I'm riding with." He motioned to the two-seater. "You're driver. I'm drone operator. Horses would be better in this hilly country, but the Council doesn't allow them. They don't want to give the Mangi ideas. Of course they don't allow ATV's with as much range as these have either, so I would just say screw their rules."

I understood the rule against bringing in horses. The Wild had horses too, the New World kinds that went extinct on our side of the Gates, not the same species we domesticated but close enough they could probably be ridden. Once the Mangi saw people on horseback, they would find ways to tame and ride the local horses themselves and that would be disastrous. They were already formidable enough. Turning them into mounted nomadic hunters and raiders could make the Wild unusable unless the Families brought in machine guns.

A truck-sized gate glided smoothly open for us. Outside, the trees were cleared for a couple hundred feet around the wall, though the grass was waist high and spindly saplings stood as high as my head. Beyond the cleared area, thick forest rose.

It felt good to be back in the Wild. Some part of me was drawn to the quiet and the clean natural scents, with the rest of me repelled by the strangeness and danger. If you grow up in a constant electronic hum, it's weird to be without it. The Gate family compounds int the Wild are the best of both worlds, with clean air, but with walls to keep out the danger. I understood why the Gate families valued their compounds in the Wild so much. It wasn't just the prestige of having something no one else in the world could have. Compounds in the Wild were also valuable in themselves.

Jerv launched his drone. "We've mapped the first two miles of our route. That's as far from the compound as the Council will let us fly drones. What we're doing now is completely off the books, but we need to know what's out there. You can't do good security when you don't know what's three miles away. A thousand Mangi could be gathering to attack, and we would never know it."

A thousand Mangi in one place was unlikely. Thirty Mangi in one place would strip the countryside and be forced to move on. Still, Jerv was mostly right. I remembered Tom Thornburg's comments. We didn't know much about the Wild and couldn't unless the Council changed its rules.

We followed a game trail into the woods. Jimmy Nelson apparently talked to Mr. Thornburg before Leah shut the Thornburg compound down, but Mr. Thornburg didn't know where the big Mangi was now. We were supposed to head into the woods and let Jimmy find us, hopefully before other Mangi or big predators did.

"What are you supposed to say to him," I asked.

"I can't tell you," Jerv said. "Council police business."

"Then why am I here?"

"Because Mr. Thornburg wanted you here," Jerv said.

Why would the Council Police want to talk to Jimmy? A Crosser back in the Wild after eight years in our world could cause a raft of problems. Way too many ideas in that head we didn't want in the Wild. But if the Council Police planned to kill Jimmy or take him back, how could I ask him to help Robinette?

Game trails, according to Jerv, avoided a lot of obstacles and made for more efficient travel, though they might not end up where you wanted to go.

"Sometimes you have to make your own trail, but usually that's a bad idea. Too many steep hills and rocky places where even ATVs can't go." Jerv pointed to the drone remote. "Animals know the territory and pick routes with the least possible effort. I can see it from the drone."

The downside was that predators and Mangi prowled the trails too and knew the best ambush spots. We were horribly vulnerable out here, and I felt that acutely. Even with rifles, or in my case a shotgun. a party this small was vulnerable to the Mangi. They could be among us before we got a shot off and fighting hand to hand even Robinette probably couldn't handle a full Mangi male, though her martial arts training might make up for the Mangi's greater strength.

I took the lead, with the others following. Jerv kept the drone ahead of us, scouting for obstacles, predators and Mangi. He had a terrain map of our side of the Gate, but it was nearly useless over here. Too much had changed in different ways in the last half-million years.

We stopped after about a mile to fire into the air and yell Jimmy's name. No response.

The trail twisted like a snake in places and turned back on itself. After enough turns, I wasn't sure which direction we were going. The direction didn't matter as much as covering ground. Jerv thought we were making progress, but even he wasn't sure. He sent the drone high over the trees a couple times to get a better view and turned away discouraged the second time.

"We've been riding half an hour and I can still see the compound's walls. We're maybe a mile from where we started if we took a straight line."

I started to see what he meant about routes on a map not remotely resembling routes on the ground. At this rate, it could take weeks to get to Don's Gate, even with four-wheelers, yet Robinette walked there after finding the Thornburg Gate closed.

"We have maybe twenty Mangi stalking us," Jerv said. "Crafty suckers. Good at using cover but they don't know about the drone."

"Jimmy?"

"Not unless he's gone native," Jerv said. "I'm not sure I would recognize him in animal skins."

"You would," I said. "He's huge for a Mangi."

I couldn't see the Mangi and wanted to but didn't stop the ATV to look through the drone's camera. Fifteen years ago, I caught a brief glimpse of a Mangi on my hunting trip and I saw a few when they tried to come through the gate at Don's but seeing a whole group in their own territory would be a treat. We stopped and fired into the air again, yelling Jimmy's name.

"They stopped getting closer but aren't going away," Jerv said.

I looked over his shoulder at the drone controller. "Not Jimmy." I was almost sure of that. "Wish we could talk to them."

The Gate families had partial vocabularies for some Mangi languages, but there were so many that it didn't make sense to learn them.

"We're working on translation apps," Jerv said. "But until they get better, they're a good way to get a spear through your gut."

We shot and yelled again, then moved on. I wondered how long this batch of Mangi could keep up with us. Not long, it turned out. We couldn't drive the ATVs fast along the forest path, but twenty miles an hour was more than enough to leave the Mangi behind.

Our next stalkers weren't so easy to outrun. Two dozen extra-large, gray-colored wolves paced us effortlessly after the Mangi fell behind, their restless noses in the air, probably smelling gas fumes for the first time.

"I don't know if they're regular wolves or dire wolves," Jerv said. "Whichever one they are, they probably weigh well over a hundred pounds."

The wolves didn't come close or threaten us, though they made no effort to hide. They just effortlessly kept pace with the ATVs, while weaving through the forest edge.

"Wolves have never attacked humans in North America," Jerv said. The cross-country star turned security guy hadn't said a word for over ten minutes, but looked as though the words were backing up inside him, like water behind a dam. He added, "In Europe and Asia, oh yeah. Wolves have been known to go into towns and break down doors if they were hungry enough. So, are wolves in the Wild more like our North American ones or like Old World wolves?"

"I vote for our North America," I said. "But the wolves get the only vote that counts."

The wolves made me wary. Maybe they were curious about these new, taller Mangi and their odd smells, or maybe they were waiting until dark to see how extra-tall Mangi taste. Our kind of humans probably got away with things in the Wild that we wouldn't ordinarily because the Mangi were not to be messed with and we looked enough like Mangi to make predators wary. How much could we depend on that borrowed fear? Not as much as I would have liked, probably.

"Mr. Thornburg and the suits have no idea how hard this trip will be or how long it might take," Jerv said. "If Jimmy is living like a Mangi, he could be a hundred miles away. A hundred miles on ATVs sounds like a half-day trip each way at most, but if it's all hills and forest, it could take a week just because we have to follow winding animal trails. You've already seen how that works. Add more time if we run into rivers with no fords for a hundred miles. For all we know, the Mississippi river, or whatever took its place in the Wild, could run between us and where he is now. Half a million years and multiple ice ages to do things different in the Wild."

He sent the drone soaring again, then swore. "The bad news is that I think I can still see the compound. The worse news is that from here I can see what looks like an almost straight trail that starts near the compound and goes to a big clearing not far from here. We could have covered all the ground we covered so far in maybe five minutes if we found that trail."

"Any good news?" I asked.

"The trail we're on twists a lot, but it ends up in that same big clearing," Jerv said. "Once we get to open country, we can pick up the pace. Forty miles an hour in a straight line instead of half that as the snake wiggles would make a big difference."

"But would Jimmy be in that big clearing?" I asked. Mangi prefer forests, though they'll go wherever food is. Jimmy wasn't a typical Mangi, though. If someone lured him back to the Wild for a hunt, he would be wary of open country. On the other hand, Mr. Thornburg knew he was in the Wild. Daddy Thornburg was too smart to bring a crosser Mangi back to the Wild, but maybe Tom Thornburg did. He said he played in the Russian Roulette hunt games. If Tom helped bring Jimmy to the Wild, what were the Council Police investigating? Mr. Thornburg might want them to kill Jimmy, erasing a trail that led to Tom, but then why ask me to recruit Jimmy?

I hate it when I poke at a mystery and not only do I not solve it, but I find more mysteries. At least I was getting paid to find Jimmy, actually by two people with conflicting goals.

The forest got thinner, gradually shading off into grassland with a few scattered trees. Elephant-like woolly mammoths tested the winds with their long trunks and shifted to put adults between us and their young but didn't charge or threaten us.

"Pick out a tree to go up if something comes at us," Jerv said. "Open country supports more animals and gives us fewer places to hide."

"Hopefully, our ATVs can outrun anything that comes after us," I said. Was that true? Maybe, on straight, level ground once we got up to speed.

The wolves had slipped away. Now they found us again and paced us easily. Did they stalk Mangi this way, or were they curious about us, noticing the differences between us and Mangi and wondering how they could use us?

I finally saw Mangi in the distance. Jerv said they had been watching us most of the trip, but this was the first I had seen of them since we stopped. They weren't trying to hide now but kept their distance. I counted a dozen, catching fleeting glimpses of white skin, with red paint outlining their ribs and around their eyes. Some had blond hair, while others were redheads or had brown or black hair. A couple had their hair spiked up in Mohawks while others were bald.

Mangi this close to a Gate Compound would probably know what guns did and assume that any humans they met were armed.

There had to be a slow, dangerous escalation in how much Mangi knew about humans and their weapons, no matter how careful the Families tried to be. If the rumors of Gate family Mangi hunts were true, those hunts would make Mangi survivors that much more dangerous. Mangi, from what little I knew of them, had long memories and a formidable taste for revenge.

The Mangi hooted at us, long deep musical calls, and brandished wooden stabbing spears—four-foot saplings with one end sharpened.

"I don't know if that's a greeting, a challenge or an invitation to a dance-off," Jerv said.

None of us knew more than a few words of any Mangi language and there was no guarantee the local Mangi could understand even those few words. Mangi used a bewildering variety of languages with few words in common.

"Staking their claim," I said. "We need to figure out how to say, 'we're passing through and we're too stupid to hunt here, so leave us alone.'"

"Or how to ask where Jimmy Nichols is," Jerv said.

The hooting went on and the Mangi added athletic dancing to it. Jerv abruptly told me to stop. He jumped off, yelled, beat his chest and did a wild break dance, then crossed his arms across his chest, squatting low and thrusting alternate legs out in front of him. "Cossack dance. I learned it in martial arts. Beat that, bitches!" He tossed himself to the ground on his back, then flipped back to his feet. "That too."

A couple Mangi tried the Cossack dance and fell on their butts.

"I thought I was kidding about the dance-off," Jerv said. "Challenging them might not have been smart. It was fun though."

I had a brief vision of this Mangi clan taking over the Wild using Jerv's moves. Not likely, but we did have to be careful what we did in front of them. Mangi were smart, able to learn from humans.

"Whatever I said, one of them is coming over," Jerv said.

The tallest Mangi I've ever seen ambled toward us, holding up a white handkerchief on a stick. He wore a deerskin around his waist and nothing else. His blond hair was spiked up in a mohawk. He walked as though his feet hurt.

"Must be an ex-servant," Jerv said. "Or maybe he trades with a family."

Tall for a Mangi meant maybe five foot six inches, more than half a foot shorter than me. I recognized the absurdly huge biceps and triceps and the "I Heart books" tattoo.

Jerv stared at the Mangi, then at me, "I don't say this much, but what the actual fuck?"

"Jimmy Nichols, I presume." I impressed myself by saying that in a perfect upper-class British accent.

"Yeah," Jimmy said. "But who are you?" His voice was weirdly high and nasal coming from that huge body, but he spoke English with no trace of an accent.

"Mr. Thornburg sent us," Jerv said.

"It took him long enough," Jimmy said. "Why did he shut his Gate down?"

The huge-muscled Mangi was a lot more intimidating in person than in the picture. The English words coming from his mouth seemed wrong, like they were dubbed. I felt baffled, with the unease mixed with the same kind of feeling I had around Marcus McFinney, half-threatened, half challenged. With the big Mangi, that feeling was more intense. This was a formidable-looking near-human.

Jerv wiped sweat from his face and whispered. "I wonder if he really does Heart books. Doesn't look like the bookworm type."

Captain Wagner rode closer, staring at the approaching Mangi. "What the hell are we looking at? That can't be Jimmy Nichols. No way he could pass as human."

Actually, with the right clothes and haircut he could have and did for eight years.

"I don't know how he passed as human," Jerv said. "But I would be extra polite if I asked him. Cauliflower ears. He's a fighter."

Some younger Gate family "nobility" staged bare-knuckle fights between Mangi, and rumors claimed they sometimes pitted Mangi against big predators, even the giant bears. I had always thought that would be effectively murder, but seeing Jimmy Nichols up close, I wasn't sure. Formidable guy.

"Nice tattoo," Captain Wagner said. "Someone has a sense of humor."

We kept our hands near our rifles. Jimmy paused about thirty feet away.

"It's weird hearing English come out of that mouth," Jerv whispered.

"Ooga booga," Jimmy said. "Is that better? Of course, I speak English. I lived in the US for eight years. And my hearing is sharper than yours. Are you here to get me back to civilization?"

Jerv and I glanced at one another. I finally said, "We may have differing opinions on that."

"Just to be sure, you are Jimmy Nichols, right? Captain Wagner asked.

"Who the hell else would I be?" He eyed her, shrugged dismissively, then turned to Jerv. "And what kind of martial artist are you?"

"Black belts in Isshin-Ryū and Kajukenbo," Jerv said. "Mixed martial arts."

The big Mangi nodded. "Not bad styles. I've fought against mixed martial artists, usually three or four at a time because one human doesn't last long enough to give the crowd their money's worth." He turned to Captain Wagner. "I don't fight human women. No offense, but they break too easy. I might make an exception for you." He turned to the Capital Police guys. "Neither of you would last more than a couple seconds. Black belt guy might last a minute or two." He waved toward me. "You, maybe thirty seconds."

Jerv looked as bewildered as I felt. "I'm not going to fight you. That would be like a ten-year-old fighting a gorilla."

"I know. You've probably heard about army guys who automatically figure out how they would kill everyone in a room. I do the same thing only just for knocking them out cold." The big Mangi paused and stepped back, then nodded. "Thornburg still doesn't know what to do with me, but he wants to keep me on his string, right? No trying to get back to my wife and son on my own." He swore in perfect English. "This isn't a tough decision. The bunch who brought me over think it's fun to drop Mangi women from helicopters, or maybe they thought threatening to would bring me out of hiding so they could shoot me. I know the Gate families don't always do things by the book, but throwing women out of helicopters is murder. Thornburg said he would take care of it, make justice happen. If he doesn't, I will. They're already down three dead and one who will probably never walk again, and we haven't lost anyone since the hunt started. If you hunt me and mine, you don't walk away."

"We aren't hunting you," Captain Wagner said. "But it's not smart to threaten people who have rifles,"

"I'm not trying to threaten you," Jimmy said. "But if I was, I would mention that I took three rifles off the mighty hunters we killed. They're on overwatch. Mangi: are all natural marks people." He stared at us. "If you aren't hunting us, and you aren't planning to take me back to civilization, why the hell are you here?" He looked wistful. "And I don't imagine you have beer or chocolate, do you?"

We shook our heads,

Jimmy shrugged. "It was worth a shot. You know who I am. Who the hell are you?"

We introduced ourselves. When we finished, Jimmy nodded. "Council Police is good, I think. I would like to report a couple murders and three self-defense killings."

"You know none of that will ever go to trial, right?" Captain Wagner asked.

The big Mangi shrugged. "If you want the law of the jungle, I can handle that. If you haven't figured it out yet, I was on the underground bare-knuckle fighting circuit back home. They call me Jimmy One Punch." The big Mangi grinned. "Dirty little secret. I pulled my punches so I just knocked out guys with one punch. I could have killed them just as easily."

He ambled the rest of the way up to us. "I was on the other side a long time. Long enough that I forgot about the quiet and the clean air, I would trade all that nature crap for a cold beer, air conditioning and watching a football game on TV in my recliner, though." He grinned, showing formidable teeth. "That's not a lot to ask, is it?"

"Maybe, eventually," Captain Wagner said. "If you tell us your story on video, we'll take it to Mr. Thornburg and maybe he'll help you go back."

"Or maybe he'll close his gate down and disappear for months again," Jimmy said.

"That wasn't his choice," Captain Wagner said. "He had a misunderstanding with the Gate Council."

"The Gate Council? Is that where all the rich guys get together and tell each other how powerful they are?" Jimmy grimaced. "Are they powerful enough to bring a poor Mangi prostitute back to life after rich young pieces of crap threw her out of a helicopter?"

"If they really did that, we'll bring them to justice some way," Captain Wagner said.

"Way too late for the ones who actually threw her out," Jimmy said. "The ones who sat and watched maybe. They all made the mistake of trying to hunt us, but I only killed the killers. Crippled one of the others, then they came after us in the helicopters. That wasn't in their rules, but they did it anyway. They didn't get any of us, but they kept trying."

"They hunted you from helicopters?" Captain Wagner asked. "The Council banned helicopters from the Wild. One of their first rules."

"What am I going to believe, the Council rules or my lying eyes?" Jimmy asked. "I was too trusting when I let them talk me into this hunt. I'm not in a trusting mood." He waved an oversized hand. "Shoo."

"We're here to take your deposition," Captain Wagner said.

"What good is a deposition if there won't be a trial," Jimmy asked.

"The Council Police have ways of handling things," Captain Wagner said. She turned to me. "You need to be out of earshot."

I drove the four-wheeler far enough away that I couldn't hear, then tried to zoom the drone camera in enough to lip read. No luck. I can sometimes lip read if I have just the right angle, but not this time. Did it matter what they said? Probably not. This whole trip was a waste. Robinette wasn't in the Wild, so there was no reason to recruit Jimmy to help her. I needed to go through the motions of asking him, but to earn my pay from his gangster friends, I needed Jimmy back. How could I thread that needle? I had no idea.

"Anything I should know?" I asked when Jerv returned from the deposition.

"Nothing you didn't already hear," Jerv said. "Gate family younger sons supposedly lured him here for a big-money fight, which turned into a hunt with him as the hunted."

"And it didn't go well for the mighty hunters." It didn't take a genius to figure that out. "Stupid, entitled rich kids against a full Mangi trained fighter with eight years in our world That's like hunting a lion with a human brain, only Mangi can capture rifles and use them."

"If you believe him, the hunt didn't go well," Jerv said. "He has major credibility problems, though. Gates are deliberately designed so they're too small to fly planes or helicopters through. You could take a helicopter through in pieces and reassemble it, but he claims they flew him to the Gate blindfolded and took him straight through on the same helicopter."

"Why are helicopters in the Wild a problem?" I asked.

"The Mangi could salvage too much from a crash." Jerv gestured to Jimmy. "Two minutes my ass. I could beat him in a fair fight."

Yeah, and I could fly by flapping my arms. I didn't say that aloud, though. "Are you done with him?"

Jerv nodded. "He's all yours."

I drove the four-wheeler toward Jimmy. I was almost there when Jerv yelled. "Do you really Heart books?"

"Books are okay," the big Mangi said. "But I'm happier in my recliner watching football on TV and drinking cold beer."

Chapter Thirteen:
Neolithic Mangi

"I hear you have a special message from Mr. Thornburg," Jimmy said.

"That I do."

Jimmy grinned, showing formidable teeth and eyed the four-wheeler enviously. "You sharing a secret she can't hear pissed off the tall police captain majorly."

"Mr. Thornburg wants you to help his daughter survive the last four months of a six-month exile to the Wild," I said. "He'll pay good money to make that happen."

"Four more months in the Wild with no beer, no chocolate, no coffee? Let me start negotiations by saying hell no. No amount of money will make me stay here another four months." He shook his head. "As I told the Council Police, his daughter isn't in the Wild anymore, so I couldn't help if I wanted to."

"How do you know she isn't in the Wild?"

"I speak Mangi, half a dozen languages, so I can tap into what's happening. News doesn't travel fast, but it travels." Jimmy shrugged. "I called in favors from before I crossed so the local Mangi tracked her but left her alone. She disappeared several days ago near where I crossed. Either she crossed or she's dead. Either way, Thornburg doesn't need me here."

He abruptly hopped into the passenger seat of the four-wheeler. "Thornburg needs to get me back to civilization. I'll show you why." He yelled to Captain Wagner and the others, "I have to show Eric something. We'll be back."

He directed me along a forest path until we reached a clearing where a huge oak tree had fallen. The clearing was overrun by saplings growing so close together a rabbit could barely slip between them, with blackberry briars wrapped around them. He motioned for me to stop. "The problem with having me here is that I've seen too much. I can live as a Mangi, but

I want the life I had over there. If I can't go back, I'll try to bring that life to the Wild. I can fill Mangi brains with a lot of ideas Thornburg and company don't want here. He needs to bring me back or kill me and killing me won't be easy."

"You don't want to back him into a corner," I said. "If the Gate families want you dead, they'll get it done."

"I just want to go home to my wife and son," Jimmy said. "Thornburg doesn't want me here. I'll show you why."

He opened a crude, but cleverly concealed gate in the tangle of saplings, an upright stick with berry briars wrapped around it, letting him swing the stick back to reveal a narrow passage through the saplings. Inside the passage, three huts with bark roofs over frameworks of sticks sat in a clearing. A sunlit garden held wild sunflowers with tiny seeds, weedy-looking plants in neat rows and watermelon vines. Strips of smoked meat sat on skewers over a small, nearly smokeless fire. A crude rope chair hung from two branches like a miniature hammock.

"I like sitting," Jimmy said. "It's a bad habit I picked up in your world." He gestured at the rows of plants. "Chenopodium and Erect Knotweed. Indians grew them before they got corn and beans. I like meat better, but the seeds make good famine food."

The other huts were empty. "Who are those for?"

"The mighty hunters brought half a dozen Mangi women crossers with them, prostitutes," Jimmy said. "They threw one out of the helicopter just for the hell of it and turned the rest loose to hunt down along with me." Anger flashed across his face, maybe from the memory of being hunted. "Hunting Mangi who have been on the other side is stupid. No amount of money can save you when you're that level of stupid." He waved a hand. "This place is a fixer-upper, but we can steal wolf cubs to raise as dogs, tame horses, figure out more crops. What do they call the time when your people started growing crops and taming animals? The Neolithic, right? We could build a Mangi Neolithic. It would be a shitload of work though. We just want to go home."

Neolithic. Not a word I expected to come out of a Mangi's mouth. "You convinced me, but the Council may do a drone strike on this place."

"Unless they got us all, that would be my signal to spread a lot of dangerous ideas I'm holding back."

#

Through the Wild Gate

When I got back to the others, Jerv raised his drone controller. "I tracked you. Mr. Thornburg will want to know about the crops."

"Jimmy just wants to go home," I said. "He showed me the village so Mr. Thornburg will get it done."

"Our side of the Gates isn't home for him," Captain Wagner said.

"After eight years over there, he doesn't see it that way," I said.

"We should burn him out," the captain said.

"Not a great idea," Jerv said. "He wasn't bluffing about having rifles on overwatch. I spotted three Mangi women in blue jeans and T-shirts carrying rifles. Do they know how to use them? I don't know."

"We can't have him running around in the Wild," I said.

Captain Wagner rolled her eyes. Okay, that was stating the obvious, though killing him or sending him back to our side of the Gates had problems too.

"He's a problem wherever he is," Captain Wagner said. "I wish to hell the families would leave the Mangi alone. Too easy to give them dangerous ideas. The 'I Heart books' tattoo is probably a joke, though."

"Maybe he wipes himself with the pages," Jerv said. "Can Mangi learn to read?"

Robinette obviously could, but she was half-human. I shrugged. "He knows what Neolithic means. He can probably read."

Jimmy apparently didn't realize that the drone was watching him. He sat in his hammock chair while three blue-jean Mangi women, all carrying rifles, gathered around him.

"Like a king and his court, or harem," Jerv said. "He operates almost like he's been in the military, but not quite. More like he's watched military movies."

How would Jerv know the difference? I had no idea, but the almost military movements made the already formidable Jimmy Nelson even more formidable.

I felt my frustration grow. Not only was this trip worthless, but the Council Police now knew that Robinette wasn't in the Wild. Maybe Mr. Thornburg could keep Jerv and Captain Wagner from telling anyone else, since they were doing a confidential investigation for him, but he would know. Should I let him think his daughter was dead, or reveal our secret? Both ideas sucked.

Jerv grinned. "You look like you've never run into a cage fighting Mangi who could break a male gorilla like a toothpick, says words like

Neolithic and Hearts books, but prefers football and cold beer. You'll get used to it." His grin broadened. "At least that's what I've heard." He stretched. "Actually, that's probably the first time that's happened to anyone in human history. And I shudder to think about what Mr. Thornburg is going to say when we get back. He won't believe us. I wouldn't believe us. On the other hand, he met Jimmy, so maybe he will believe us."

We started back, taking the more direct path Jerv found. To add insult to the already wasted trip, a turkey sized bird dashed into the trail, directly for our four-wheeler and jumped, sailing over me and landing in Jerv's lap. Jerv folded over, gasping, while the bird staggered on, landing on the other side of the four-wheeler. It stopped long enough to glare at us and give an outraged squawk, then ran on.

Jerv rubbed his stomach. "Idiot bird. That will leave a bruise. Nothing major damaged, though. Thanks for asking."

I tried to keep from laughing but couldn't. "So, turkeys over here can fly."

"I wouldn't call jumping six feet and landing in our four-wheeler flying," Jerv said.

"It was six inches from taking you out of the gene pool," I said.

Jerv winced. "I already have kids, but six inches over would have topped off this crap-fest of a day." He grabbed the drone controller, which had fallen, and wiped the screen. "And the controller broke."

#

"The drone footage should save our butts with Mr. Thornburg," Jerv said. "At least it will if that fool turkey didn't screw up the data chip."

That almost started me laughing again. "Did you get the turkey strike on video? I really want an instant replay or ten."

Jerv glared at me. "That turkey hurt. You won't think it's funny when one lands in your lap."

"I don't think anything that happened to us this last hour will happen to anyone else in the entire history of the world," I said. "What do we do now?"

Jerv eyed the drone controller. "If the data chip still works, we show Mr. Thornburg a video of the village. Then we wait while he changes his underwear." He shrugged. "If Thornburg is as smart as I think he is, he'll freak out. Mangi Neolithic. Trying their hand at farming and villages. That's disturbing. The Council will have a flock of kittens when they find out. They'll send a boatload of security people to hunt down this crew before other Mangi imitate them. Except we can't tell the Council because we're doing a confidential investigation."

"We can tell Mr. Thornburg and hope he can handle it," I said. Part of me wanted to leave Jimmy One Punch and his crew alone to make as good a life for themselves here as they could.

Jerv probably saw the distaste on my face. He shook his head. "It's a slippery slope from little gardens to strip mining, tearing down rain forests to make extra soft toilet paper for our pampered butts, plastic garbage islands in the ocean and World Wars. If the Mangi go down that slope on their own that's one thing. A bunch of kids with too much money and not enough brains sending them down that slope is a whole other thing."

He had a point, but it wasn't my call anyway. The Gate families would probably crack down hard when they found out about Jimmy's village. Maybe they were already trying. Someone, probably the Council Police, had been hunting Jimmy. But if the Council Police were hunting for the tall Mangi, wouldn't Jerv and Captain Wagner know?

"It would be easier to just let him go home," I said. "He's been on our side of the Gates eight years with no problems. That's his home now."

Some of Jimmy's comments still puzzled me. What did the bit about throwing a Mangi woman out of helicopters mean? The young 'nobility' undoubtedly conned Jimmy into a Russian Roulette hunt with him as the hunted. Despite their rifles, it didn't take a genius to figure out that hunt went very badly for the hunters. Three dead? They were lucky any of them survived. The big Mangi was formidable.

"The families still don't allow helicopters in the Wild, right?" I asked.

"Not even for the Council Police," Captain Wagner said. "And there are times we could really use them. But what happens if one crashes? Way too much metal the Mangi would love. Plus, helicopters start a slippery slope, toward commercializing the Wild and the Council knows it."

Did Jimmy's hunters really bring him in on a helicopter? It didn't seem possible, yet why would he lie about that? Did his helicopter claim trigger the Council Police investigation? Probably. Helicopters in the

Wild weren't something the Council Police could ignore. Did Marcus and company use a helicopter to get Robinette to where she was stranded? She was unconscious when they took her through, but she might have seen something that would tell us. Nothing I could do about that now, though, so I forced myself to relax and enjoy the Wild's extra-clean air and quiet.

The wolves paced us for a while, then sniffed the air and trotted away.

"Not as curious this time," Jerv said. "Our novelty wore off extra quick. Nothing to see here. Just Mangi riding metal horses that smell like burned gasoline."

The air still felt cleaner than back home, though noticeably less so when we got closer to the Compound. Despite the families' stringent efforts, their Compounds in the Wild still had a small, local impact on the air. I took in deep breaths while we were still far enough from the Compound, wishing we had more time in the Wild, but also anxious to talk to Robinette and wary of approaching twilight. With the shortcut, we should have plenty of time before dark, but none of us wanted to risk a night outside the Compound's walls.

It was late afternoon when we got back to the Compound. Mr. Thornburg took the broken drone controller and huddled with Jerv and Captain Wagner, telling me to wait until he finished with them. I wandered over to watch the rebuilding work. Contractors restrung electric wire and installed a backup generator by the Gate corridor. I wondered where the contractors thought they were. Some isolated rich people estate, probably. Most people who served the Gate families in the Wild never knew they had been there.

The Council Police finally finished and escorted me to Mr. Thornburg's office. It was a huge corner office that overlooked the now barren gardens. It was still sparsely furnished, with a card table and three folding chairs. The table and chairs still managed to look expensive. Mr. Thornburg. swore when I told him that Jimmy refused to help Robinette, then frowned, "It may be too late for that now."

I remembered that Jimmy told the Council Police that Robinette had disappeared, which probably meant Mr. Thornburg thought she was dead. I wanted to tell him that Robinette was safe, and opened my mouth to do it, but closed it with the words unsaid. Until Robinette decided to tell her dad, her location would stay a secret.

Through the Wild Gate

I noticed something change in Mr. Thornburg's face. He seemed more distant, almost hostile. Did he suspect I was hiding Robinette? What would I say if he asked me directly? No idea.

I hastily changed the subject. "Jimmy just wants to live in the suburbs, drink beer and watch football. If it was up to me, I would let him."

"That's what we figured," Mr. Thornburg said. "But there is a big difference between not bothering him when he's on our side and deliberately bringing him back." He suddenly looked tired and old. "You're a private detective, so you know this stuff. Possession really is nine-tenths of the law, even Gate family law. Once he was on our side of the Gate and had been there awhile, he had possession. Someone would have to make a case for sending him back or killing him. Sending him back would be stupid because he could teach the Mangi a ton of things we don't want them to know. Killing him would hack off organized crime. We aren't afraid of them, but we don't screw with them when we don't have to. Now that he's back in the Wild, though, I would have to make a case to send him to our world. That's not an easy case to make because he is a risk on our side too." He grinned, "But if he somehow ends up on our side again, he's back in possession. Somebody has to make a case for sending him back."

None of that makes much sense, but it is the way the law works. I wondered if the possession bit worked for Gates too. Outside, teams of gardeners planted flowers and garden vegetables, staking Mr. Thornburg's claim that reopening his Gate was permanent.

"If I find out who brought a martial arts trained Mangi with eight years of experience in our world back to the Wild, I'll tear out their intestines with my bare hands," Mr. Thornburg said.

"Even if it's your son Tom?" Sometimes my mouth moves faster than my brain. I hastily added, "Not that I have any reason to think he's involved."

Was that true? Tom talked about being in Russian Roulette hunts. Hopefully he wasn't stupid enough to get involved in this one, but I couldn't rule it out.

"The Council knows about Russian Roulette hunts and Mangi fights in general and doesn't approve, but usually doesn't interfere, as long as they're among consenting adults and no heirs are involved," Mr. Thornburg said. "And yes, I know Tom has been in a few of the hunts. If it was up to me, I would shut hunts and Mangi fights down entirely, especially Mangi fights to the death. Dead Mangis have friends who start blood feuds and eventually some Mangi clan will decide that the Gate families are part of the feud too. Maybe they couldn't do much to us, but Mangi have memories like elephants, and they'll wait a lifetime looking for revenge."

Jimmy lived in our world for nearly a decade. His English was nearly perfect. Before I met him, I wondered how a full-blooded Mangi could make it in our world. After all, Robinette had to work to look human and she was only half-Mangi. Jimmy should be as conspicuous as a shaved gorilla. After seeing him in person, most of those doubts went away. He had English and human body language down perfectly. If I met him on the street, I would be intimidated, but wouldn't wonder if he was human. What else could he be?

Mr. Thornburg knew about Mangi fights and Russian Roulette hunts, but the ones he knew about might be just the surface layer, with more violent and dangerous ones deeper underground. The Council Police monitored everything that went through the Gates, though.

If the Council knew about every plastic bag and candy wrapper that went through a Gate, how could they miss a helicopter and a huge Mangi? Corruption? The system was only as good as the bored guy watching the Gate and not making much money compared to the vapid, frivolous new nobility they saw around them. I didn't have much opportunity for corruption at Don's Auto, but I felt the boredom and resentment toward Gate families. Resentment and envy could help guards justify accepting bribes and glitching security cameras that were supposed to keep them honest.

Still, the Gates were supposedly designed so helicopters wouldn't fit through without some disassembly. Even if someone could fit a smaller model through, if Jimmy's story was true, the helicopter would have to carry at least him, a Mangi prostitute and someone to throw her out.

"Jimmy talked about a helicopter," I said.

Mr. Thornburg nodded. "And not a small one. I used the investigation to go behind the Council's back and reopen my Gate. Did I have the right to do that? Arguable, but now it's a fait accompli. Anyone who tries to shut it down again has to bring their case to Council court. I wrote most of their rules and have very good lawyers, so the Gate will

Through the Wild Gate

stay open for the foreseeable future. It took a while to get all that done, though. Maybe too long for Robinette."

"But there is a real security problem."

Mr. Thornburg nodded. "We have no records of Jimmy Nelson coming back to the Wild. That would be bad enough, but if someone brought him over by helicopter, we obviously have major holes in our security."

"Or somebody else developed Gates," I said.

Mr. Thornburg nodded. "That's the nightmare scenario. The Council police should spot any effort to build a gate before it happens, but they should also have spotted Jimmy coming back, especially by helicopter."

"Are you planning to bring Jimmy back?"

"You don't need to know," Mr. Thornburg said. "But I'll tell you anyway. He'll stay until I'm sure Robinette isn't alive somewhere in the Wild. Easier to keep him here than to get him back."

"What about his village?"

"It doesn't worry me. A lot of Mangi know about farming, Mangi servants see our vegetable gardens, though we don't hire them to work in them. Most Mangi near family Compounds don't try farming because it doesn't fit into their lives. If they don't keep moving, they hunt out all the game locally, so they can't just add a little farming to their lives. Horses and dogs would fit in very well, so we have strict rules against bringing them. With farming, the Mangi have to make a choice. Who in their right mind would stay in one place and dig in the dirt when there are mammoths to hunt?"

"Why did we choose farming?" I asked.

"I don't think hunters chose to be farmers," Mr. Thornburg said. "Our ancestors probably just drifted into it and eventually populations got so big we didn't have a choice. We'll have to shut Jimmy and his friends down, but it isn't urgent. Their ideas aren't contagious because other Mangi don't want to do what they're doing."

When I got home, I told Robinette about our adventures. "At least your dad is trying. You think we should let him know where you are?"

"I starved in the Wild for over two months while he screwed around. He can wait."

"You'll have to talk to him sometime."

"I'll do more than talk when the time comes, but I'm not looking forward to the conversation."

Dale Cozort

I told her about Jimmy One Punch and his village. "He seems to be making a life over there. We should leave him alone and see what happens."

"It would be nice," Robinette said. "I wish I had run into him in the Wild, though he might have wanted a high price for his hospitality and been coercive if I wasn't interested. Plus, he makes me look bad. Harvard graduate genius girl wanders around eating bugs while some ex-boxer Mangi jump starts civilization."

"At least he Hearts books."

Chapter Fourteen:
Mangi in the Suburbs

I called Mike Dickey and asked if he knew anything about Jimmy Nelson.

"Why are you asking?"

I thought about telling him about our brief expedition and its weird ending but decided not to trust him with that information. "Missing person case. I can't tell you more."

"Rumor mill only works if you feed information in when you take information out. Tell me something interesting."

What did I know that he didn't? Quite a bit, probably, though Mike had ways of knowing things he shouldn't. "Do you really know anything about Jimmy?"

"Nothing solid, but a step or two better than making crap up." He paused. "Not planning on giving me anything?"

"Tom Thornburg hates Marcus McFinney with a fiery passion but hides it when McFinney is looking. Thornburg gave McFinney a look that should have turned him into a flaming crater, then went all expressionless when McFinney turned around."

"That's thin stuff, but it's good to know. Having McFinney playing bedroom games with his twin sister has to grate on little Tommy."

"Not so little anymore, but not someone you want watching your back."

"I figured that out from your bear fiasco. Jimmy Nelson is a full Mangi, a crosser. He got across early on, before they got good security at Don's. Local gangs put him in underground bare-knuckle fighting. He got the nickname Jimmy One Punch, because that's all it usually took. He's tall for a Mangi and with a little work he can pass for a really ugly human. He's gone native. He speaks English like he was born here. He likes beer, hot dogs, football, apple pie and television. He even drives a Chevrolet. He has a human wife and a son, who is half-human. The

Blackwood family knows about him, but local organized crime wants to keep him and he's too dangerous to put back in the Wild with everything he knows, so the Blackwoods tolerate him. He keeps a low profile outside the underground fighting circuit. I don't think the other families know about him. Is he missing?"

"Sort of." Most of that I already knew, but at least it confirmed that the grapevine mostly knew what it was talking about.

"How did you find out about him?" Mike asked.

"A client," I said. "Any reason he would go back to the Wild?"

"Nope. Like I said, he's gone native. He's living the good life here."

Not anymore, I thought.

"What kind of idiot would get in a ring with an oversized full-grown male Mangi?"

"One who needed money and thought he was tough," Mike said. "Jimmy fought in mixed martial arts cages against two or three guys or fighters wearing brass knuckles. Even then, fights didn't last long. He earned that Jimmy One Punch nickname."

Did Jimmy going back to the Wild have anything to do with Robinette? Maybe. Based on what Jimmy's wife told me, Jimmy disappeared a couple of weeks before Robinette got stranded. That timing seemed too close to be a coincidence, but how were the two connected? Did Mr. Thornburg talk to him before his Gate got closed? Probably. How else would he know about the big Mangi?

Jimmy grew up in the Wild and could probably survive there, especially with modern weapons, so Mr. Thornburg's idea of having him help Robinette would have probably worked. But who was hunting him?

Jimmy might be another piece to the Robinette puzzle, but I had no idea how he fit.

"Here is a freebie," Mike said. "Robinette Thornburg wasn't the only Gate family member to disappear recently. Rumor mill claims that two guys from two separate families went missing a few months ago."

"Before or after Robinette?" I asked.

"Probably before. The families are keeping it very quiet. Someone may even be faking social media post to keep their friends from noticing they're missing."

"Important people?"

"Not by Gate family standards. They're all younger sons, a long way from inheriting, and the families aren't too unhappy they're gone."

"How reliable is that rumor?"

"Mid-range," Mike said. "Don't trust it with your life, but it's more likely to be true than not."

Where did the missing younger sons fit in? I remembered Jimmy saying that he killed some of the hunters. Missing younger sons. Dead hunters. It fit, but that didn't mean it was true. What other explanations might there be? If the two disappeared after Robinette, Robert Thornburg might have kidnapped them to exchange for Robinette, except if he kidnapped family members as leverage, he would have chosen people the families wanted back.

If Mike was right, the two disappeared before Mr. Thornburg would have a reason to kidnapped them anyway. Still, the missing younger sons went missing close to when Robinette did. The timing could be a coincidence, but my private eye instincts told me that was unlikely. The missing family members were probably pieces in the puzzle and reinforced Jimmy's story.

I had one lead to follow, though it was a long shot. Jimmy's wife was doing a sketch of the men who lured Jimmy into the hunt. If the sketches were good enough, maybe they would help.

#

When I got off the phone, I turned to Robinette. "Any reason the young 'nobility' wouldn't shanghai a full-grown Mangi with Martial Arts experience into their idiot Russian Roulette hunts?"

"Other than self-preservation? No. What could go wrong hunting someone almost as strong as a gorilla and as smart as a man? Actually, they're so bored and pampered I don't think fear would stop them. The Council would probably stop them if they knew about it, though. How would they get a Mangi through a Gate?" She took a deep breath. "I'm still stalling about talking to Dad. Tell me I'm a chickenshit and I need to get this over with."

"You're anything but a chickenshit, but you do need to talk to him." I remembered that Jimmy told the Council Police that Robinette wasn't in the Wild anymore. "You may be talking to him soon whether you want to or not."

She nodded and reached for the phone. As she did, the doorbell rang. I looked out the peephole and swore. "Your dad is here with a crap-ton of security people." A crap-ton equaled a dozen men and women. "You can have your heart to heart in person."

Chapter Fifteen:
Thornburg Family Reunion

I'm not sure what I expected when Robinette opened the door. Would she rip out Robert Thornburg's guts before his security stopped her?

Robinette jerked the door open. "Hi dad. It's been a while."

He opened his arms as if to hug her, then stopped. "Two months and fifteen days." He glared at me. "I figured it out when I heard that Robinette disappeared from the Wild about the same time she tried to come through the Gate at Don'ts. I just couldn't figure out why you didn't tell me." He turned back to her. "I guess you came through that first night instead of turning back and someone faked the video. Why didn't you come to me?" He turned to me. "Why didn't either of you tell me?"

He waved for his security people to back off and stood in the doorway, looking exhausted, and suddenly, old.

"We figured that if you didn't keep me from being stranded there the first time you couldn't or wouldn't stop me from getting sent back."

"I can defend you," he said savagely. "I'm on the inner Council, a founding member. I chose the Gate families and set up the rules."

"Yet your Gate was shut down and our mansion in the Wild was stripped, with Mangi crapping in the halls and not even plumbing left," she said. "I looked at that and figured you lost your power. Are you even still on the Council?"

His face went expressionless. "Officially, I'm suspended. I was stupid. I trusted your sister." He shook his head slowly. "I still don't get it. I planned to give her everything she tried to take, and she knew it."

"You didn't make her think you might change your mind?"

"No. She wasn't the perfect choice, but she was the best choice I had." He took a deep breath. "But you're back. How did you make it all those months?"

She shrugged. "Two months and change? I lost track of the days.

Through the Wild Gate

I'm tough and wanted someone to pay for stranding me. How did you know I was here?"

"I didn't, but it was worth checking, especially after I found out you weren't in the Wild. You had to be either here or dead." He glared at me. "I would have checked sooner except I figured Eric here would know he needed to get you where I could protect you."

"That didn't work out so well last time," Robinette said. "I went home and ended up buck naked, tied up and in the Wild. And now I hear you decided to make me a mother without my permission."

Mr. Thornburg stared at her. "Make you a mother? Sorry dear, but that won't work for you. You're too different."

"Like a mule," she said. "But with enough money, test tubes and genetic manipulation, it might work. I'm not your lab rat, though. If you tried that, I would scratch your eyes out."

"Where is this coming from?"

I told him. When I finished, he leaned his head back and laughed. "You two believed that crap?"

"Not entirely," I said. "But the Council did and Leah either did or pretended to. Your son Tom was leaning toward believing it. So it's not true?"

"After I told Robinette about her mother and she blew up at me because she couldn't have kids, I did a little research, but the risks of exposing the Wild or of getting a severely handicapped child were way too high. I dropped the idea so fast it had skid marks on it. It probably wouldn't get past the sperm meeting the egg anyway." He turned to Robinette. "And if I got serious about it, I would ask you."

Was he telling the truth? Probably, but he was quite capable of lying with no outward signs. He might not bother lying to me, but if he really planned to do this, he wouldn't want Robinette to know.

I couldn't tell if Robinette believed him or not. Her fists were still clenched, her knuckles pale. "If the test tube baby thing was just a passing thought, why did I end up in the Wild?" She asked. "And why didn't you find me?"

"I knew where you were," he said. "I just couldn't do anything about it."

She got that incinerate on the spot look. "Why couldn't you do anything about it?"

"You deserve an explanation." His eyes flicked to me. "Mind if I come in, Eric?"

I wasn't thrilled with the idea. "That might lead to broken furniture," I said. "I like my furniture."

He turned to Robinette. "Willing to hear me out?"

"I'm not excited by the idea." She took a deep breath. "But I won't break Eric's furniture."

He stepped inside, waving off his security people again.

"Have a beer?" Robinette turned away briefly, a mix of fury and sadness on her face. She worked hard, visibly for composure, looking calm when she turned back.

Mr. Thornburg dominated the room, a tall man, stomach flat as mine had been at nineteen. His hair was thick, though peppered with gray. "Raising you with my other kids wasn't popular among Gate families," he said finally. "They think Mangi are hopped-up apes. I wanted you as my daughter and forced it through the Gate Council. I had to agree to a test, though. You had to get a college degree by age twenty-two, which nobody thought was possible."

"I hit that out of the park."

He smiled. "Yes, you did." There was pride in his voice. "The families went along with me because they figured you couldn't make it through college, and I would have to send you back to the Wild. Hell, most of them didn't think you would make it to adulthood. Most hybrid kids don't. But you lived and got a college degree. A lot of people in the Council were looking for an excuse to send you to the Wild or kill you outright because you're a danger. If you got in an accident and needed blood, we would have to scramble to keep some smart doctor from figuring out something was badly wrong."

"So they were waiting to pounce."

"Yes, but I didn't think they would have the guts. I went hunting in upper Michigan and came back four days later with you gone, the Gate closed and me suspended from the Council. I didn't notice you were gone at first, then got private detectives and figured out where you probably were. Without a Gate I couldn't do much except hope you remembered Don's and lived to get to it."

"The Council never told you why they suspended you?"

"Just bullshit about imminent danger to the families and that you were exiled to the Wild for six months."

"Six months?" Robinette's face darkened. "Nobody raised here could last six months. I was starving after two months--lost a quarter of my body weight. Why didn't they just kill me?"

"They can't kill Gate family members without a trial and a unanimous vote of twelve randomly chosen Council members," Mr. Thornburg said. "But the six months was designed to kill you."

"Which is why they left me unconscious and tied up," Robinette said.

"Tied up wasn't part of the deal," Mr. Thornburg said. "They had authority to exile you, but not to leave you helpless. Of course, nobody would have known about the tying up if you died there."

"It happened," Robinette said. "The vultures almost had me before I got loose."

"I hate to ask this, but is there any way you could last four more months there? I have some ideas, but I may lose in the Council. We do have an ace up our sleeve if you have to go back. I hid some provisions near my Gate."

"Nothing you could send would get me through four months alone. It would be more merciful to put a bullet in my head," she said. "I would do it myself before I went back."

"Hold off on bullets," Mr. Thornburg said. "I have ideas that should work."

"They had better involve a lifetime of showers, toilet paper and brushing my teeth."

"Yes, but some of them may put you in a lot of danger. Let me see what I can do." He stood abruptly. "Rest. Get your strength back. Enjoy modern life." He turned to me. "You're back to bodyguard. Full pay for guarding her. I'll have people on an outer perimeter but watch yourselves."

He walked out. Robinette took a deep breath. "Do you believe him?"

I didn't entirely, though I couldn't remember him straight-out lying to me. He didn't always tell me everything when I was his bodyguard, but he didn't lie. "Has he ever lied to you?"

"Just a tiny bit," Robinette said, her voice bitter. "Until I was twenty-one, I thought I was all human, just weird. I thought I could have a family, enjoy old age with my grandchildren. But nope. I'm sterile. Remember when I said I called him a bastard? That was when he told me the truth. I didn't know the Wild existed until then."

"You really blew up at him when you found out you couldn't have kids?"

"Yes, but I got over it. There was nothing either of us could do about it."

The blowup made McFinney's story more plausible, but I still didn't believe it. What Mr. Thornburg said about risks rang true. If Council members were already looking for an excuse to get Robinette, they might not have looked at Leah's evidence too carefully.

"Does Leah hate you enough to screw up her inheritance to get to you?" I asked.

"I've never given her any reason to," she said. "She made everything a rivalry, which I almost always won, but I didn't rub it in."

That didn't necessarily mean anything. Sibling rivalry can go deep and irrational.

I felt as though a huge burden was off my shoulders. Whatever happened now, it would be between Mr. Thornburg and the other families, not a ridiculously uneven struggle with Robinette and me pitted against the most powerful men in the world. Still, even Mr. Thornburg might be overmatched if the Council was united against him.

"Any idea what your dad's planning?"

She shook her head. "Them leaving me tied may give him an opening. The tying was probably my sister's idea. She gets into ropes and handcuffs, or so I hear."

"Any other lies from Mr. Thornburg?" I asked.

"Wasn't that one enough?" She drained her beer. "At least I don't have to worry about birth control. As to other lies. I don't remember any. He *is* a bastard, but not usually a liar."

"So maybe he didn't try to treat you like a lab rat. And maybe the Council did make him agree to send you back if you didn't make it through college."

"Probably. He steered me ways that helped in the Wild. No survival training, but rough camping trips, hiking, botany, including edible plants. Martial arts. I was as ready as anyone could be except snake-eater wilderness survival types." She stared at her empty beer bottle. "I was still lucky as hell to make it two months and that was drawing down fat stores, eating bugs and bluffing fricking mountain lions off their kills. I'm seriously not going back."

#

The next two weeks, Robinette ate a lot, worked out and slept a lot, alone. I took the couch, not because she kicked me out but because she was exhausted. She came to the couch some nights and wrapped her arms around me. The first time, she said, "I want you to hold me, nothing else."

I held her a lot of nights and felt her growing stronger, rebuilding lost muscle. Her muscles were far harder than any other woman I've held, including top-notch female athletes. If she couldn't make it in the Wild, I couldn't imagine anyone who could. Jimmy Nelson maybe, but he was all Mangi and he grew up there.

What was Robert Thornburg planning? It had something to do with Robinette being left in the Wild tied up. It probably also had something to do with honor. The Gate families are gutter rats with ancestors smart and lucky enough to get rich. They are vicious enough to keep and expand those fortunes but as Tom mentioned, they think of themselves as modern-day nobility. Honor is big among them, though they would cheat a starving man out of his last penny. Yeah, not nice people. Still, if daddy Thornburg manipulated their twisted version of honor to keep his daughter alive, great.

Mr. Thornburg pulled me off guard duty and told us the other families knew where Robinette was and had agreed to leave her alone, until a Council hearing. "Possession is nine-tenths of the law, and they don't have her anymore, which means they have to convince the Council to take her instead of okaying a fait accompli. I may win at the hearing or delay a decision until the other side gives up."

He said that we could go out now, but cautiously. That was a welcome break from cabin fever, though we only went out together, in daylight, to heavily traveled areas. When we went out, Thornburg's security tracked us, as did someone else. Professional. Lots of resources. The Council or maybe the hostile families. They just watched, not making contact. We didn't see Leah or Tom or Marcus McFinney. The tails I picked up at Jimmy's house vanished shortly after Mr. Thornburg visited my apartment.

We didn't go from suspecting Robert Thornburg of planning unspeakable things to trusting him, but we followed his guidance, warily. He understood Council politics in ways Robinette and I couldn't hope to.

Robinette kept getting stronger. She also spent a lot of time on the Internet, reading about edible wild plants, improvised shelters and wilderness survival in general.

"Planning to go back?" I asked.

"Planning to survive if I do go back." She turned back to her research. "I knew a lot more than I realized about how to survive over there. Dad slipped in enough survival training that I'm not learning a lot more now that I'm working at it. I don't think it's possible for someone raised on this side to make it over there on their own."

Her getting sent back to the Wild seemed unlikely at this point. Before, the Council thought sending Robinette to the Wild was a death sentence. Now that she survived two months there, they wouldn't be sure the Wild would kill her. If she survived over two months, they might think she could survive indefinitely. That wasn't true but they probably didn't know how close to starving she was when she came back.

"If they want you dead, they'll kill you outright this time instead of trying to let the Wild do it."

"They'll want to kill me, but they have rules, and Dad will hold them to those rules." She turned back to her research. "Going back for the rest of the six months is a real possibility, though I would like to think I would force them to kill me rather than letting them send me back."

The Council rules would not stop an 'accident', though with Mr. Thornburg on our side that kind of accident would be more difficult to arrange.

I had almost forgotten about Mike. The corrupt cop called me a couple times to brag about his exploits, real or imaginary, and to pass along tidbits of family gossip.

"I hear Marcus McFinney is getting too big for his blue jeans," Mike said. "He's hooking up with Leah Thornburg, the acting head of a Gate family and thinks that makes him a force. The Blackwood family is looking for ways to cut him down to size."

"They probably don't have to worry about him," I said. "Leah likes her bad boys, but from what I've heard she changes them out like she changes shoes."

"She sort of runs a Gate family but doesn't control the Gate," he said. "She probably thinks she needs him for now, but he brings a ton of baggage and Robert Thornburg is using that baggage against her in the Council, trying for a full comeback, taking his Council seat back and keeping his Gate open. Can he pull it off? I don't know. He's the master of Council in-fighting and rules-lawyering, plus he knows where the bodies are buried, literally in some cases, so maybe."

He heard rumors of Mangi hunts, with the younger Gate family members using the same rules for Mangi that they did for their Russian

Roulette hunts, and suspected those rumors were partly true. "I could see them trying that with Jimmy Nelson, but I'm pretty sure the Council would put a stop to that. Jimmys too dangerous. He might well kill the lot of them and then he would be running around the Wild with everything he learned over here."

That was exactly what I thought had happened, but Mike was right about the Council being very unhappy about bringing Jimmy across to do the hunt. Still, I knew he was in the Wild, so he had to have gone through a Gate to get there. Maybe the Council Police didn't have as much control as they thought they did.

"I've heard rumors of people hunting game animals, and Mangi, from helicopters," Mike said. "That's from people I would ordinarily believe, but I don't believe it. That would go against Council policy enough that I can't see anyone thinking they could get away with it. I wouldn't want to try hunting Jimmy Nelson with anything less than a helicopter, though."

Jimmy mentioned helicopters in his rant, but the Council would never authorize them in the Wild. A crash could leave any survivors far from rescue and the Mangi would find the wreckage a treasure trove of unique material and ideas. Could someone smuggle a helicopter through without the Council knowing? It would take bribing guards and probably taking the helicopter apart to make it fit through the Gate. Guards would know that letting something that big go through would get them fired and probably dead if they got caught. No way a helicopter could get through without the guards being in on it.

Evette, Jimmy's wife, called and told me that the watchers were gone, then asked if I knew any more about Jimmy. I couldn't tell her much more than I had in person, but she lingered on the line, apparently lonely. I wondered how Jimmy was doing. Probably fine. If anyone could survive in the Wild, it would be the big Mangi. Unlike Robinette, he had Mangi he knew to watch his back, was well-armed and grew up in the Wild. Still, if someone with helicopters was hunting him, he was in danger.

Evette was almost done with her sketches and said she would email them to me in a day or two.

Other than those calls, we remained isolated, living a normal, even boring existence. Robinette offered to take the couch, but I declined. With her tension gradually relaxing, she flashed back to the Wild a lot of nights and came to the couch, clinging desperately to me until the terror subsided. How she held herself together over there, I don't know, but the experience left her terrified as well as angry.

The terror didn't lower my opinion of her toughness. She was, in most ways, a modern, human young woman, forced to live alone in the Wild for over two months, surviving by her wits, her next meal and drink of water always iffy, vulnerable every time she slept, with no one to help watch for predators. The slightest misstep, even a twisted ankle or infected cut, could be fatal, while a broken leg would be a death sentence.

Our times on the couch together were comforting, not sexual. She had mentioned a childhood crush at one time, and I wondered what I would do if her embraces turned sexual. A physical relationship now would make an already precarious situation worse. Would that stop me from joining in? I wasn't sure. Fortunately, she was focused on healing and getting ready for what the Council would throw at her.

Part of me was happy in that limbo, because when the lull ended, matters could get far worse. Part of me felt the danger hanging over us and wanted to face the Council, to know what they were going to throw at us and deal with it.

The lull lasted two weeks, then Robert Thornburg showed up at my apartment. He looked tired and discouraged.

"Did you work your angle?" Robinette asked.

"I set it up," he said. "I know all the loopholes in the family charter because I wrote most of it, but the other side knows the charter too and closed off most of what I was trying to do. I had to get creative and if we go through with this, you'll be in a great deal of danger. Are you willing to fight to keep from going back to the Wild for the rest of the six months?"

"I would fight an army."

"You won't have to fight an army, but you will have to fight." He wouldn't tell us anything else about his plan. "I'm out of good options and if what I try works, you could end up dead or crippled," Mr. Thornburg said. "But you'll have a fighting chance to stay."

"Chances of me not going back are a hundred percent," Robinette said. "I may die, but I'll die here."

"This can only work if it's a surprise," Mr. Thornburg said. "Dress in your business best. We're going in front of the Council tomorrow at noon, both of us and the stakes are as high as they come." He smiled at Robinette. "Bring your 'A' game." He turned to me. "You're coming too." He left before we could ask any questions.

Chapter Sixteen:
A Council & A Trap

Robinette was going to have to fight. What kind of fight? A physical one? Who with? Robinette and I sat together on my couch after Mr. Thornburg left and tried to figure that out. Marcus McFinney was a possibility. I remembered the Council's supposed love of duels. Was Mr. Thornburg planning a duel? From what little I knew, duels were officially over honor, though in reality they were probably more for spectacle or to settle scores. Robinette claimed duels were always held in the Wild because no one except the Council had jurisdiction there. The challenged had their choice from a list of weapons and duels could be to first blood, until someone couldn't stand up to fight anymore or to the death.

In the morning, Mr. Thornburg stopped by with his security entourage and picked up Robinette and me. They blindfolded us for the last part of the ride. When the blindfolds came off, we were in an imposing room that looked like the US Senate chambers, with a courtroom vibe thrown in. The room didn't shout power and wealth. It calmly and confidently made both clear.

Five chairs sat on a raised platform at the front, one of them empty. "The inner Council." Mr. Thornburg pointed to the empty chair. "Mine." His tone was flat. "And I'll have it back, just not yet."

On one side of the platform, a witness chair sat inside a low fence. Uniformed Council Police guarded the room.

I wondered about the police. Robinette claimed the Gates were officially a Continuity of Government operation. Did the Council Police have actual police powers on our side of the Gates? They might, but I wondered how much power they had over the Gate families. The families had their own security, and an actual police force was an obvious threat to family independence. Maybe that was the point. How else could the Council enforce its rules? These were fabulously wealthy people, used to doing whatever they wanted. Council rules had to have teeth to them if the families wanted to keep the Wild the way it was.

How effective were the Council Police? I had no idea. Jerv and Captain Wagner seemed effective enough, but they let me go on their investigation when a semi-disgraced family leader asked them to. Mr. Thornburg was a special case, though, because he picked most of the Council Police and for at least some of them, their loyalty was apparently more to him than to the Council.

A half-circle of sixteen chairs faced the five raised ones. Outside that circle a raised stand with stadium-style seats gave room for a few hundred spectators, with the lowest seats high enough that anyone who tried to jump down would break bones. The only ways down were narrow stairways guarded by Council Police.

Above the stadium-style seats were three stadium-style enclosed boxes, apparently for members of the Families and their guests. Marcus McFinney was in one of the boxes, along with Leah Thornburg. The Council police escorted Mr. Thornburg's party, including us, to the same box. I eased forward between Robinette and McFinney, but she just smiled a feral smile and said, "Later."

The Council chairman, Jericho Blackwood, called the Council to order. He wore another expensively tailored black suit with a white bow tie, apparently his trademark. He seemed relaxed, in control, but I sensed a tension in him that set off alarm bells in my head. If something had this man rattled, I had to be on my guard.

The Council did mind-numbingly boring crap long enough that I almost dozed off despite the cloud hanging over Robinette. It was my normal sleep time and I had to fight waves of drowsiness.

I snapped back to attention when Chairman Blackwood moved to review the matter of Robinette Thornburg's exile. Mr. Thornburg's lawyer immediately called Marcus McFinney to the witness chair. He didn't get sworn in the way a witness in a courtroom would have, but Chairman Blackwood said, "As a witness before the Gate Council, you will give truthful and complete answers to all questions. You have no right to avoid questions on the grounds of self-incrimination here, and if you claim faulty memory and the Council decides that you are trying to avoid the question you will be severely punished. Any untruthful, incomplete or evasive answers will result in severe penalties, up to and including permanent exile to the Wild or death. Is that clear?"

McFinney agreed, while I mentally said, "Oh crap." Yeah, the Gate families did what they wanted and little things like the US Constitution didn't seem to bother them.

"If a question is improper, I will stop you immediately," Chairman Blackwood said. "If I don't stop you, don't look to your lawyer. Just answer." He nodded to Mr. Thornburg's lawyer. "Your witness."

Mr. Thornburg's lawyer was a small man, not overweight, but flabby, with a long, dangling double chin about an inch wide hanging below his mouth. The chin wobbled when he walked or talked. I found myself staring at it and had to refocus on his questions. He was saying. "The two sides have agreed to stipulate that on the date indicated on the document in front of you, you, working with Leah Thornburg, temporarily exiled Robinette Thornburg to the Wild, based on Ms. Thornburg's role as acting head of the Thornburg household and invoking emergency powers due to an imminent threat to the Families. The stipulation also states that you alone performed the actual exile and that neither you nor Leah Thornburg communicated with anyone else, due to the extreme urgency of the situation. Do you agree with that stipulation in full?"

"Yes, I do."

"That's all we needed," Mr. Thornburg whispered.

The lawyer pulled out a sheet of paper. "This is a signed and notarized statement from Robinette Thornburg that says she woke up in the Wild after being drugged, and was at that time tied up, both hands and feet. Do the emergency powers allow you to leave a person in temporary exile tied up?"

"I didn't—"

"Just answer the question," the chairman said.

"No, it does not."

"Doesn't it in fact specifically forbid leaving a temporary exile incapacitated or restrained, with severe penalties, up to and including death for anyone who violates that rule?"

McFinney turned visibly even more pale than normal. "Yes."

"Did you, in fact leave Robinette Thornburg in the Wild, with her arms and legs bound?"

McFinney looked trapped. "No, I did not."

"Given Robinette Thornburg's sworn affidavit, I ask Chairman Blackwood to rule that Mr. McFinney has cast aspersions on Ms. Thornburg's truthfulness and honor."

"I so rule," Chairman Blackwood said. Leah rose halfway out of her chair, then abruptly sat back down.

"Does the person whose honor has been questioned wish to respond?"

Robinette immediately stood. "I do, your honor. I demand a duel, with the stakes being the remaining time of my exile in the Wild. If I lose, I will go back. If I win, Mr. McFinney will serve the remainder of that term."

"The challenge is recorded and will be considered a just and valid challenge of honor unless Mr. McFinney's employer objects at this time. As Mr. McFinney's employer and as chair of this Council, I have to recuse myself, therefore there is no objection, and the challenge will be considered just and valid. A duel will be scheduled at the Council's convenience."

McFinney glared at him but didn't say anything.

"Mr. McFinney, as the challenged party, you may decide among authorized forms of duel, subject to the approval of the Council. You have two days to choose the form of duel and tentative rules. After the challenger approves, rule changes can only be made with the consent of both parties. You may return to your seat."

I stared at the witness chair, stunned at the speed of Mr. Thornburg's coup and torn between hope and fear. Marcus McFinney didn't move for several seconds, his face expressionless. Finally, he got up and marched up the stairs, his eyes straight ahead.

When he got back to the box, Marcus glared at Mr. Thornburg. "You think you're clever, don't you? All you've done is put your half-ape daughter back in the Wild with her arms and legs broken."

Chapter Seventeen:
Getting Ready to Rumble

As a railroading, the brief legal clash was brilliantly done and over before the opposition could get their minds around what happened. It also offered the Council and their families a unique and interesting duel, which would be unpopular to stop. The opposition on the Council also probably expected Robinette to lose, which muted their protests.

"That looked almost too easy," I said, once we were back in the car. "Are you sure we didn't just fall into a trap?"

"It looked easy because I put everything in line," Mr. Thornburg said. "A lot of people could have jolted it off the rails, but I gave them reasons not to. Think about all the dogs that didn't bark."

I thought about the way the brief legal encounter played out and realized he was right. Mr. Thornburg had stage-managed the entire affair, playing off the Blackwood family's growing concern over their overly powerful and ambitious head of security so the Blackwood family didn't object to the damning language in the stipulation document or to the duel itself. As chairman, Jericho Blackwood undoubtedly knew ahead of time where the questioning was going, at least in general. This wasn't justice by any means, but it did the job, if the goal was to put Robinette in a duel with Marcus McFinney.

The more I thought about it, though, the less I liked that goal. I turned to Mr. Thornburg while we filed out of the Council chamber. "This literally gives her a fighting chance but wasn't there a better way?"

"It was the last thing in my bag of tricks," Mr. Thornburg said. "I don't want to send her into this, but it was that or have them send her back by force or try to. You heard her say she would rather die, and I believe her."

I believed her too, but I was also keenly aware of the downside. "Don't underestimate Marcus McFinney," I said. "He's a big, strong guy with a good martial arts background. He wouldn't last two minutes against Jimmy Nelson, but Robinette is half human and a lot smaller than McFinney. McFinney could beat her and might very well break bones. That's not much better than sending her back tied up,"

"That's why I wouldn't have done it this way if I had any choice," Mr. Thornburg said. He turned to Robinette. "But it does give you a chance. If you win, nobody from the Gate families will dispute your right to stay here."

"Then I'll just have to win," Robinette said. "I'm stronger than anyone I've ever met. I'm a black belt in two kinds of martial arts and I've spent two months in hell. He put me there. I'll take that sucker down."

I felt a fierce wave of protectiveness. "Can you name someone to fight in your place? I'll fight him."

"Five years ago, you would have won," Robinette said. "And you're still a very strong man, but he's almost ten years younger than you and a lot faster. Sorry, but I have to do this myself."

That stung, but she was probably right. Mid-thirties isn't old, but it's near retirement age for most boxers and martial artists.

"Age and treachery beats youth and enthusiasm," I said. I didn't really believe it, though, not in this case.

"I can beat him," Robinette said. "I'm half Mangi and I have two months of rage to unload on that bastard."

I didn't meet her eyes. Yes, Robinette was by far the toughest woman I had ever met, but McFinney weighed over two hundred pounds, twice her body weight. That was problem enough, but he knew hundreds of dirty tricks from his mixed martial arts days. I wished briefly that we could put Jimmy Nelson into that ring. "Either of your black belts in Mixed Martial Arts?"

"We did some, but it wasn't the main focus," Robinette said. "It's settled. I'll do it. When?"

"We'll know in two days," Mr. Thornburg said. He turned to me. "What kind of duel do you think he'll choose?"

"He probably doesn't know how good she is with a gun, so he'll steer clear of that. Knives maybe, but unless he's really good with a knife he could end up sliced up too. The old saw about knife fights is that the winner goes to the hospital. If they're allowed, he'll probably go for bar fight rules. No weapons that are specifically designed as weapons. Street clothes. You fight until one of you can't stand up. No tapping out. All holds are legal. Maybe the ref steps in if one of you is about to die, or maybe not. If the rules don't forbid it, you can do it."

Those were brutal rules, but Mr. Thornburg said they were allowed in Family duels if the challenged party wanted them. The color gradually drained from his face as he apparently realized how brutal this fight could be. There was an option where the ref would stop the fight to prevent broken bones or joint damage and one where they wouldn't.

"Eye gouges allowed?" I asked.

Mr. Thornburg sighed. "In some types of duels. Blinding. Stomping." He swore. "I shouldn't have agreed to the fight, but If I back out now, they'll claim we forfeited and send her back."

My anger surged. This wasn't a fight. It was a license for assault, then murder. Sending a badly beaten woman to the Wild *was* murder. "She can't win," I said.

Robinette glared at me. "I thought you were on my side."

"I am but blowing glitter up your skirt doesn't help." I hated this, but someone had to tell her. "You are the strongest, toughest woman I know. You could beat almost any man you meet, including me. Against a dirty, experienced MMA fighter more than a foot taller than you, who outweighs you two to one, you probably won't win. He has reach on you and will have zero qualms about hitting you. Ever watch boxing matches where one guy has a couple inches of reach advantage?"

She shook her head. "I don't watch boxing."

"A two-inch reach advantage means a boxer can hit at will and the shorter person pays a price to get close. If the taller person is fast on their feet, the shorter person rarely gets a punch in. That's two inches. He'll have six inches or more of reach on you. He can keep out of range and hit you at will." Her arms were long for her body, but her legs were short. If Marcus was smart, he would use mostly low kicks and jabs to wear her down, never letting her get her hands on him. "Shorter reach means you pay a price every time you try to get close enough to throw a punch. Steel-toed boots make that price much higher. Figure he'll have what amounts to steel clubs on his feet. Human, or even Mangi, heads can't take hits with steel clubs."

"And there is nothing I can do?"

"You can cut the ring off and try to trap him in a corner. If he kicks at your head, try to grab his foot. If he gets close, grab him and take him down. You are stronger than him, but that only helps if you get a grip on him. If he's overconfident you may get a hold on him and take him to the ground. If you do, finish him because you may not get another chance."

"We're getting way ahead of ourselves," Mr. Thornburg said. "We don't even know he'll pick that kind of duel."

That was true, but it was the kind of fight he was used to and good at, and probably his best chance to win. "I would be thinking about how to win that kind of fight. He's a thug, so it would come natural to him."

She nodded. "And what you said to do makes a lot of sense. Sounds like I have a chance. I just have to fight smart."

That wasn't what I was saying, but I continued. "He is carrying twice your weight, so every second he's moving but isn't hurting you, he gets a little weaker and slower. That may help if you survive long enough. Every missed kick or punch tires him. If you block a punch or kick, make the block hurt." Martial arts would have taught her that, but it didn't hurt to remind her. "If his arm or leg is close enough to hit you, you can hit it. Every block should throw him off balance or have you grabbing his arm or leg."

"It's winnable," she said.

"He'll have nasty tricks up his sleeve," I told her. "Street clothes could include steel-toed boots and belts with heavy metal buckles he can use as a whip. He can have heavy rings on his fingers, like brass knuckles."

Mr. Thornburg looked sick. "I was trying to give her a chance. She's so strong I thought she could beat him."

"I can," she said. "I'm smarter and tougher than him, and I know what months in the Wild are like. They'll carry him into the Wild when I'm, done, because he won't be walking."

I didn't believe that, but I had a few days and a very motivated pupil to make it happen.

#

As I expected, McFinney chose bar fight rules and scheduled the fight for five days after he chose the type of duel. That was close to as long as he could wait without forfeiting, which hopefully meant he wasn't confident about the outcome. It also meant that he had almost a week to come up with dirty tricks.

Mr. Thornburg found videos of Marcus McFinney's mixed martial arts fights. Bad news. The guy was a thug, but smart. He could take a punch or fight on the ground, but rarely had to. His long kicks usually dominated fights. God was he fast. He was only a few years short of thirty now so he might have lost a little speed. Most martial artists do at his age. We couldn't count on it, though. We couldn't find any video from his last two years.

I studied the rules again. Heavy boots and belts weren't forbidden. Hair pins were. Guns, knives and clubs were out, as were laser pointers and a list of edged and throwing weapons, including rocks. I wondered what they left off the forbidden list to give Marcus an edge. I didn't spot anything. Neither did Mr. Thornburg's security people. Mr. Thornburg brought in specialists for some training, but I did most of it. Robinette learned fast and already knew a lot about martial arts. If anyone her size could win, she would. That was the problem, though. Her size left her at a huge disadvantage.

We tried steel-toed boots for Robinette, but they slowed her too much. I did find steel-toed tennis shoes. Never knew they existed. Hopefully Marcus wouldn't know either. Heavy rings wouldn't help her much because if she got in a clean shot to the head, it would probably end the fight anyway. We sparred a lot, and she was as strong as I figured, driving me back when I held punching pads for her.

The sparring uncovered a problem. Mangi are ambush predators, fast in a sprint, with packs wrestling thousand-pound bison to the ground and killing them. That takes enormous grip strength and tough bodies, surviving bison kicks that would kill normal humans. Our ancestors made their living a different way, chasing anything that ran from us until the prey couldn't run anymore. Endurance hunting. While Robinette was much stronger than a man pound for pound and could run far longer than most humans, she didn't have the endurance an elite human athlete would. She had to end the fight early.

She had a pleasant surprise too, though. She could jump from a standing start unbelievably high and far. From a run, holy crap her leaps covered ground fast. That was an ace to remember, but a leap leaves you committed, and a smart fighter can get out of your way if he knows it's coming or make you pay for committing too soon, adding your momentum to the force of his kick or punch.

Belts might let Robinette make up for his reach advantage, but she didn't have time to master using one as a whip. I had her wear one with a sharp metal tip in public and was rewarded when Marcus asked to modify the rules to outlaw belts. Mr. Thornburg got a modification outlawing rings in exchange for no belts. Score one for our side.

The rules didn't ban dirty tricks before the fight, but if either fighter was killed or permanently crippled before the fight, their opponent would go to the Wild.

Fight day came on like a freight train. I alternated between hope during our training sessions and despair when I watched videos of Marcus fighting. I felt my tension rising while the days counted down and tried not to let my fears infect Robinette. Then it was fight day.

I got an email from Evette with her sketches attached. Normally, that would have been at the top of my agenda, but with the fight on my mind, I just printed the sketches out and stuffed them in my pocket.

The fight was in a gym in the Wild of course, ironically in the Thornburg compound, but with Marcus's people in charge of setting up the venue.

Mr. Thornburg brought me along as a bodyguard and as Robinette's coach, though I had to go in blindfolded. No one outside the Gate families and a very few close retainers got to know the exact locations of the Gates.

When the blindfold came off, I was in a hall leading to the Gate. Uniformed Council police stood at the Gate with metal detectors, waving the detectors over everyone, including Gate family members and their security. I recognized Jerv and Captain Wagner among the police. Jerv waved and looked as though he wanted to say something to me but was too busy. The Council Police allowed each family member to carry a handgun and a single magazine and each of the families brought three armed bodyguards.

The hall looked more complete than it had been last time I was here, almost back to where it had been when I was a bodyguard here. Still, the recovery wasn't complete. It had been stripped and vacant for months and nature wears down the works of man in a hurry if we stop fighting back.

The duel apparently captured Gate family imaginations, because most of the families were there. I recognized all four of the people from the inner Council chairs, including Chairman Blackwood and most of the other sixteen Council members from the brief legal maneuverings, along with a couple hundred family members and servants. Younger family members apparently decided this was a time to show off. The women mostly wore skimpy, impractical designer dresses and shoes that wouldn't have looked out of place in a Hollywood awards ceremony, with elaborately styled hair.

"You drew a crowd," I told Robinette. "And all the women want to steal your spotlight."

Mr. Thornburg apparently heard that. "We're bloodthirsty bunch, I'm afraid. Power corrupts and there is lot of power here. Half the thrill of the Wild is that we can do things our lesser rivals couldn't get away with. And we can do it in clothes that cost enough to feed most of Africa." He shook his head. "They're thirsting for my daughter's blood, hoping McFinney cripples her. That's part of why the Council flipped my way. They think it will backfire on us, on her." He turned to Robinette. "I believe in you, but I wouldn't send you out to entertain this bunch if there was any other choice. They will mostly be on his side, a real human beating a half-Mangi because he's tougher and smarter. His size and his dirty tricks won't turn them against him. You'll be fighting most of the crowd along with him, no matter how you look or how you fight."

"Don't let them take you out of your fight," I interjected. "If you have to claw or bite, do it. Anything legal, if it helps, do it. And almost everything is legal."

This was my third time in a family compound in the Wild, the first being in this same compound fifteen years ago. The Thornburg compound was a carefully disguised fortress, with high, but ornate walls surrounding a castle-like central building and several outbuildings.

The Thornburg outbuildings were carefully sited to leave fields of fire open, but the design was subtle enough that it took a discerning eye to notice what the designers had done. This revived compound kept the same defenses, but the high walls around the compound were topped with tangles of barbed wire and strands of electric wire. We headed to the sports center, smaller than the main house, but large enough for a full gym and an Olympic-length pool.

I passed a wary looking security guy. He carried a military style rifle and his eyes never stopped scanning the walls. "Expecting trouble?"

The Mangi sometimes raided family mansions, usually smash and grab affairs to grab random goods or vegetables from the large, flourishing gardens.

"Mangi camped in here while the gate was closed," the guard said. "We chased them out, but they got a taste of being out of the wind and rain and they like it." He shifted, still eying the wall. "They kept trying to sneak back in, so we asked for a hunt to thin them out but instead, last week we got a bunch of kids with hopped up paintball guns, trying to scare them. Mangi will face down a sabretooth tiger. They don't scare easy."

What, if anything did the Mangi and the hunt have to do with Jimmy Nelson and his village? If they went up against Jimmy Nelson, the kids were lucky they weren't dead.

Kids with paintball guns going up against Mangi was so ridiculous that I found it hard to believe that even Gate family younger sons could be that stupid.

Leah Thornburg walked by, wearing a dark green dress slit up to her thighs on both sides and matching green spike-heeled shoes. "The paintball hunt would be my brother Tom's idiot idea. No common sense in the guy. No stomach for fighting either. He's too big a wimp to even watch his half-sister get her half-ape butt kicked, even though he's been waiting for someone to do that for fifteen years." She turned to Robinette. "I wasn't lying or trying to frame our darling dad. He really was going to use you for his Frankenstein baby experiments. Your eggs were already on the way to the lab when we found out about the scheme."

"Why bother lying now?" Mr. Thornburg asked. "Your plan failed. You lost."

"I haven't lost anything. Robinette lost. Do you think winning this fight will end this? The Frankenbaby thing just proves once again that she's a threat to the Families. They'll find some way to kill her or send her back to the Wild. The only issue is how much damage you'll do to our family before that happens. But this will end today. You'll see why in a minute."

We passed the pool and turned left into the gym. When I saw the cage where the duel would happen, I understood why Leah was so confident.

Marcus got to choose the cage size, something everyone on the Thornburg side, including me, overlooked. When I saw the cage, I realized that we screwed up badly. Stupid mistake, and one he took full advantage of. The cage was an unpleasant, maybe fatal surprise. far larger than normal, ridiculously large, giving him more room to keep out of

Through the Wild Gate

Robinette's way. I searched the rules. They didn't spell out cage size or anything else about the venue. I swore. Score one for them. The cage's size made a tough fight even tougher.

Was there anything else about the gym that spelled trouble? If there was, I couldn't see it.

I hoped Marcus would charge in, expecting an easy fight. We promoted that by dressing Robinette in matching light pink shorts and top, along with custom dyed pink steel-toed tennis shoes and elaborately styled dyed blonde hair with pink ties. She looked good, very human, very feminine, the result of expensive tailoring and makeup, as though she was going shopping. That was partly for the audience, most of the Council, hundreds of people from the Gate families and their security details.

"You drew quite a crowd," I said. "Enough wealth here to equal half the world's GDP."

That might have been an exaggeration, but not by much.

Robinette looked down at herself and grimaced. "I look like a mugger's dream."

"That's what we're going for," I said. "Marcus won't buy it, but he may hold back on the dirtier stuff. He has to live with the Families if he wins and stomping Bambi is never a good look."

She hugged me, her hair smelling faintly of shampoo, then turned to Mr. Thornburg. "Wish me luck."

He nodded. "You can do this. Luck has nothing to do with it."

I stared at the oversized cage and wished there was something else I could say or do, but the outcome was out of my hands now.

Robinette stepped into the cage and the door slammed closed behind her, the sound echoing, the cage now complete. Marcus was, as expected, wearing heavy boots. He was grinning, but the grin looked forced, fragile. Not a good thing. Mangi have a fearsome reputation for strength and ferocity, so despite the pretty in pink bit, he was taking this fight seriously.

Leah sauntered over to us, her high heels clicking in a sudden silence as the crowd waited for the bell. She stood too close to me, nearly touching. "You did a good job of making her look human. Too bad she isn't. I always wanted a little sister."

"You have one," I said. "You couldn't ask for a better one." I stepped back. "What are you doing here?"

"There is something you really need to know," she said. She closed the distance, then leaned close as if to whisper in my ear. Instead, she kissed me on the cheek. "It drives little Miss Pretty in Pink crazy when she sees me close to you."

I stepped back. "You need to go away." If Robinette saw the kiss, she didn't react.

The bell rang, the only time it would ring in this fight. This would go until one of the fighters couldn't stand up.

Marcus moved near the center of the cage and waited. At least the big ring gave Robinette room to gain momentum. She trotted toward him, then sprinted and leaped, trying to end the fight in the first seconds. Marcus scrambled to get out of her way, but she grabbed his arm, the momentum swinging him off-balance. She kicked a leg out from under him, throwing him to the ground. I felt a surge of hope. She landed on him, aiming an elbow to the stomach with her full weight behind it. He got his arms in the way, deflecting most of her power, but still grunted when the elbow deflected into his stomach.

"Keep a grip!" I yelled.

She grabbed his arm again and threw two freight-train punches into his gut. She drew back for a punch to the head, but he jerked his legs up, curling them around her punching arm and kicking her in the face. Two legs against an arm stopped her punch and threw her backward. She grabbed his thigh and twisted, sending him to his stomach. She still had her grip on his other arm and levered it straight. He kicked for her head. She still gripped his arm, but her hand was slipping. She kicked the back of his elbow, which cracked audibly, but he slipped free and was on his feet, backpedaling.

Leah was still close to me, but she was concentrating on the fight now, her hands gripping the chain links, body tense and shouting something I couldn't make out over the crowd noise. Someone started a chant of "Marcus, Marcus." It beat against my ears.

McFinney's kicks would have knocked out most humans and they left Robinette's face bloody. She also looked wobbly, which I hoped was an act. Marcus was too busy trying to get his elbow working to notice. That elbow would need surgery.

She hurt him, but now he knew how fast she could charge. If Robinette tried it too often and from too far, she would exhaust herself. Her fast charges changed the fight, though. If he got close enough to kick her, he wouldn't have time to avoid her charges. But if he didn't get close, he couldn't hurt her. For now, he simply backpedaled to stay as far from her as he could.

She motioned for him to come to her. That wasn't about to happen. So what now? He was a dirty fighter, who helped write the rules for this fight and design the cage they were in. He would have an ace in the hole, something beyond steel-toed boots and the extra-large cage. I was missing something. What?

The gym lights suddenly went out, then a spotlight came on, blinding Robinette. She tried to get out of the light, but it followed her. The audience booed. Robert Thornburg yelled, "Get those lights back on."

Someone yelled back, "No rules against spotlights."

Beside me, I realized Leah was booing.

Marcus ran and kicked Robinette in the side of her unprotected head, then threw thunderous punches to her jaw and face as she went down. The lights came back up as he kicked her in the side, the kick lifting her into the air. I found myself sprinting toward the cage door. Security guys stopped me.

The gym echoed to the chant of "Marcus! Marcus!" The crowd was on its feet, clapping and chanting.

Robinette was down now, not moving. Marcus raised his foot for a stomp to the back of Robinette's neck. She rolled, took the stomp on her forearms, then kicked upward with her steel-toed sneakers to his groin. He had a cup on, but the kick from below must have gone under it. His face went purple. The chant faltered.

A groin shot doesn't always take the fight out of a man, as Marcus proved. He dived on Robinette, pinning her arms with his body, and slamming punch after punch into her face with his good arm. She was already groggy and any of those punches would have knocked me out. She tried to pull her arms loose, then when he shifted his weight to stop her, she bit his shoulder, strong teeth tearing flesh. She spat blood into his eyes, then when he recoiled, she jerked her arm free and punched him again and again, each punch like a sledgehammer. He slumped, his head bouncing on suddenly limp neck muscles.

The referee ran to stop her, but she twisted Marcus's good arm out of its socket and stomped the side of one knee before the ref got there. She stepped back, her face bloody, wobbly but ready to fight if Marcus got up. He rolled to his side and tried to push himself up on his bad elbow, then screamed long and high. His body went limp, and he rolled onto his back, not moving.

The crowd went pin drop silent. I glanced at Leah and surprised a huge grin on her face. She stared at me for a second, then whispered, "She's family." Her face went cold and expressionless, as if the moment never happened.

The referee waved his hands over McFinney. "That's it! Fight is over."

Robinette staggered back to the fence after the fight, then pushed past me without a word. Leah nodded curtly. The audience shrank back from her. She wobbled through them, to a restroom. When she came out, the blood was gone from her face, her makeup and hair carefully back in place, though bruises were developing under the makeup. She gave me a hug, then turned to Mr. Thornburg and said, "Dad, I want to go home now."

The lights abruptly went out again.

Chapter Eighteen:
Bad Luck Times Three?

I braced for an attack, remembering what Leah said about the Families not letting Robinette live, but no attack came. A few seconds later, the lights came back on.

"Triple redundancy on electricity to the Gates," Mr. Thornburg said. "I put that in the rules."

The lights went out again but came back within seconds. We hastily left the gym. Leah came with us. I kept an eye on her, not sure if her reaction when Robinette won was genuine. The hall was crowded with security teams formed up around Gate families and talking urgently on their radios. Family heads yelled for younger family members to form up around them. The armed security kept hands near their still holstered sidearms.

"No storms," Mr. Thornburg said. "Why did we lose power?"

My bodyguard instincts took over. Main power and backup power were both apparently out. That didn't have to mean an assassination attempt, but the odds went up with each outage. The lights went out again, leaving only battery-powered emergency lights.

"The Gate is on battery power now," Mr. Thornburg said. "It should stay up for seventy-two hours, even without solar power flowing into it, but we won't have electricity anywhere else in the compound until a generator or main power comes back. We should get through the Gate now."

"That may be what they're waiting for, sir," one of his security people said. "Two independent power sources going out smells like someone trying to herd us."

I nodded. If the Families wanted to kill Robinette, the confusion of a hasty exit would be the perfect time.

A muffled explosion came from outside. I resisted the urge to look out the gym hallway's high, small windows, but a security guy did. "Hallway to the Gate is blown to hell and burning. The explosion took the Gate offline."

"It's a kidnapping," Leah said. "Someone stranded us here and they'll ask for a crapload of ransom."

I stared at her. Could that be true? An enormous amount of wealth was concentrated here, but so was an enormous amount of power.

"Nowhere in the world they could hide after they took the money," I said. The Families would track them down relentlessly, using all the power of the governments they dominated. Still, the ransom idea explained the sudden power failures, each on top of the last. What else could?

"Do the generators or batteries depend on one another?" I asked.

"No," Mr. Thornburg said. "The Council checked. Main power and two independent generators went down, then the battery backup exploded. We still have solar panels, but not many batteries to store the energy. More batteries for the solar were on the way. Those outages had to be intentional, and it probably isn't about Robinette. No one would risk getting stranded here." He turned to Leah. "Why aren't you with Marcus?"

"Not much I can do for him. He'll need surgery, then rehab." She turned to Robinette. "And you did have to kick him in the family jewels."

"Cleaning up the gene pool. Just one of the many services I provide." Robinette put a hand through my arm and leaned her head on my shoulder. "Why couldn't you let me go home?"

"I'm not stopping you," Leah said.

"You didn't do this?"

"I'm not an idiot."

"You couldn't prove that by me," Mr. Thornburg said. "You had everything in the bag, but you risked it all on a kamikaze play. Maybe this is your backup plan."

"Stranding myself in the Wild? No thanks." Leah stared out the window. "You understand that we'll be here tonight with no electricity, which means no lights on the wall, no cameras to warn us about a Mangi raid and only a few rifles. How many security guys with rifles do we have?"

"Six," Mr. Thornburg said. "And each family has three guards with handguns. That should be enough to handle the Mangi."

Through the Wild Gate

Would it be enough to handle Jimmy Nelson and his crew? Probably, but if the big Mangi attacked now, he could do serious damage. Did he take out the power? Could he? I didn't see how but knew not to underestimate the big Mangi.

Jerv and Captain Wagner rushed over. "You think Jimmy Nelson is behind this?" Jerv asked.

"The thought crossed my mind," I said. "But I doubt it."

"Who the hell is Jimmy Nelson?" Leah asked.

Jerv told her, ignoring or not seeing my finger across the throat gesture. He didn't mention why we went to the Wild earlier, but Leah would probably figure out most of it. I shrugged. The secret was out now. Not much we could do about it.

"Think he would help us?" Leah asked.

I hadn't thought about that possibility. "Maybe, if we could get him back across or give him enough beer."

"No one here would have beer unless it was imported and expensive," Leah said. "And we're fresh out of Gates."

"How long before someone can open a Gate from the other side?" Robinette asked.

"A new Gate?" Mr. Thornburg shook his head. "A week to get it open and three days for testing."

Council Chairman Blackwood yelled to get our attention. "Council meeting in the main house in five minutes. Security, get lookouts on the walls. With the Gate down, we could be on our own for over a week, so we need to know how much food we have and probably quite a few other things. Mr. Thornburg isn't officially back on the Council, so he'll be in charge of figuring out what resources we have here. It's his Gate, so he'll have a head-start. If we pull together on this, it shouldn't be much worse than a camping trip."

That was a more organized response than I expected, and I felt vaguely disappointed that the most powerful people in the world didn't panic in this unexpected situation.

"Ten days," Mr. Thornburg said. "What does that buy that makes it worth pissing off the most powerful people in the world? They can't strand us here permanently. If we had to, we could walk to the nearest Gate."

"With this bunch?" Robinette laughed. "How far to the nearest Gate?"

"A hundred miles," Mr. Thornburg said. "They can send help, though. Off road vehicles could make it in less than a day if they pushed it."

I thought about our experience traveling in the Wild and doubted that. Travel in the Wild was slow and tough.

"The Council doesn't allow off-road vehicles except for the Council Police," Leah said. She smiled viciously. "Otherwise, we could have them here. That doesn't sound too smart now, does it?"

"What are you grinning about?" I asked. "You'll have to walk out too if things go south."

"Yeah, but it's almost worth it to see pompous old men hoist by their own rules. They'll break the rules, of course, but the hypocrisy is fun to watch, too." She shook her head. "It might be fun if I didn't have to live through it and if I didn't have a horrible suspicion that someone plans to drop another shoe on us."

"We would normally have a year's supply of food and water for a hundred people," Mr. Thornburg said. "Part of the Continuity of Government requirements. But somebody let the Council shut down the Gate and take all that stuff. We started replacing it, but I don't know how far we got."

I wanted to talk about asking Jimmy for help but didn't want to discuss it in front of Leah. Could we trust her? No. At best we could work together warily at arm's length if we had a common goal. We might have a common goal right now, but would that last?

"What they've done so far just annoys a bunch of very rich people," Robinette said. "How do they gain from that? How could they turn this from annoyance to threat? And who are they?"

"Could they be short sellers?" Leah asked. "They're almost as big a bunch of snakes as the Council and they could make a boatload of money betting that our company stocks go down." She shook her head. "Stocks would go down, but when we got back, we could look at who bet big and have our suspect list. Anybody smart enough to strand us would know that. But if it isn't ransom and isn't short selling, what is it?"

I had no idea and that worried me. I couldn't care less about the other Families or Leah. Getting stranded in the Wild would be justice for them. Robinette and maybe Mr. Thornburg I did care about, though. Robinette needed to live her life without having to deal with this crap again.

"Water and sewage," Mr. Thornburg said. We stared at him. "Those are things that will bite us. We may run out of toilet paper before the end of the week unless we're careful. We haven't restocked for this many people, so we'll go through supplies fast." He shrugged. "They asked me to figure out what we may be missing. Those are the important things. We'll also have to ration flashlights."

"Too bad they made everyone turn in their cellphones on the other side," Robinette said. "We would have plenty of flashlights until the batteries ran down. But no, we can't have cellphones over here because someone might take pictures."

No cellphones in the Wild actually made sense in my opinion. I thought back to Leah's questions. She had some good points. Stranding the Families in the Wild made them more vulnerable than normal, but they still had several dozen bodyguards and people on the other side of the Gates to rescue them. It would take more than destroying the Gate to force family members on the other side to pay ransom. Leah was right. Another shoe had to fall. It was the only thing that made sense. I stared at the ornate concrete wall that separated this compound from the rest of the Wild and wondered what it would be.

Chapter Nineteen:
The Other Shoe Falls

"Don't drink the water here," Mr. Thornburg said about an hour later. "It will give you the roaring, projectile trots."

He told us why and I had to shake my head at the sheer stupidity of the situation.

Water in the Wild was pollution free but harbored nasty bacteria. The compound had a reverse osmosis filter system, but it required electricity. Normally, when electricity went off, the system stopped bringing in new water, so the existing supply wasn't contaminated. When the electricity went off this time, some genius noticed the dwindling water supply and manually turned the valves back on, letting unfiltered water in. That contaminated the whole supply, leaving nearly two hundred people in the compound with only what little water they brought in water bottles. We had some soft drinks and alcohol but not enough to replace the water. Most soft drinks make you thirstier anyway.

"We can't last a week without water," Robinette said. "Dehydration kills you fast."

"How did you make it drinking the water here?" Leah asked.

"I drank the water, got really sick and spent two weeks wishing I could die. I was too stubborn to give up, though. My immune system eventually got the upper hand, but I'm a hell of a lot tougher than any of these people. Either we get clean water, or we'll have a crapload of trouble and I emphasize the crap part of that."

Was that the other shoe whoever stranded us here expected to fall? Maybe they figured we would run out of clean water and the idiot who contaminated our supply was just a bonus. Or maybe whoever opened the valve was working for the other side. The contaminated water was a devastating blow, but was it fatal? Probably not. Even if we had to drink that water and got sick, most of us would survive long enough for help to get to us, though we might wish we didn't.

"We can boil water," Mr. Thornburg said. "But we'll have to collect firewood to do it."

Collecting firewood would be a problem. Security cleared trees and brush away from the compound to keep lines of fire open. We would have to go out past that cleared zone to get wood and it would be an ongoing operation to keep enough and to ration what little we had among people who were used to getting anything they wanted.

Some younger family members treated the stranding as a party. Someone hauled out old furniture, antiques from the look of it, and used it for a bonfire, then got into the alcohol stocks and sat around the fire, getting drunk. I expected the Council or Mr. Thornburg to break it up, but they just put the alcohol in a locked room under guard and posted guards to keep the partiers from adding more furniture to the fire.

Leah strode by the partiers, sneered and walked over to Robinette and me. "If we're going to burn antique furniture, we should at least boil water over it. We should stop the party, but Dad always said to choose your battles. Those people have no survival instincts."

"And you do?" Robinette asked.

"I'm not half-animal like you," Leah said. "But I know we're in a lot of trouble." She pointed to her feet, which were now in tennis shoes instead of green spiked heels. "I traded my shoes for these, and the girl thought she was getting a great deal."

"Still full of charm," Robinette said. "Why don't you walk away while you still can?"

"Because, half-sister dear, we have to work together if we plan to make it. We have to get out of this compound and through the Wild to another Gate. You're the only one here who could lead us, and you'll need people with you who know they can't do it without you." She waved a hand at the partiers. "None of them are smart enough to figure that out. The Council members are smart enough, but they're too old to keep up. They wouldn't go anyway because they think someone will rescue them if they stay here."

"Why can't they stay here?" Robinette asked. "Water is a solvable problem. Just don't be stupid."

"I don't know what else is going to happen but stranding us is pointless if we can just wait to be rescued."

That was true, of course. It had been nagging at me since the stranding, though Leah took my thinking a step further when she said that we had to get out fast.

"This won't help make my case with you," Leah said. "But Marcus needs to be in a hospital."

"The deal was that the loser went to the Wild," Robinette said. "Then again, the winner and loser both ended up in the Wild, so maybe it doesn't matter anymore."

I have to admit that I hadn't even thought about Marcus McFinney since Robinette left him lying in the cage after their duel. Maybe if I was a better person, I would see him as a badly injured guy who needed help. I'm not that good of a person, though.

I glanced around the Compound. Grim-faced security guys paced along the walls, carrying rifles. Most of the Gate families still clustered by family, with security around them, but with younger members either joining the party around the bonfire or staring at the partiers enviously. It was later in the evening than I had realized, with the walls casting long shadows over the compound.

"Getting McFinney to a hospital would take a lot more forgiveness than I have," I said. "The guy tried to kill Robinette, went beyond his instructions to do it. May have raped her too."

"He better not have had sex with my sister," Leah said. "With or without her permission. I would stuff him down a woodchipper. How can rape be a maybe?"

Robinette explained. When she finished, Leah shook her head. "I don't buy it. He's a tough guy, but I scare the crap out of him."

"Did you tell him to leave me tied up?" Robinette asked.

"Mr. Blackwood himself ordered Marcus to leave you tied up," Leah said. "Nothing in writing, though. And Blackwood left him dangling on that horse crap honor thing." She turned to Robinette. "Blackwood figured Marcus would cripple you, but he hoped you would get in some good shots, enough to leave Marcus with permanent injuries so the Blackwoods could ease him out as head of security and give him a nice pension. Either way, Blackwood would win." She laughed. "This is the snake pit I've been training for all my life. I'll fit right in though."

She was probably right about fitting in on the Council, but I couldn't imagine Mr. Thornburg giving her any power after her attempted coup.

"None of us will make it unless we move fast," Leah said. "We should sneak out tonight, bluff our way through the guards with light backpacks and handguns if we can get them, then hike toward the nearest working gate as fast as we can walk. It's dangerous as hell, but the other side, whoever they are, won't expect it and maybe we can get a lead on them before they figure it out."

"What about predators?" I asked.

"Didn't I read someplace that big, fierce predators are rare?"

"Not rare enough," Robinette said. "They're curious and they cover a lot of territory. I would worry more about the Mangi, though and the distance we would have to cover. What makes you think this mysterious 'other side' will do anything? How could they even have people over here?"

"I don't know," Leah said. "There has to be more to this, and it has to happen fast, because people on the other side will be competing to be the heroes that rescue the Families." She paused. "Actually, that could be the point. Strand the Council, let them get worried, then ride to the rescue." She shook her head. "I'm overthinking it. Sometimes you can be too cynical, though it isn't easy around this crowd."

#

"That's the longest conversation I've ever seen you two have," Mr. Thornburg said. He marched over, staring at the partiers. It was already dark enough that the flames sent ragged flickering shadows across low vegetable gardens. The partiers trampled tomato vines, squashing them into a muddy green paste. Mr. Thornburg took one step toward the party, then shook his head and muttered, "That's my furniture they're burning. Our next generation, God help us." He turned back to Robinette and Leah. "You two, on the other hand, aren't brainless. Have you decided to shake hands and be friends?"

"It's more like two scorpions agreeing not to sting each other for now," I said. "That's about the best you can expect."

"Was Leah being reasonable? She's always at her most dangerous when she seems reasonable. People start believing she's smart enough to play in the Council games and mature enough to wait until she's ready to ease into it."

"I had no choice." Leah shrugged. "But you'll never admit what you tried to do, because then everyone would know you've lost whatever judgement you had, instead of just suspecting it."

"We could have another replay of "he did" and "I didn't"," Robinette said. "But it's pointless. Neither of you can prove it, not from here. And, unless one of you secretly shut down the Gate, someone took advantage of our drama to put us all in danger. So, let's put that crap aside and figure out who is screwing with us."

Mr. Thornburg nodded. "Our drama is on hold, for now. As to who is screwing with us, the choices are limited. They knew details about how Gates work and our backups that only security and immediate family know."

"Does that include the latest Mrs. Thornburg?" Leah asked.

Mr. Thornburg shook his head. "None of my wives knew Gates exist. They just knew I had an isolated secret getaway. Security never let them outside the wall the few times they were at my Compound. My current wife has never been to the Wild."

At least one of his ex-wives, Clara Wolf, did know about The Wild, though I had no idea how she found out about it. I wondered if she was still alive. If she was, she might well be a prisoner in The Wild even as we spoke.

"Secrets as big as the Gates are hard to keep," I said. "Organized crime knows you have some ace in the hole. Police at the high end and especially federal power agency like the FBI have some of the pieces and might put them together. Maybe the FBI has been building a case against the families for years and took advantage of this duel to wrap the Gate family thing up. They could strand the political powerhouses here and roll up your assets on the other side while your people waited for orders. Then they could open a new Gate and give us all perp walks." I felt a certain amount of satisfaction while I outlined that theory, but I didn't really believe it. It would be a dose of well-deserved karma, but probably wasn't about to happen.

Mr. Thornburg didn't buy the idea either. "We have ears too many places. What would they charge us with anyway? Our houses on this side are perfectly legal, actually required by law. I can't get into why that's true, but it is. It's amazing what you can hide in obscure line items of the federal budget. Our lawyers would have their cases thrown out in five minutes, then have them arrested for endangering national security. We do some things in The Wild that wouldn't be legal back home, but nobody has jurisdiction over here. Even if they could arrest us, politically and economically, charging us would be a disaster. If they won, they would have a stock market crash that made 1929 look like a pothole. If they lost, we would chase everyone in their command chain out of government and bankrupt them."

I didn't doubt that the Gate families had enough power to do everything Mr. Thornburg said they could, but that much power in private hands might push elements in government to find ways to rein the families in, out of self-defense if nothing else. Gates could also be a national security issue if hostile countries figured out how to make them, or a huge asset if US spy agencies had them.

I couldn't rule out government action, but it seemed unlikely. The Gate families were powerful, smart and ruthless. They were also careful to stay within the letter of the law, or get laws changed if they needed to.

If not law enforcement agencies, who? Could someone else have discovered how to create Gates? Gates were decades-old technology, but not cheap to create or maintain and as the Gate at Don's proved, they took some experiments to become practical. Did anyone outside governments have the resources to secretly create Gates? Wealthy companies or individuals who didn't quite make the cut as Gate families? Some might be close enough to Gate family circles to figure out the secret. Once they knew about the Wild, they would want to be in the very exclusive club. Maybe, but I didn't buy it.

Organized crime? Maybe they got enough information from disgruntled ex-security people and crossers to figure out what the Gates were and then infiltrated or bribed someone and pieced together enough to launch an attack.

Gates were tempting targets. If organized crime had Gates, they could do a crapload of illegal stuff in the Wild, including smuggling, prostitution, hiding bodies, dumping waste and setting up drug labs. The list went on and on. Did they set up this stranding? If so, what would they do next? Force the Families to give them Gate technology? Maybe, if they didn't already have it.

"Who stranded us matters," I said. "Organized crime would need people over here. Law enforcement could wait."

What about the Families themselves? They had everything reasonable people could want, but the Council's rules or not being part of the inner Council could grate on some of these status-obsessed men and women. I thought about asking if anyone on the Council seemed unhappy but at this level the players would be good enough at hiding their emotions that Mr. Thornburg and Leah probably wouldn't know.

"Any families not here?" I asked.

"Three," Leah said. "But they are second tier, with older leaders and no ambitious heirs. They probably aren't behind this."

That left increasingly unlikely possibilities. Foreign intelligence agencies? Disgruntled security people or technicians? All were remote possibilities though I couldn't rule them out and neither could Leah or Mr. Thornburg.

What about Jimmy Nelson? The big Mangi was probably still close to the Compound. If part of his crew were ex-servants, they might know more about how the Compound worked than anyone realized. Maybe they found out about the influx of families and security and thought the families were gathering to hunt Jimmy and company. That would give Jimmy motive, but how could he get into the Compound with all the security? I didn't rule the big Mangi out completely, but he probably wasn't behind the stranding.

Thinking of Jimmy, even if he wasn't behind the attacks, he was probably still lurking somewhere near the Compound. Was he close enough to notice that there were no lights on the walls? Probably. The sky glow from the compound had to be visible for miles, normally. What would he think when that glow didn't show up at nightfall this time? Would he be curious? Maybe he would see it as an opportunity. He might already know exactly what was going on in the Compound and how vulnerable we were.

I turned to Mr. Thornburg, ready to warn him about Jimmy, but one of the partiers stood up abruptly, holding his throat and making choking sounds.

Leah shook her head. "Choking on his own barf. These are our future movers and shakers."

The guy started twitching, almost as if prompted by her words, then fell on his side, still twitching. The other partiers laughed, but then two more started choking.

"We need a doctor," Mr. Thornburg yelled.

Two, a man and a woman ran over. By the time they got there, most of the partiers were choking and twitching. The twitching didn't last long before they were still.

"They aren't trying to ransom us," Leah said. "They're trying to kill us."

Chapter Twenty: Invisible Attack

The poison, apparently in the alcohol, was deadly and acted fast. Two of the partiers survived, probably because they didn't drink enough for the poison to be fatal. The rest, thirty-one young men and women, lay dead by the charred furniture that had been their bonfire. Security hauled the bodies into the gym once the doctors gave up on them.

I was braced for an attack, but the sudden deaths still stunned me. Over thirty wealthy, powerful young people, not many years from taking over financial empires and political power, were dead in the dirt, their deaths coming in minutes. Families were suddenly without their next generation, their heirs. The surviving Family members also seemed stunned, probably the first time many of them had seen sudden death. The survivors hustled back to tight, distrustful family clusters with their security around them. Families who had lost members demanded answers. Mr. Blackwood handed that hot potato off to Mr. Thornburg, who handed it to me.

I felt the deaths hard. Didn't expect that. Not logical for me to care. I didn't know the dead and wouldn't have liked them if I did. Idiots, the lot of them. Someone stranded them in the Wild. What do they do? Burn antique furniture and get drunk, Still, watching them die, helpless to save them, shook me.

I borrowed gloves from the doctors, then inspected the alcohol bottles. Most were already open, with seals so mangled I couldn't tell if they had been tampered with. The unopened bottles had intact, genuine-looking seals. Someone with the resources to penetrate Family security could print genuine-looking seals, though.

"Who could get at the alcohol?" I asked.

Not many people, it turned out. This was a stash brought in since the Gate reopened and kept locked up for guests. Only one servant had access to it. He looked terrified when I questioned him. He claimed that he had only opened the alcohol closet once in the last month, to restock and replace unopened bottles after the paintball hunting trip.

Leah had been listening to the interview. She suddenly swore. "That sneaky rat bastard."

I turned to her. "You know who did this?"

"Maybe. Not a name I want to mention without more proof, though."

"This has gone beyond offending people," I said. "Someone is killing people and they probably have something nastier than poisoned alcohol coming. What's next? Poisoned food?"

"Poisoned alcohol may be all they needed," Leah said. "We can't trust anything liquid, and we'll die of thirst before help gets here."

She refused to say anything more about her theory. Did she really have someone in mind? If she didn't, she was a very good actress. She also seemed thoughtful and subdued. "We really need to get out of here and fast. If I'm right, we're all supposed to die here. Only way this could work." She eyed the tight circles of families and their security people. "With this lot, you may think they're mourning, and maybe some of them are a little, but most of them are calculating. Who inherits now? Can the younger brothers or sisters step up their games enough to handle the power? Does the head of the family need to dump his old wife and find another one young enough to give him an heir?"

"Why do you want to be part of that crap?" I asked. "Why not dump it all and do something you really want to do?"

"Who says I don't want to do this?" She grinned. "Power is an addictive game. Life would be boring without it." Her grin widened. "Power lets you screw with people. I can make my half-sister nuts just by standing a little too close to you and twirling my hair or touching your arm." She stepped back. "But we don't have time for that now."

She circled back to her idea of making a dash for the nearest open Gate. That made a kind of sense, but even with young, fit people it would take a week of hiking through hostile country to get there. What would we find if we made it? Would whoever stranded us expect us to try for a Gate? If so, what precautions would they take? With most of the Council stranded here, how much power could plotters seize back home?

Also, I didn't trust Leah. She hated Robinette, always had. What would she do when our backs were turned on the trip or especially when we got to the Gate?

I talked to Robinette and Mr. Thornburg, outlining what Leah said and what she wanted to do.

They agreed that someone needed to get help. Leah, Robinette and I, with a few security guys would be logical picks, Leah because she was sort of on the council, Robinette because she knew the country and me to keep the sisters from killing each other.

"Getting to another Gate will be harder than you can imagine," Robinette said. "On a map, the next Gate is maybe a hundred miles away, but we'll be twisting and turning, climbing hills, wading through rivers and avoiding swamps. We know what the countryside is like on our side of the Gate, but we have no idea what it's like here."

I remembered our brief trip to find Jimmy. She was probably right.

"But you made it to the Gate at Don's Auto," I said.

"In two months, and in mostly flat, open country," Robinette said. "Have you looked outside the walls? This is hills and forest. We could wander for days and end up back where we started."

"Are you saying we shouldn't try?"

"No. I'm saying to be ready for a lot more adventure than we want and a crapload more walking."

She was right about the country. Our brief expedition was enough to tell me that. We didn't have a lot of other choices, though.

#

We slept in shifts in a dark corner of the gym that Thornburg security took over, with too-thin wrestling mats between us and the gym floor. Jerv and Captain Wagner joined us, both looking lost. The only light was from battery-powered emergency lights scattered around the gym. I wondered how long they would last. Hopefully quite a while. Gate families could afford the best.

Marcus McFinney sat in a wheelchair across the gym, in a pool of light near the Blackwood family but apart from it, outside the circle of Blackwood security people. He glowered in our direction, though he probably couldn't see us in the darkness. I half-expected Leah to go over to him, but she didn't. She didn't look at him, just made her place in the near darkness next to Mr. Thornburg.

"You should see how McFinney is doing," Robinette said.

"I'm not that big a hypocrite," Leah said. "Halfway through the fight, I realized I wanted you to win."

"Oh come on," Robinette said. "You don't expect me to believe that do you?"

I remembered the expression I surprised on Leah's face at the end of the fight. Sibling relationships are weird.

"It's true," Leah said. "Just for a minute or two, though. Then I remembered how annoying you are."

"There's the Leah I know," Robinette said.

"And they squashed us together in one corner of the gym so we can't get away from each other," Leah said. "We don't even rate one guest room for the bunch of us. That's a big step down from Dad being on the inner Council."

Mr. Thornburg pushed himself up on an elbow, glaring at her. I expected him to say something about her actions that helped put us here, but he turned away.

Robinette put her mat on top of mine, smiled at Leah, then snuggled next to me. "I have a little of the Thornburg viciousness," she whispered. "Enough that I like reminding her that she's sleeping alone and I'm not. Plus, two mats under us are better than one."

Leah sat up. "I want to see Jimmy Nelson. Didn't security guy say he had drone video?"

"Sitting right here," Jerv said. "And I'm with the Council Police, not Thornburg security."

"Do you have the drone video?"

Surprisingly, he still had the drone controller, now repaired. He brought the video up. Leah leaned her head on his shoulder. "Ooh shiny. I can feel the testosterone through the camera. I wonder how Jimmy Hard Body would be in bed."

"You have a boyfriend who needs to be in the hospital," Robinette said. "And Jimmy's married."

"Doesn't stop a girl from wondering. Oh, come on. You would wonder too if you saw him."

Jerv had been uncharacteristically quiet. He turned to me and said, "I'm glad I only had one sister. Sister rivalries get vicious."

"And brother sibling rivalries don't?" I laughed. "I was never as happy as when I beat my older brother at something. That didn't happen much, though."

"Why don't you go see how McFinney is doing," Robinette asked.

Leah shook her head. "I don't want to know."

Through the Wild Gate

"Not knowing doesn't make him Schrodinger's Dirty Fighter. He'll either walk again or he won't. No uncertainty."

Leah glared at Robinette. "He would be useful about now if you hadn't beaten him half to death."

"In case you didn't notice, he was trying to kill me at the time."

"He never had a chance," Leah said. "You could take on a grown male gorilla at even odds."

"Not even close. I'm stronger than most men, even big ones, but nowhere near as strong as a full-blooded Mangi, much less a gorilla. Besides, you claim you were on my side during the fight."

"A moment of weakness," Leah said.

"The McFinney fight is over," I said. "We need to concentrate on staying alive. Any ideas?"

Mr. Blackwood stopped by. He glanced at Mr. Thornburg. "This isn't a secret, but don't spread it more than you have to. I've been on the Compound's main radio to the closest working Gate. They're stripping down a couple helicopters so they can get them through the Gate. They'll have to put them back together and test them, but once that happens, we'll be back to civilization in half a day." He glanced at me. "You may not have heard, but Gates are designed so most helicopters won't fit. You have to partly disassemble them and put them back together. That's a feature, not a bug. We designed it that way. That doesn't seem as smart now as it did when we set that up."

Still, helicopters coming to the rescue seemed too easy after the series of attacks that stranded us and left the young partiers dead. I couldn't tell for sure in the semi-darkness, but I thought Leah and Mr. Thornburg looked skeptical too.

"How long will getting the helicopters apart and putting them back together take?" Leah asked.

"I have no idea," Mr. Blackwood said. "Maybe a day or two. Hopefully less."

After he walked away, Leah said, "I don't want to sit here for a day or two with a target on my back. If we don't have to get help, let's at least get out of the Compound. We can gather firewood. If we're unpredictable, we're harder to attack."

"That makes sense," Mr. Thornburg said. "We can organize it in the morning."

The security people were on their radios, coordinating the

Compound's defenses. Was Jimmy lurking outside? If so, he knew something was very wrong in the Compound, though he wouldn't know exactly what. What if the big Mangi got himself shot? He wasn't bulletproof and the guards were jumpy tonight.

I thought about asking Mr. Thornburg to tell the security people Jimmy might be coming, but I couldn't guarantee he would be friendly. What if he found out the Council was trapped here? He would probably say, 'Good!' and walk away. I would probably say that myself if I wasn't trapped with them.

If Leah was right about another attack, was it smart to wait until morning to leave? That gave whoever was orchestrating the stranding time to screw with us. Travelling in the Wild at night was entirely too dangerous, though, so we had to wait. We would have more than enough challenges in the Wild without wandering around in the dark. Before we settled in for the night, we gathered backpacks full of items Robinette figured would be useful if we got cut off from the Compound, including hatchets, metal pans to boil water and two handguns from the Thornburg security guys. We wanted rifles, but when we asked Mr. Thornburg, he shook his head. "They won't let you have them and asking for them might get the trip vetoed."

The night dragged, with the unfamiliar surroundings, hard gym floor and distant emergency lights keeping me awake. This was the time I normally worked, too, so my body stubbornly fought sleep for what felt like hours. I must have slept eventually, though, because I woke to sunlight filtering in from small, high windows.

Nobody from the other Families offered to join us in our trek, but none of them tried to stop us. The deaths last night still had the families in tight, defensive huddles, hoarding what little food and water they brought with them. Mr. Thornburg tried to get them to cooperate with us on gathering firewood and finding water, but for now no one would help. That would have to change, or they would all die of thirst. Hopefully, they would figure that out.

We went out through the main Compound gate, shoving it open and closed manually because the normal electronic mechanism wasn't working. Neither was the electronic lock, which meant that the Mangi could shove the gate open and be inside without even breaking the lock if they got to the wall.

Mr. Thornburg sent Jerv and Captain Wagner from the Council

Police with us, Jerv smiled when he got to the gate. "Second time out of the Compound. We're a team now."

Captain Wagner just eyed Robinette and Leah. "These two aren't best buds from what I've seen. Will we have to waste time keeping them from killing one another?"

"Truce until we get through a Gate," Leah said. "After that, you don't have to care what we do to one another."

I got ready to head into the woods, but Robinette put a hand on my shoulder. "Wait." She raised her hand. "Footprints. Somebody got close to the wall, probably last night." She studied the tracks. "No more than two days old."

That meant somebody visited either last night or the night before. With the lights and cameras out last night, that was probably when the prowlers visited.

Robinette still wore her 'pretty in pink' outfit with the steel-toed tennis shoes, her T-shirt still stained with dried blood spots she couldn't wash out.

"Mangi," Robinette said, not long after we got to the forest. She didn't point but lifted her arm in the direction she saw them. I didn't see anything but took her word for it. We were on a game trail, with woods crowded close on both sides of us.

"They're tracking us," Robinette said. "Not that we can go anywhere unexpected in forest we don't know."

"Deja vu all over again," Jerv said. "I feel like I'm in a time warp. Next, the wolves will show up and then we'll spot Jimmy or a Mangi woman in blue jeans and I'll do a dance-off against them." He grinned. "I still think I could take him. Muscles aren't everything."

After seeing what Robinette did to Marcus, that seemed delusional, to say the least. I shrugged. "At least he figured you would last longer than the rest of us."

Officially, we were out here to collect firewood and water, but we also wanted to scout for incoming threats, and maybe contact Jimmy, so we went deeper into the woods than we had to for firewood.

We didn't have the drone up yet, so I tried to spot the Mangi without being obvious about it. I couldn't see them. I took Robinette's word for it. After two months in the Wild, she was head and shoulders above the rest of us on just about everything involving the Wild. She quickly demonstrated that by stopping briefly to cut saplings a little over an inch thick with straight sections about six feet long and sharpened points on one end of each of them.

"I would have killed to have a hatchet the last time I was here. The spears don't look like much, but if you keep the pointy end between you and something hungry it will slow them down enough that the rest of us can help you." That was good advice since we didn't have rifles.

When we got to a creek, Robinette gathered flat stones the size of her fist and distributed them. "Good for killing rabbits once you get the hang of it, and yes, you'll eat fluffy little bunnies if you get hungry enough. Grasshoppers and crickets too."

We cautiously filled our metal pans with creek water, boiled it and filled water bottles once the water got cool enough, then passed what was left around with each of us draining part of the water without touching the pan with our lips. The now lukewarm water tasted great after a thirsty night.

When we put out the fire and got moving again. Leah cut in front of Robinette and linked her arm in mine. She put her chin on my shoulder, leaning in so her cheek touched mine, then whispered. "Let's see if half-sister dearest still has the schoolgirl crush on you." After a couple seconds, she added, "Probably, but she's good at hiding it. That's no fun." She lifted her chin off my shoulder, but still pressed her body close to mine and slid her hands into my jeans' pockets, tracing her fingers along the tops of my thighs.

"You're getting a little personal there," I said. I squirmed when her hands drifted toward intimate territory.

"Don't take it personally. This is for my sister's benefit."

"I thought you two had a truce until we get back."

"No fighting. Sniping is okay," Leah said. "It had better be because I've been doing it so long that I couldn't stop if I wanted to." She took her hands out of my pockets, though. "Why do you have sketches of my brother Tom and one of his worthless friends in your pocket?"

"I didn't know I did." It took a second, but then I remembered stashing the sketches Evette, Jimmy Nelson's wife drew of the rich young guys who lured Jimmy to a big money fight. "Well crap on a stick. Your brother is a blithering idiot."

"An idiot? Not really," Leah said. "He's a coward and he's lazy, but he's smarter than I am, maybe as smart as Robinette. He was going to be a Gate technician, but dropped out because it was too much work. You don't get into that program unless you have serious mental horsepower, though. Why do you think he's an idiot?"

I told her about the rich young guys who lured Jimmy Nelson into what sounded like a Russian Roulette hunt, but with Jimmy as the designated victim. "The hunt went to crap, which was totally predictable. Jimmy probably killed some of the hunters and got their rifles. Now he's loose over here, with almost a decades' worth of ideas from our side of the Gates. And when I asked Jimmy's wife to make a sketch of the rich young guys, she drew your brother."

"Wow! He is so screwed. Even Dad couldn't save him if the Council finds out. And that's before Dad lost a lot of his power."

"So, like I said, he's an idiot."

"He's a coward," Leah said. "Too afraid of what his friends will think to stop things he knows are bad ideas. He's still one sneaky, vicious bastard. Smart too. He's my twin brother, after all."

I took the sketches from Leah. One was definitely Tom.

The others caught up to us. Captain Wagner asked, "Who is a sneaky, vicious bastard?"

"Everyone on the Council," Robinette said. "And especially my darling sister. I don't know about the smart bit."

"I saw the hands in the pockets bit," Jerv said. "If you two want to go into the woods and have sex, feel free. We're all adults here. Just avoid poison ivy. We'll go on, but you can catch up."

I felt my face get red. Robinette glared at us. Leah grinned. "I thought I was being sneaky with the hands in his pocket thing. Only my sister was supposed to see it." She brushed her body against mine, then pulled back. "Another time, maybe. We need to chat about my brother Tom."

We decided to stop briefly. We were all hungry because we had to treat all the food in the compound that we didn't bring in with us as though it was poisoned. The canned stuff probably wasn't and the people who stayed would undoubtedly have to risk eating it, but last night no one had wanted to try.

I worried about the lurking Mangi and Jimmy. Hard as it was to believe, with all her strength, Robinette was only half Mangi, not as fast or strong as the real thing.

Robinette slipped between Leah and me. Leah grinned at her but stepped back. Her grin ebbed away, leaving her silent and subdued for once. She was out of her element and seemed to know it. The Capital Police seemed more confident. They had been out here once and survived. I wondered how much stamina Captain Wagner, the bulky Council Policewoman had. She seemed okay, but if we really tried to hike to the nearest Gate, would she be able to keep up? Jerry seemed to have almost unlimited energy but still seemed to have trouble keeping his mouth shut, despite increasingly obvious hints that we needed to stay quiet. My rounds at Don's gave me a lot of stamina too, though the rough ground stressed muscles in my knees and ankles that I wasn't used to using.

"Brother Tom doesn't confront people with power," Leah said. "He knows I'm the heir and he has never challenged that. He has his trust fund and his bunch of loser spare heirs and that's enough for him. This Jimmy Nelson hunt thing could take that all away. I wonder what brother Tom will do when he figures that out."

"Double down on trying to kill Jimmy Nelson, probably," Jerv said. "If he kills Jimmy, his problem is solved."

"And if a Gate magically appeared right in front of us, our problems would be solved too," I said. "But I wouldn't count on either of those things happening."

"I don't trust the bit about helicopters coming to rescue us," Leah said. "But I hope it's true. If we have to find help on foot, by the time it gets here, the survivors will be splitting the bones of the dead and eating the marrow." She grinned. "I could see Dad as one of the survivors if it came to that." She stared into the forest on both sides of the trail. "Whose bright idea was this? Okay, mine, but why didn't anybody who knew what they were doing stop me?"

"Because we have a chance out here," Robinette said. "And I wanted you to get a taste of what I went through. Remember, I did this walking with no shoes and no water bottle and no hatchet and nothing to boil water in."

"On flat, open land. Still, I get it. You're a badass."

"No. The point is that I made it through two months of this crap because I wanted revenge. Now I'm not even sure who to take that revenge on. Well, other than McFinney and he was just dirty deeds for hire."

"So you don't know who to kill now. Yeah, that sucks," Leah said. "But we have to survive before you can get your revenge."

"Actually, I have to survive to get my revenge. I'm not sure you're necessary."

"And this is why they sent the Council Police, to make sure you both make it back," I said.

"And why Mr. Thornburg didn't give either of them guns," Jerv said.

We kept hiking, with Robinette reclaiming her place beside me. She found edible berries and some plants she swore were edible but that tasted like they should have been coming out instead of going in. The plants at least stopped my hunger pangs. My stomach decided that if I was going to send that kind of foul crap its way it would hold off on asking for anything.

So many things would have helped us, but they were all on the Council's don't bring to the Wild list. Horses, GPS, even dogs and an undamaged drone. They would have all helped. A drone would give us a bird's eye view of where we were going instead of wandering along trails that met some animal's needs but might go in a circle. We had a compass, but it didn't help much unless we left the trail.

We picked up animal stalkers, a dozen oversized wolves who kept their distance and rarely showed themselves, but paced us. I wondered if it was the same pack that stalked us the first time we came through. They seemed much more menacing this time, without ATVs and a rifle in easy reach. I wondered if they sensed our unease or maybe even registered that we didn't have long guns with us. Wolves were smart. Were they that smart? Wolves in the Wild might be smart enough, even if the ones back home weren't.

A little after noon we heard the unmistakable sound of helicopters flying over, headed for the Compound.

Chapter Twenty-One:
Helicopters at Noon

We only saw the helicopters briefly, fleeting glimpses through the trees. The Wild absorbed their sounds, cushioned them. The Wild went on. The noisy intruders just passed through.

I stopped, letting the others catch up. The wolves paused too, in a loose circle around us, ears cocked toward the fading helicopter sounds, noses testing the air.

"We should go back," Leah said, her voice uncharacteristically uncertain.

Heading back was logical, but I hesitated too. Why? Too many unanswered questions. I stretched my back. The wolves eyed me but didn't move. Leah put a hand on my shoulder while she took off a shoe to dump out a pebble. She stood too close, still holding my shoulder. Robinette rolled her eyes but didn't move between us.

Where was Jimmy? We were close to where we met him before, near the edge of the plains. We were still close enough to hear radio messages from security at the Compound, Was Jimmy close enough to hear them? He might have taken radios from the hunters he killed. If so, he was probably smart enough to listen if they hadn't run out of battery power.

If Jimmy knew the Council was stranded in the Wild, what would he do? Despite his fighting ability and the Mangi he led he probably couldn't take the Compound without getting most of his Mangi killed. Mangi walk away from wounds that would kill a man, but bullets to a vital organ would kill them just as much as they would kill a man. Besides, Jimmy just wanted to get home to his wife, his TV and his beer. He needed the Council to get there.

Leah finally let go of my shoulder. "Your mind is racing. I can almost hear the gears grinding."

I nodded curtly and tried to put myself in Jimmy's place. The big Mangi wouldn't trust the Council, of course. He probably thought they were hunting him too. How much did he know about how the Gate families worked? Less than I did, probably. He might suspect a feud was going on between Gate family factions but wouldn't know enough about that feud to use it.

What would Tom Thornburg do? If he killed Jimmy Nelson before the Council found out about the hunt, Mr. Thornburg could probably cover for him. Tom could have been trying to kill Jimmy from this Compound as soon as it reopened. Instead, he went on a ridiculous paintball hunt against the local Mangi, if that's what he was really doing.

"Want to share?" Leah leaned against a tree, fixing her makeup.

"I'm thinking about Tom," I said.

"My chickenshit brother? Maybe you aren't just eye candy. Tell me more."

I tried to collect my thoughts. A lot of things didn't add up about the hunt for Jimmy Nelson. How did Tom get the big Mangi through a Gate? How did he cover up the rifles he lost in that hunt? How did he cover up the dead family members? How could his crew drop a Mangi woman to her death from a helicopter when helicopters weren't allowed in the Wild?

"Crap! He has his own Gate," I said.

"Tom?" Leah nodded. "Probably. When I heard what Jimmy Nelson said about the helicopter I pretty much knew. Tom knows the technology from studying to be a Gate tech. He gets way too much money from Dad, but always seems broke."

"Our brother Tom?" Robinette cupped her hands to her forehead. "Him and his loser friends. Why not? They all have more money than they know what to do with and Tom knows enough about how Gates work to piece the rest together." She ran her fingers through her unruly dyed blond hair. "On the other hand, that's a big project for a bunch of losers. Could they really pull it off and keep it secret?"

She had a point, especially about keeping an unauthorized Gate secret.

The helicopter sounds faded away completely, leaving only wind ruffling through the trees and squirrels chattering. I felt a sudden urge to get back to the Compound, mixed with my earlier reluctance, but I focused on Tom's Gate.

"What does his Gate, if he has one, have to do with Robinette getting stranded?" I asked.

"Maybe nothing," Leah said. "Or maybe Tom was afraid Dad would find out about the Gate and wanted us at each other's throats so we wouldn't compare notes."

That sounded weak, though Mr. Thornburg knew about Jimmy and was investigating how he got back to the Wild. Tom running a secret gate seemed unlikely, though Leah and Robinette both seem convinced, and they knew Tom better than I did.

"He didn't fight to inherit because he already had a Gate," Leah said. "But I can't believe his bunch of losers kept it a secret for long."

They couldn't, not for long, but the secret Gate was probably no more than a couple years old. Tom wouldn't know about the Wild until he turned twenty-one, then he had to learn how to design a Gate, buy remote property and build the Gate, making it wide enough to fit helicopters through.

"Tom is lucky he didn't run into Jimmy Nelson on his paintball game," I said.

"The paintball game was probably a cover for a more serious hunt," Leah said. "I'm not sure how that worked, though. They couldn't hunt him from helicopters close to a Compound." She turned toward the Compound. "We should go back." She still didn't sound convinced.

"We should," I said. "But you don't really think so. Why?"

Leah shrugged. "Maybe I'm scaring myself. Are they really coming to help? They could be the other shoe dropping."

The helicopters coming this quickly was unexpected. I knew they were on their way. I was just surprised that they cut through Council regulations that kept helicopters out of the Wild so quickly and got them through the Gates. Someone made things happen fast. Were they allies of the Council, coming to the rescue or the same people who stranded the Families here?

I turned to Leah. "You said you had a suspect for who was behind the strandings. It's getting close to crunch time. Are you thinking Tom?"

"It pretty much has to be him, but he couldn't organize his way out of a paper bag, much less stage a coup against the entire Council."

"Holy crap on a stick," I said. "You think your brother Tom not only has his own Gate, but is the mastermind behind all this?"

"The thought crossed my mind," Leah said. "If Dad really didn't try to give Robinette a Frankenkid, someone had to fake the evidence I found. Tom could do it. Why though?"

"If Robinette was dead and you and your dad were at each other's throats, he would probably inherit," I said. "That's motive."

Leah shook her head. "On paper, maybe, but he would never really have power outside his bunch of loser younger sons. The Council might give him a seat, but they wouldn't trust him with a Gate. He would be probationary on the Council, and they would stall giving him control of the Thornburg Gate." She brushed her blond hair back from her face, then turned decisively back toward the Compound. "Dad has a trust set up for him with more money than he could spend in a lifetime, though he's been going through it like water. If he didn't have a Gate and wasn't really on the Council, what would he gain from inheriting?"

"More," I said. "Not much of what the Gate families do makes sense, but they keep doing it because they want more. You're built that way. Maybe he is too. You could back off on inheriting and live a good life. No stress. All the money you need. Why don't you? You want more, even though you know more comes with stress and heart attacks."

"And the way you think puts you on night shifts at Don's Auto," Leah said. "Why live a crap life if you don't have to? People who want more become kings and presidents and heads of corporations. People who coast on what they have lose it all to people who want more." She shrugged and settled herself into a ground-eating pace. "That's the way the world works. Satisfied people are future peasants."

"If Tom thinks the way you do, he has all the motive in the world," I said. I hesitated, then followed her. Robinette made a point of linking her arm in mine. I shook my head. "Plenty of motive. Ability to make big plans happen? That I can't see."

Robinette leaned her head on my arm. "Our brother Tom would only fight if he's cornered, about to lose everything. Corner him, though, and he'll fight like a rabid weasel. Did you make him think he's cornered?"

Leah shook her head. "I was going to inherit, and he had his little posse of loser younger sons and all the money he could spend. He seemed happy with that."

"But you still think he has a Gate and he's behind all this crap."

"That's what my logic tells me," Leah said. "My instincts say my logic is screwed up. I have to be missing something."

"If your brother Tom has his own Gate and brought Jimmy through it, he is trapped," Jerv said. "If Jimmy testifies to the Council, the Council will find the Gate."

That made sense, but it still didn't feel right. "I guess we'll find out." I picked up the pace, heading back for the Compound. Jerv and Robinette followed.

Captain Wagner yelled, "Aren't we going to talk about this? Who put you in charge?"

"I did," Leah yelled, but she circled back. "We go back, get close and watch. If this is a real rescue, we ride to civilization."

"And if it's a trap?" Captain Wagner asked. "How will we know without sticking our heads in it?"

That was a good question. I nodded. "If the helicopters are a trap, how will they spring it? What will they do once they spring it?"

Were these Tom's helicopters or the ones Chairman Blackwood told us about? If they were Tom's, what would Tom and his friends do when they got there? Even with helicopters, they couldn't take on the Gate family security. These weren't gunships. Parts of the Compound doubled as shelter from Mangi attack and would probably stop anything short of a cannon.

"I walked how many miles just to walk back?" Captain Wagner asked. She grumbled until she got a radio message from Council Chairman Blackwood. "He says to come back right away. We're slated for the first ride out."

#

I didn't know what to expect when we got back to the Compound, and I knew the others felt the same uncertainty. We listened for gunfire on our way back and looked for signs of fighting when we entered the Compound. Council Police were still on the walls, though, and two helicopters sat just outside, with Council members standing bored outside them, still in their dress clothes from the duel, now wrinkled.

The helicopters were larger than I expected, transport models. Mr. Blackwood stood outside one, smiling. He waved a hand toward the helicopter. "Once you're settled in, they're ready to go. Since you volunteered to go out for firewood, you should be on the first flight. Everyone else on the first flight is on the Council or security, so you're privileged."

Through the Wild Gate

I approached the helicopters warily. Captain Wagner asked, "Are you sure these are the helicopters you expected?"

Mr. Blackwood looked puzzled, "What else would they be? The other Compound confirmed that they were on their way. I know the people running them. Let's get this show in the air. I'm on the second flight out, so we need to get you to the Gate and get the helicopters back before dark. Our weather gurus think we'll get thunderstorms later today, so get moving."

Unexpected storms were a major problem in the Wild, with no satellites to warn us. Weather people could give educated guesses, but those guesses didn't help much.

We reluctantly got in the helicopter. Mr. Thornburg was already there, in the back, sitting uncomfortably in a sling chair. Five other Council members and Marcus McFinney were also there, crowded into the seats, along with security people. McFinney glared at Leah then turned away. All the seats were taken, so we made do on the floor. Leah crowded in next to her dad. "Is everything okay with this flight?"

"It breaks Council rules and I wish they took more time to test the helicopters after they reassembled them, but yes, we should be okay."

The helicopter engines revved up, making conversation nearly impossible. The rescue still seemed too easy. What was the point of stranding the Council if they could radio for help so easily? Still, the Council members had armed security with them, enough to protect them against any threat I could think of.

The helicopter clawed its way into the sky. I forced myself to relax. At this point we were committed. Either we would make it to a Gate or yet another shoe would fall.

A case of water bottles sat at the front of the cargo compartment, with a sign that said, "Take one." Leah glanced at the bottles, then at me and made a finger across the throat gesture. I nodded. After our experience with poisoned alcohol, I wasn't about to drink anything I wasn't sure of. A few of the Council members did drink, but most of them and their security people didn't. If the water was a trap, it wasn't going to catch many people.

I still felt uneasy. According to Jimmy, Tom and company had helicopters in the Wild. Were these from the Council or from Tom and his friends? What if they were from Tom and friends? Did he think rescuing the Council would get him off the hook for a secret Gate? Maybe that was the idea. Put the Council in danger, then come to the rescue. If he thought that would work, though, Tom was naive. If the Council didn't exile him to the Wild, Mr. Thornburg would certainly cut off his trust fund or reduce it to a pittance. Maybe he would have to work for a living. Graveyard shift at Don's Auto Body? Maybe. That would be karma, though I pitied whoever had to work with him.

The stresses of the long day and disturbed night crept in, though my mind kept racing. One of the Council members closed his eyes, with his water bottle halfway to his lips. The bottle tipped, dripping water down his shirt. Nobody reacted. I felt a sudden flare of alarm. Was the water poisoned? Most of the Council members and security members were asleep, but most didn't drink the water. Leah's head was on Mr. Thornburg's knee. She slid off and flopped prone to the floor. I tried to get up but couldn't. Robinette was already on the floor. I tried to yell something, but only a croak came out, lost in the engine noise. The other shoe was falling.

My head felt heavy, then suddenly my eyes were inches from the floor, with everything fading to black.

#

I was face down on the helicopter's floor when I came back to myself, cheek on the gritty floor. My hands and feet were tied, with a rope between them that forced my ankles up behind my back toward my wrists, straining my shoulders back and forcing my back into a painful arch.

I raised my head and turned it slowly, still groggy. The floor was littered with Council members and their security, all tied up like me. Tom Thornburg and another young man knelt in a narrow corridor down the center of the copter, working over a Council member, apparently trying to revive him. Tom stood up. He yelled over the engine noise, "We lost him. That makes two."

The other young man shrugged. "Less fun that way, but not all bad." He seemed shaken despite his words.

Robinette lay beside me, eyes closed, her curly hair spilling across her face. I wanted to reach out to her, to hold her and protect her, but I couldn't. Leah was on the other side of Robinette, next to her father, her dark green dress around her thighs.

Tom glanced at me and gave me a slow, ironic thumbs up. He had a wild look in his eyes, part predatory, part scared. He grinned, but the grin looked forced. "We're committed now, even if we weren't before."

I glared at him and tried to roll onto my side, facing him.

Tom leaned over me. "I bet you were worried about the water. We figured people would be, so we used gas, a little too much for a couple people. You'll have a headache, but no long-term damage from the gas. The fall, though, that will kill you."

He walked away and closed a hatch behind him. Leah struggled to a strange awkward parody of sitting, bracing herself against the side of the helicopter. I tried to sit up like her but slammed down on my face.

"Don't worry about sitting up," Leah said. "Sitting when you're tied like this takes practice." She grimaced. "First time I've been tied up by my brother. though. I'm kinky, but not that kinky." She winced. "I'm also not into dying. 'The fall will kill you.' He plans to dump us out the helicopter like Jimmy claimed they did the Mangi prostitute."

I stared at her. "Us being you and me?"

"Us being everyone in the back of this helicopter, including Dad, the Council members and their security. He's already killed two Council people. He can't let any witnesses live. He has to kill us. He's cornered rat dangerous and not thinking straight, but he really doesn't have a choice."

I shook my head and was sorry I did. I felt a sharp pain that mostly went away if I held my head very still. "That worthless, spoiled, cowardly kid is planning to kill the richest, most powerful men in the world? How does he expect to get away with it?"

"No laws in the Wild except Council rules." Leah struggled with the ropes, then shook her head. "I've been tied up a time or two for recreational purposes. Tom did it right. Who is going to prosecute him if the Council all falls out of helicopters? Would throwing us out even break any laws?"

I tested the ropes around my wrists and ankles. They were tight. I always carried a pocketknife, but it was gone, not that I could have reached it anyway. "You're taking the idea that you're dead rich woman sitting pretty calmly."

Leah grimaced. "I have a good poker face. Inside, I'm really hoping there isn't a hell and I'm afraid I'll break and beg that smarmy bastard for my life. Why aren't you all emotional? I know you don't have a good poker face."

That was a good question. Whatever drug Tom used lingered in my head, muffling my emotions, but mainly I didn't believe, down deep, that Tom would kill us.

One of the Councilmen, a balding, bearded guy with broad shoulders and a wrinkled ten-thousand-dollar suit, apparently heard enough of what Leah said to figure out what was happening. When Tom stepped back in, the Councilman yelled at him to come over. Tom stood at the hatch, a mocking half-smile playing over his lips. "Have some last words?"

"I have more money stashed in secret accounts than anyone could spend in twenty lifetimes," the Councilman said. "More than the British royal family. Let me go and it's yours."

"Then you hunt me down and take it back," Tom said. He gestured to one of his friends, strapped himself to a sling chair, then pointed to the Councilman. "We have our first domino to fall."

Tom's friend stared at him. "We're really going to do this?"

"It's way too late to back out now."

The two opened a large side door, letting in gusting wind. I thought I heard distant thunder over the engine noise. Tom and his friend grabbed the rope between the Councilman's bound arms and feet like a handle and dragged him toward the door. The Councilman kept talking, his voice getting faster and higher. He flailed against the ropes and his words turned into a scream so high his voice didn't sound human. He kept thrashing, the screams turning into sobs as Tom and his friend dragged him to the door.

I found myself yelling, "No!" I could barely hear my own voice over the yells and screams of the other bound men and women, many of them just waking up.

Tom and his friend pushed the Councilman out the door, with Tom losing his balance on the final shove. He grabbed the side of the doorway and teetered for a long second, then pulled himself back in. Everyone abruptly shut up. In the relative silence, we heard the Councilman screaming as he fell, screams fading until they were lost in the engine's roar.

"I guess I could go the way that poor sap did," Leah said. "But I want to keep a shred of dignity."

Tom whirled and strode over to her, bending down to put his face at her level. "Really, sister dearest? Want to be next?"

She glared back. "Do it, but you'll still have raisin-sized balls."

Maybe physical courage was Leah's Island of decency, or at least part of her I could respect. I wondered if the knockout drug stripped away filters to leave raw emotions in some, like the thrashing Councilman and isolated others, like me and maybe Leah, from what we should be feeling.

In any case, bound as she was, Leah faced her brother, with no sign of fear. Finally, he turned away. "I'll drop you last, let you watch everyone else go."

He left through the hatch, leaving the side door open and the wind blasting through, adding to the engine's roar and buffeting our faces.

I should have felt horror, adrenaline coursing through me. Instead, I felt detached. If I closed my eyes on the way down, I thought, death would be quick and painless.

Many of the prisoners were still unconscious. They gradually woke up. Leah told Robinette and Mr. Thornburg about Tom's role in taking us prisoner and what he did to the Councilman, talking over engine noise and a babble of crosstalk.

When she finished, Mr. Thornburg looked stunned, physically sick. He took a deep breath. "I wondered what he was doing with his money, but I figured he would learn hard lessons if I left him alone."

"We're the ones who will get the hard lessons," Marcus said. He had apparently been listening. "Don't give a balless sociopath a lot of money being a big one."

We glared at him.

Tom opened the hatch. "Everyone awake? Time for the next act. Who wants to be next? If you want to be next, thrash around." He turned to Mr. Thornburg. "Any words of wisdom, Dad?"

"The Thornburg line will be extinct within a month if you go through with this. You can't handle the avalanche that you're starting, and I won't be there to save you."

"Don't stop now," Tom said. "Tell me how I can't even manage my own trust fund and how I'm such a loser that you would make your half-Mangi bastard heir if you had to choose between her and me."

"Neither of you could handle being the heir," Mr. Thornburg said. "Her because she's a decent person, you because you aren't smart enough. You don't know how much you don't know. How do you expect to get away with killing dozens of the richest, most powerful men and women on Earth?"

"Dropping them on their heads from five hundred feet should do it," Tom said. "We won't even have to hide the bodies, and dropping people out of helicopters in the Wild isn't a crime. There isn't even a name for it. Defenestration maybe? But that's throwing someone out of a building."

"Sure, you can kill us, but then what?" Mr. Thornburg asked, his voice clear over the wind and engine noise. "That many powerful people disappearing will crash the stock market and destroy Gate family political power. You'll start a quiet, vicious economic war to replace the Gate families and grab their assets. You and your spare heirs will lose everything then die, because you don't know how power works at this level. Do you even understand that we're legally an arm of the federal government, a continuity of government operation and that the Council Police are federal law enforcement?"

"Tom and his little friends aren't smart enough to understand that," Robinette said. "I don't think they even have a plan. This feels like a cornered rat move. They're stuck at twelve-year-old thinking, killing their parents because the parents cut off their allowance."

Tom's friend put a hand on his shoulder. "Your family drama can wait. We have a thunderstorm coming in. If you're going to throw people out, do it, then we can set down or try to outrun the storm."

Tom turned back to Robinette. "We're circling over short grass. You might live if we dropped you into trees." He smiled coldly. "Everything would have been okay if Dad had thrown you back in the Wild with your mother. You would already be old and toothless, if you were still alive. I'll save you until just before Leah, let you watch everyone else go over the side." He turned and strode back through the hatch.

What Robinette said about them might be true, but it didn't make Tom and his crew any less dangerous. Even if they were improvising desperately, they were deadly.

The reality of what was happening hit me like a fist to my jaw. It penetrated my drug-induced calm and suddenly I understood the Council guy's thrashing, pleas and screams.

Leah seemed shaken, too. Maybe the danger was sinking in for her too. Every move the helicopter guys made pushed them further along a desperate, murderous path, one that could only work if they killed us all.

Tom returned. I tried to read his face but couldn't. He wore a fixed grin that somehow seemed fragile. Was he as terrified as he should be? Was it better for us if he was calm? It probably didn't make any difference. He was committed now.

Robinette seemed calm, as calm as Leah had earlier. She struggled around so our faces were close. "You did your best to save me. I wish I hadn't dragged you into this. And I wish I could feel your arms around me again."

I could barely hear her over the engine noise and more Council members frantically offering Tom fantastic amounts of money if he let them go. He ignored the offers. His friends dragged a security guard to the door. A few seconds later his screams faded into engine noise and distant thunder.

Leah closed her eyes when the scream started, then opened them when it faded. "I won't scream. I won't give him that satisfaction." She struggled to stay sitting. "We all die because my brother is a moron. He keeps doubling down. If the Council found out he had a secret Gate they would have taken it away from him and made sure he didn't have enough money to do it again, but they wouldn't kill him. Now, they wouldn't hesitate. Either they die or he does."

"If I wasn't dying with you, I would cheer," McFinney said. "Your whole system is rotten. I hope the Gate families kill each other to the last pampered piece of watery shit woman and child."

"Yet you took our money," Mr. Thornburg said. "And you killed people in duels for our entertainment or because the families told you too."

"And you played my games to get close to the power," Leah said. "You're part of the system, no better than the rest of us." She shifted uncomfortably in the ropes. "Only people here who don't deserve to die are Eric Carter and my sister. And Robinette's not really a person—just an ape who is really good at monkey see, monkey do."

The helicopter engines kept roaring. Tom and his friends dragged out another security guy, then another, moving faster. I watched them go with a sick feeling in my stomach. People were falling, flailing and screaming, to their deaths, and we couldn't stop it. We would be falling soon. I felt more helpless than I could ever remember feeling, unable to stop the macabre string of falling bodies. My hands and feet strained against the ropes without conscious thought until they trembled from exhaustion, the effort wasted. What else could I do, though? Nothing to lose.

Tom and his friends went through the security details first. I wondered briefly if he planned to terrify the two remaining Council members and Mr. Thornburg by killing their security people, then make them some offer. What could they give him, though? As he pointed out to the now-dead Councilman, if anyone in the helicopter lived, they would hunt him and his friends anywhere they fled and the Gate families had enough power that he couldn't hide, couldn't escape. Killing us all was the only way out for him.

#

I finally struggled from my stomach onto my side on the helicopter floor, face inches from Robinette's. My knees and shoulders ached from being tied so long. How did Leah manage to sit up? I still had no idea. I could barely stay on my side.

Tom and company went through the security details quickly. A couple guys tried to chew through the ropes holding the people next to them, but Tom and company threw them out first.

I try to wrap my head around the idea of Tom Thornburg, mastermind, but it still seemed ridiculous, even as he systematically hurled security people to their deaths. However unreal it felt, Tom Thornburg had rendered the richest men and women in the world helpless, stripped away their security, and was systematically killing them.

What about the rest of the Council? Were they on the other helicopter, meeting the same fate?

Only three Council members remained now, counting Mr. Thornburg. The other two, a man and a woman, both in their fifties and still in the expensively tailored clothes they wore to the duel, didn't say anything. The woman closed her eyes, as though shutting them would keep out the world.

Tom helped throw each of the security people overboard, staying strapped to the helicopter by a long rope. Four of his friends switched off helping him.

One of those friends looked terrified every time thunder roared. "Lightning is going to knock us out of the sky. Karma."

"Shut up and get this over with," Tom said. His fists were clenched, knuckles white.

Finally, only the two Council members, the Thornburg family, McFinney and me were left. The Councilman broke his silence when Tom grabbed him, pleading and thrashing. He screamed on the way down, the sound quickly lost in the wind and engine noise. The councilwoman kept her eyes closed but said something too soft for us to hear. When Tom bent down, she jerked around and clamped her teeth on the meat of his hand. She held on desperately, tearing into the hand, while Tom and his friend punched her unprotected face, then clubbed her with their sidearms.

Tom kept screaming. Leah yelled, "Bite the sucker off! Take off fingers!"

I struggled against the ropes, tried to roll toward them, desperate, with nothing to lose. The woman's jaws clung desperately to Tom's hand, kept clinging long after she should have been unconscious, stayed tight while kicks and punches rained down on her, with Tom screaming again and again, but finally she went limp. Tom pulled his hand free and kicked her in the ribs and head repeatedly, blood dripping from his torn hand. He finally shoved the limp and probably lifeless body out the door.

"She's dead, but she still won," Leah said. "When my time comes, I'll go after something more painful than a hand."

Tom staggered through the hatch, clutching his hand. His friend hesitated and muttered, "This is crazy."

"If there's a God, he'll knock you out of the sky," Leah said. "He has a thunderstorm to do it. Even if there isn't a God, you're idiots to fly in this crap."

"Still a chance to back out," Mr. Thornburg said.

The guy shook his head. "We've all killed at least one Council member. We can't back out now."

"Talk Tom into doing something that gives us a fighting chance, and if I make it, I'll do what I can for you," Mr. Thornburg said. "Get him to land because of the storm if nothing else. Give us a chance."

"What do you have in mind?"

"I don't know. A hunt, maybe."

"You would still die and there are worse ways to die than this." He paused, then turned and strode through the hatch, closing it behind him.

Were there worse ways to die? Maybe. At least falling to our deaths would be quick. I turned to Robinette and searched desperately for some way to save her.

"I'm going for a castration bite," Leah said. "I think I can do it. It won't save us, but if it's all I can do, so be it. Maybe I'll end the Thornburg line forever. The world would be better off without us."

One of Tom's friends came in and closed the big side door. "Change of plans. We have a friends and family special just for you."

We felt the helicopter descending, then jolt to a landing. The engines shut off, leaving a sudden silence except for thunder muttering. Tom's friends opened the big side door and dragged us into a football-field-sized stretch of ankle-high grass. Tom joined them, his torn hand wrapped in gauze and his face pale.

"New plan," Tom said. "One of you gets to survive. All you have to do is kill all the others in front of multiple cameras, up close and personal, with a pocketknife. If you can do it in ten minutes, you do what we tell you the rest of your life or go up on murder charges, but you live. If you try to cut any of the others loose, we shoot you and go to the next volunteer. Any questions?"

"Yeah," Leah said. "Who would have jurisdiction for a murder in the Wild?"

"The new Council," Tom said. "The one we'll form once the dust settles."

"Good luck with that," Leah said. "What the hell? I'll volunteer. We're all dead anyway."

"Any other volunteers?" Tom asked.

McFinney volunteered. I hoped Robinette would. If any of us could turn this around with just a pocketknife and a thirst for revenge, it would be her. She shook her head though. "I'm not your puppet. If I have to die, I'll die cleanly."

What if I volunteered, grabbed the knife and tried to take one of them with me or tried to cut Robinette loose, then charged them? It wouldn't work, but we had nothing to lose. Thunder still rumbled. If we stalled long enough for the thunderstorm to roll in, maybe the storm would raise our chances from near zero to minuscule.

"I'll do it," I said.

"He'll kill whoever volunteers anyway," Mr. Thornburg said.

"And miss watching them dance on my strings?" Tom asked. "Nope. The offer is genuine. We won't kill you or strand you. And since my sister volunteered first, she's up."

So much for a wild try for freedom. Helpless rage welled up in me. "Why don't you just kill us?"

Through the Wild Gate

"Because I want to see if my sister has the guts to kill you," Tom said. "For all her tough girl crap, I don't think she does."

Tom cut Leah loose, then tossed a pocketknife in the dirt beside her. "You have ten minutes to kill them all."

Leah struggled to her feet, knife in hand, and staggered toward Robinette, opening the knife. "First one isn't really murder. Just an ape Daddy dressed up and sent to Harvard to show how powerful he is." She knelt over Robinette, knife poised. "Any last words, little sister?"

Robinette lunged for the knife hand with her teeth but caught a sleeve instead of flesh when Leah jumped back. Leah dropped the knife and suddenly Robinette had it in her bound hands. She slashed the rope between her hands and ankles, then the one around her ankles.

"Enough!" Tom yelled. "Drop the knife or we shoot you both."

Robinette paused, knife in still-bound hands. Something roared, far too loud for a rifle and suddenly flames poured from the helicopter. Lightning strike? The sound wasn't right.

Robinette rolled up to a sitting position, got her hands in front of her and was suddenly on her feet, zigzagging toward me. She slashed the ropes around my wrists and pushed the knife into my hand, then ran on.

I slashed the rope around my ankles and surged to my feet, then promptly fell sideways, my legs refusing to cooperate. A bullet whined over my head, way too close. I dropped the knife when I fell and scrambled to find it in the grass. I found a fist-sized rock instead and aimed it at the nearest rifleman's head. My shoulder betrayed me too, sending the rock into the dirt a foot in front of the guy. It took a lucky bounce into his shin, sending him hopping.

I found the knife and charged Tom's nearest friend, zigzagging and expecting a bullet. The guy fired from the hip, squeezing off shots as fast as he could pull the trigger in an arc that emptied the magazine before the arc reached me. I crashed into him, punched him in the groin, grabbed his now-empty rifle, then his sidearm. I slammed the rifle into the side of his head, then stomped his groin when he fell. I fired the sidearm at the nearest rifleman, saw him fall, then looked for another target. There weren't any. Two guys were down, with Robinette carrying their rifles and sidearms. Leah had Tom flat on his back, squatting on his chest with his arms trapped under her legs, hitting him in his unprotected face hard enough to make his head bounce against the hard ground.

I stood gaping, my mind struggling with the sudden reversal of fortunes. I expected yet another shoe to fall, some twist from the mastermind, apparently Tom Thornburg, but he stayed on the ground, with Leah trying to beat him to death.

I cut Mr. Thornburg loose and handed him the empty rifle. He glanced at it. "These things work better with bullets."

"We'll find ammo. Want to rescue your son or let Leah beat him to death?"

"Help me save the helicopter first."

The helicopter was still burning, with debris from a recent explosion in the cockpit. Mr. Thornburg grabbed a fire extinguisher, while I tried to smother the fire with an emergency blanket. We finally got it put out, then turned back to Tom and Leah.

She had Tom tied up in the same arched-back posture he tied us in. She turned to us when we strode up. "He's alive, hopefully with a concussion. He claimed that if I stopped hitting him, he would tell me the real mastermind behind all this. He fainted, or pretended to, before he gave me a name."

"Avery Blackwood," McFinney said. He used an empty rifle as a cane, with one arm hanging limp. "It has to be him."

"Your boss?" Robinette asked. "Chairman of the Council? Why?"

"He was going broke.".

Chapter Twenty-Two:
Final Confrontation

With the threat of imminent death gone, I took a deep breath of the Wild and savored it. My body needed that clean air. After the long helicopter ride when I thought we were all dead and the brief, brutal fight, my muscles felt weak as warm butter. I still didn't understand what happened to give us our chance. An explosion in the helicopter's cockpit with the copter powered down seemed unlikely, yet it happened and at the perfect time to distract Tom and his crew and give us our chance.

"It was a bomb," McFinney said. "The only thing it could be."

Looking at the damage, I had to agree. With the helicopter powered down, nothing else could have caused that much damage. A lightning strike? This didn't look like a lightning strike and no other lightning bolts hit nearby.

If the pilot and copilot had been in their places, the explosion would have decapitated them and the helicopter would have crashed, killing everyone aboard.

"It was Blackwood cleaning up," McFinney said. "He probably promised Tom Thornburg and his idiot friends seats on the Council, but then he sent them out, supposedly to kill us, but really to die with us. All of Blackwood's big-name rivals on the Council would die, making him undisputed leader of the Council. He could push through rules that let him make money in the Wild and get rich again."

I shifted restlessly, my knees and shoulders still stiff. Thunder still rumbled, getting closer. "We may want to continue this conversation later."

Mr. Thornburg nodded. "In a second." He turned back to McFinney. "I saw no sign the Blackwood's needed money. And if anyone should know it would be me."

"Blackwood's the only one who makes sense," McFinney said. "Your idiot son didn't dream this up on his own. Who selected the people who went on this helicopter? Blackwood. If they died, who would benefit?"

"Blackwood," Mr. Thornburg said. "The strongest opponents of developing the Wild are gone now except me, and I would have died if the copter crashed. But I still don't think the Blackwoods are out of money."

"Somebody set the bomb." McFinney shifted restlessly on his improvised cane. "If it wasn't Blackwood, who was it?"

None of us knew. We turned to more urgent matters. The helicopter landing and gunshots attracted curious carnivores, including bears, wolves and Mangi. They surrounded us in a loose circle, eyes and noses probing the air.

Tom's pilot was alive, though battered from a brief fight with Robinette, and he thought he could fly us out, despite the damage, which was mostly to the pilot's seat.

The pilot winced when he saw the seat. "That would have been the upper half of my body if we hadn't landed."

He didn't know who backed the spare heirs, beyond Tom, but said Tom hinted at powerful allies. "Whoever it was, they used us like yesterday's diapers."

I felt like pounding the guy's face in, but the copilot was dead, so he was the only one who could fly us out. I half-expected him to try to use that power, but he seemed cowed by defeat and especially by the explosion. Leah sat next to him in the shattered co-pilot's seat, not that she could do much if he tried to fly us somewhere we didn't want to go.

The rest of us sat in the back, in the same compartment where we had been prisoners, but with the hatch open and the gas canisters disconnected. Even with those precautions, my legs balked at taking me into that compartment. I stood at the door and breathed deeply. "Maybe we should walk."

"Fifty miles," Robinette said. "And whoever is behind this would have days to get ready for us."

My mind knew she was right, but my body resisted. When I finally went in, I had a nearly overwhelming urge to run back out. I controlled it and sat in a web chair between Robinette and Mr. Thornburg. Tom and two of his surviving friends were on the floor, backs arched by the ropes between their bound hands and feet, looking terrified.

The thunderstorm I had hoped would save us finally roared in, bringing in rain that pounded the helicopter roof and lightning strikes way too close. Tom and his friends shifted restlessly but remained silent.

McFinney glared down at them. "I vote we toss them out. What do you think, Tom? Isn't tossing people out of helicopters fun? The screams. Watching them flail? Knowing that at the end they go splat?"

"Enough," Mr. Thornburg said. "I'll handle this from here." He said that calmly, barely audible over the storm, but his voice held authority. McFinney shut up. Mr. Thornburg turned to Tom. "There will be no bargaining. Try bargaining and we'll do what Mr. McFinney's suggested. You will give a full and truthful account of everything you know that relates, no matter how remotely, to you dropping Council members off the helicopter. When you're done, I'll decide whether to intervene with the Council on your behalf. Chances of that are slim and will go away with any falsehood or omission I detect. The truth may not save you but lies will kill you."

Tom nodded and started his story. Mr. Thornburg recorded it on Tom's smartphone, brought in through Tom's Gate in defiance of Council rules. A lot of it we had already guessed, but some elements were new. Tom had toyed with the idea of building his own Gate, but never went beyond talking to his friends about what he would do with one until Mr. Blackwood approached him. Blackwood heard about Tom's interest and offered to invest in the Gate in return for access to it.

"Blackwood said he could make it legal," Tom said. "He gave me your communications codes and had me vote remotely as you on the authorization."

Tom ended up paying for most of the Gate, draining all the money he could from his trust fund and borrowing against what he would get in the future. He opened the Gate two years ago and charged his friends for access and increasingly risky hunts. Meanwhile, Mr. Blackwood sent helicopters through on mysterious flights.

When the hunt for Jimmy Nelson went so badly wrong, Tom and his friends tried to cover it up, but Jimmy went to the Thornburg Gate and talked to Mr. Thornburg, who started an investigation, Blackwood found out about the investigation and ordered Tom to get the Gate shut down. Tom went to Leah with the evidence that got Robinette exiled and the Gate shuttered. Jimmy was still out there, but Tom and company had more time to find and kill him.

"You planted the evidence," Mr. Thornburg said.

"No. I found it," Tom said. He hastily added, "I'm not lying. If anyone planted it, it wasn't me." His head sagged to the helicopter floor.

"Could you untie the rope between my wrists and ankles? I can't hold my head up much longer."

"If it gets too painful, we can fix that," McFinney said.

Tom claimed that he didn't know about the explosions the stranded the Families, but assumed Blackwood was behind them. Blackwood had Tom and his friends bring the helicopters in, then pulled Tom aside and told him to gas and kill everyone Blackwood assigned to the helicopter. The helicopters were already equipped with gas cylinders to subdue Mangi lured in with the promise of a ride then used in fights against bears or other big carnivores.

Blackwood promised the spare heirs seats on the Council for their efforts and Tom and his friends were desperate enough to believe him.

That still left Blackwood's motive unknown. Was the Blackwood family nearly bankrupt, trying to use the Wild to stay afloat?

The worst of the thunderstorm passed, letting us take off. After all the stresses of the last few days, I fought to keep my eyes open through Tom's story. I squirmed in the uncomfortable seat. We were far from safe, riding in a damaged helicopter in the Wild, hopefully between thunderstorms and with a pilot we couldn't trust. Still, with Tom helpless and his story spilling out, the nightmare felt close to an end. I fought against complacency. The mastermind, whether or not it was Blackwood, was still out there, probably desperate if he knew we were alive.

"If the Blackwoods have money problems, they're hiding it well," Mr. Thornburg said. "But when you've been wealthy for a long time, you can pretend you still are for years. Banks keep loaning you money because they know you're rich, and as long as you have cash flow you can hide losses. The family could be a burned-out wreck financially, but if they keep up appearances they can keep going." He turned to McFinney. "Did you see any sign they were hurting financially?"

McFinney shook his head. "Someone was smuggling things in from the Wild and I figured it was the Blackwood family because they shut down my investigation, but if they were strapped for cash, I never saw signs of it."

We flew on. Robinette leaned close, her hands on my shoulder. "We still have a long way to go before we're safe."

I nodded and raised my voice over the engine noise. "But at least we aren't tied up, waiting to get thrown out the helicopter."

My mind shied away from that nightmare time, time when I was sure we were dead, time when the rich and powerful died horribly. Would their bodies even get buried? Probably not. Scavengers would get to them before we could. Whoever was behind that, whoever was pulling Tom's strings, they had to pay.

#

We landed at the nearest Gate Compound, one that belonged to the Hardwick family, according to Mr. Thornburg. That was the first time I had heard that name, but Mr. Thornburg said they went way back, getting rich in cattle, then oil before going into finance. Their Compound had the obligatory wall, but with twists to make it look more like a fairytale castle than the more utilitarian Thornburg Compound. Murals covered the wall and outside gate, with a mix of Disney-inspired and Lord of the Rings-inspired artwork all in vivid greens, blues and yellows.

Grim-faced guards with M-16s spoiled the theme. They didn't quite point their weapons at us but were clearly ready for a fight. Mr. Thornburg told them why we were there, violating Council rules with the helicopter. He abbreviated the story to the point it was deceptive without saying anything technically untrue, conveying urgency that got us through the Gate and into a fleet of cars with a minimum of fuss.

Mr. Thornburg was on a borrowed cellphone, in a borrowed suit that managed to look tailored, rallying his security people and allies before we settled into the cars. Robinette and I sat together in a borrowed stretch limousine the length of a city bus, with Mr. Thornburg and Leah facing us. Despite our adventures, Leah managed to look fresh, with her makeup and hair perfect. She had grass-stains from her knees up her thighs at least as high as the slit in her dress showed, though and had trouble keeping her eyes open.

I had grass stains too, plus a rip up the side of my jeans from mid-calf to mid-thigh. Robinette's hair was in disarray. She pulled it back into the same sloppy ponytail she wore when she came through the gate. I smiled at her. "Still need saving? I don't think I've saved you yet."

"You've saved me a dozen times. I'll need at least one more."

"Blackwood is probably across already, staging the other half of his coup," Mr. Thornburg said. "I don't think he handled the other helicopter-load of Council members the way he intended to handle us. One helicopter crash could be an accident. Two is an open coup. He might get away with it, but it would signal that the Council can be changed by killing members. If he has any brains, he doesn't want that."

Blackwood's strongest opponents were all on our helicopter anyway, so most of them were dead now. Five dead Council members changed the balance a lot and Blackwood probably brought his allies from among the rest of the Council home first if he could.

Mr. Thornburg turned to Leah. "What do you think of our chances on the Council?"

"Against Blackwood? There are enough people who will side with whoever they think will win that it could go either way. We'll win in Council if we look like we'll win."

"And how do you suggest that we look strong?" Mr. Thornburg asked.

"Is this a quiz? Do I get a Council seat if I get the right answer? I hear they have vacancies."

"If this was a quiz, you failed," Mr. Thornburg said. "I asked the wrong question. The Council isn't Blackwood's weakness. If he did this to move wealth from the Wild, he is in deep crap financially. So we hit him in the finances. How would I do that?"

"Find excuses to pull in his loans from banks we control," Leah said. "Dump stocks in his companies and take huge, short positions, betting his stocks will fall. Plant bankruptcy rumors with friendly financial pundits."

"That's a start," Mr. Thornburg said. "I have accountants studying his companies, looking for overvalued inventory and other accounting tricks that hide losses. They're also trying to figure out when and how he got in financial trouble. I hope we're right about him being bankrupt, because if he isn't we'll lose a ton of money."

After the desperate physical struggles of the past few days, all that seemed mundane, boring, but it would probably decide the winner in this struggle. That felt wrong, a battle in a realm I barely knew existed and didn't understand.

"This needs to end in a fist fight or guns blazing," I said. "Not accounting and finance crap that makes peoples' eyes glaze over."

Leah sneered. "Fists are the way you settle bar fights."

"Really?" I pointed to her knuckles, skinned and bruised from pounding Tom's head. "Your fists disagree."

She grinned. "Hitting him felt good. My hands hurt like hell now, though."

"Would you have cut Robinette's throat if she hadn't grabbed your sleeve with her teeth?" I asked.

"She would never have gotten close enough to grab me if I didn't want her to," Leah said. "Don't get me wrong. I would have happily sliced her throat open and laughed while she bled out, but getting her loose was our only chance."

"I don't believe you on the throat cutting bit," I said. "I saw you when you thought McFinney would win."

"And now you think I have a soft side." Leah grinned. "So cute and so naïve. I'm demoting you back to eye candy. How do you survive in the PI business? Oh yeah, by moonlighting at Don's Auto."

Mr. Thornburg stayed on the phone while the limousine drove on, working his financial magic in a flood of cryptic conversations. He took a brief break and turned to us. "Blackwood is claiming we're all dead. He's trying to install the current Mrs. Thornburg on the Council. That means he knew about the bomb and still thinks we're all dead. I want him to keep thinking that until his finances are smoking ruins, which should be happening now if everything I set up works."

"And you timed it to hit about the time we reach the Council chambers," Leah said. "I'm impressed."

"Don't be impressed until I pull this off without triggering Great Depression 2.0," Mr. Thornburg said. "With all the dead Family heads, that's a real risk. This is the finance equivalent of a gunfight next to leaking gas tanks."

We pulled into an underground garage under the Gate Council chambers. "I have Council Police I hired primed to go, but I don't want a gunfight," Mr. Thornburg said. "I want the Blackwood family off the Council and his family bankrupt or downsized to a fast-food franchise. His role in killing Councilors should never come out, just hang over him to keep him from fighting back, Violence is a bad precedent and we've already had too much. I want the most boring coup ever."

I had the feeling Mr. Blackwood would have his say on that, but I understood. Bring in guns to overthrow a government, even a secret one, and those guns never entirely go away, never completely give up their power.

Mr. Blackwood was at the podium, delivering a eulogy for the dead Council members, who he apparently thought included Mr. Thornburg. The empty chairs where the dead Council members once sat seemed to dominate the room. A sparse crowd was in the balcony, some still in the wrinkled clothes they wore to the duel, though their hair and makeup was now perfect again.

The color drained from Blackwood's face when he saw Mr. Thornburg among the Thornburg security people, along with the Council Police. He stumbled to a stop.

"Don't stop on my account," Mr. Thornburg said. "You were saying good things about our fellow Council people, including me. You might want to pause for a moment to check your financials, though."

"What would I find?" Mr. Blackwood asked.

"That your façade is broken. Your family has been a burned-out ruin for seven years, borrowing and spending yourself deeper in debt to keep up appearances." Mr. Thornburg grinned. "You did a good job. You even fooled me. Once I knew, though, everything fell into place. You are melting down, losing everything."

Mr. Blackwood grabbed a tablet computer. He stared at it, swiping from screen to screen, his face expressionless, left hand clenched on the podium, knuckles white. He finally looked up. "Why?"

"I know what you did, not all of it, but enough." Mr. Thornburg gestured to Mr. Blackwood's calf. "You carry a snub-nosed revolver in an ankle holster, according to Marcus McFinney. You'll want to get it out."

"Why? So you have an excuse to shoot me?"

"No. So your family can live on, comfortably upper-middle class."

Blackwood stared at him. "I can give up my Gate, pull out the deposit and use the money to stop the meltdown."

"Your daughter could. You couldn't. The Gate deposit would be tied up in investigations that last until the last remnants of your wealth was gone and then probably get forfeited."

The two men stared at each other, with the surviving Council members silent. Finally, Mr. Blackwood said, "If I take the gun out, one of us is going to die."

Mr. Thornburg nodded. "What I'm doing to your holdings is on a dead man switch. Unless I stop it, your family loses everything, and your daughter goes to jail for fraud."

"I'm not going to kill myself."

Mr. Thornburg shrugged. "That's your choice."

Mr. Blackwood eased the revolver out of its holster and stared at it, then sat it on the podium and stared at the tablet computer, flipping between screens. Finally, he looked up. "You're a bastard. I hope you burn in hell." He took a deep breath. "My daughter gets the Gate deposit and a chance to salvage things?"

"Not everything, but enough."

Mr. Blackwood stared at the pistol. "How do I make sure?"

"In your mouth, angled up," Mr. Thornburg said.

Mr. Blackwood took a deep breath, then addressed the room. "Consider this a Do Not Resuscitate Order."

He put the revolver in his mouth and fired, then fell, the revolver still in his hand, the gunshot echoing.

#

"And that's how they do it in the big leagues." Leah said. Despite the nonchalant words, she sounded subdued, Mr. Blackwood's body still lay on the floor, with Council Police paramedics surrounding him. They didn't work over the body, just felt for a pulse and began the cleanup.

If Mr. Blackwood had friends on the Council, they laid low during the confrontation and they continued to do so.

Mr. Thornburg turned to the remaining Council members. "Since we probably don't have a quorum and definitely don't have a chairman, let's declare this session paused while we mourn the members who actually did die in a helicopter crash and sort things out."

That sorting amounted to the Thornburgs smoothly taking over the Council. Five seats were empty with no surviving close relatives to take over, along with Mr. Blackwood's seat. Rather than selecting new families to buy into those Gates, Mr. Thornburg opened those Gates up to an auction among the remaining families, shrinking the Council to fifteen, but giving the families who bought a second Gate two votes. Tom's secret Gate was already Council approved as an emergency Gate, not linked to any family but administered by Blackwood, Thornburg took it over and made Robinette administrator, though she didn't get a seat on the Council. I'm now her head bodyguard.

No one knows what happened to Tom, though I can guess. Mr. Thornburg quietly let Jimmy Nelson back through to our world and cut Tom off from his trust fund. Jimmy's ties to the underground fighting world undoubtedly left him with plenty of ways to hide a body. -The long months Tom and company hunted him gave Jimmy plenty of motive to track down Tom and make him disappear.

Clara Wolf/Thornburg apparently believed Robinette about the Gate families being part of federal continuity of government plans. She stopped trying to break her prenuptial agreement, and according to Mike, she went back to dating rich old men.

Does all of that make for a perfect ending? Nope. The Gate families still secretly control our world and the Wild, with that power concentrated in fewer hands now, and dominated by Mr. Thornburg, with his ruthlessness and islands of decency and with Leah waiting in the wings to take over. Mangi still die too young, of things we could easily treat, their bodies already worn out when they should be starting their lives.

What happened to Robinette's mother? We still don't know. Probably long dead. Mangi life in the Wild is harsh.

Who framed Mr. Thornburg for trying to give Robinette a Frankenbaby? That turned out to be Robinette, though she didn't mean to. After her argument with Mr. Thornburg, she looked seriously into finding some way of having children, before her anger cooled down and she realized it was a bad idea. She forged her dad's signature on a couple documents while she was trying to make a child happen. Tom found evidence of the attempt and used it, a convenient club that put Robinette out of the picture and set Mr. Thornburg and Leah against each other.

Robinette and me? I love the girl and I think she loves me, but neither of us have quite decided if it's a romantic love or a big brother/little sister kind of love. We'll figure that out eventually.

Mike is back at Don's. He says he misses having someone he trusts to back him up. I hope to hell I never go back there. Guarding a rogue Gate is a crap job, scary as hell when it isn't boring.

Final Notes

I hope you enjoyed Wild Gate. I haven't decided if this novel is a one-off or the start of yet another series. There is certainly room in the fictional universe for more stories, but as of yet I haven't decided to pursue them.

If you enjoyed this story, you're likely to enjoy my novel ***Char,*** which has some similar elements or ***The Necklace of Time,*** which has a science fiction background like Wild Gate, but also has strong elements of mystery. Fair warning on Necklace: If you haven't read any of my Snapshot novels it may take a couple chapters for you to figure out what is going on. I think it's worth the effort and the feedback I've gotten generally supports that.

Both of those novels, plus a dozen more of my novels or collections are available in paperback and e-book. For details, just do a search on Dale Cozort on Amazon.

You might also consider being on my mailing list. It's free and you can opt out at any time.

I send out updates on new books, appearances and discounts on current books very sporadically, no more than once or twice per year, along with insights into how books came about, what I'm currently working on, etc.

If you would like to be on the list, just send a message titled: "Please Add Me To Your Mailing List" to: DaleCoz2@gmail.com

If you no longer want to be on the list, just send a message titled: "Please Remove Me From Your Mailing List" to the same address.

Finally, if you enjoyed this novel, please rate and if possible, review it. Ratings and reviews help drive how visible Amazon makes a novel, as well as giving potential readers a better idea of what they are getting into.

Printed in Great Britain
by Amazon